THE MODERN LIBRARY
OF THE WORLD'S BEST BOOKS

THE CRIME OF SYLVESTRE BONNARD

TURN TO THE END OF THIS VOLUME FOR A COMPLETE LIST OF TITLES IN THE MODERN LIBRARY

THE CRIME OF
SYLVESTRE BONNARD
(MEMBER OF THE INSTITUTE)

By ANATOLE FRANCE

TRANSLATION AND INTRODUCTION
BY LAFCADIO HEARN

THE MODERN LIBRARY

PUBLISHERS   ::   ::   NEW YORK

MANUFACTURED IN THE UNITED STATES OF AMERICA
FOR THE MODERN LIBRARY, INC., BY H. WOLFF

INTRODUCTION.

—

"LET us love the books which please us," observes that excellent French critic, Jules Lemaître — "and cease to trouble ourselves about classifications and schools of literature." This generous exhortation seems especially appropriate in the case of Anatole France. The author of "Le Crime de Sylvestre Bonnard" is not classifiable, — though it would be difficult to name any other modern French writer by whom the finer emotions have been touched with equal delicacy and sympathetic exquisiteness.

If by Realism we mean Truth, which alone gives value to any study of human nature, we have in Anatole France a very dainty realist;—if by Romanticism we understand that unconscious tendency of the artist to elevate truth itself beyond the range of the familiar, and into the emotional realm of aspiration, then Anatole France is betimes a romantic. And, nevertheless, as a literary figure he stands alone: neither by his distinctly Parisian refinement of method, nor yet by any definite characteristic of style, can he be

successfully attached to any special group of writers.
He is essentially of Paris, indeed;—his literary train-
ing could have been acquired in no other atmosphere:
his light grace of emotional analysis, his artistic epi-
cureanism, the vividness and quickness of his sensations, are French as his name. But he has followed
no school-traditions; and the charm of his art, at
once so impersonal and sympathetic, is wholly his
own. How marvellously well the author has succeeded in disguising himself! It is extremely difficult to believe that the diary of Sylvestre Bonnard
could have been written by a younger man; yet the
delightful sexagenarian is certainly a young man's
dream.

M. Anatole France belongs to a period of change,—
a period in which a new science and a new philosophy
have transfigured the world of ideas with unprece-
dented suddenness. All the arts have been more or
less influenced by new modes of thought,—reflecting
the exaggerated materialism of an era of transition.
The reaction is now setting in;—the creative work of
fine minds already reveals that the Art of the Future
must be that which appeals to the higher emotions
alone. Material Nature has already begun to lure
less, and human nature to gladden more;—the knowledge of Spiritual Evolution follows luminously upon
our recognition of Physical Evolution;—and the hori-

zon of human fellowship expands for us with each
fresh acquisition of knowledge,—as the sky-circle expands to those who climb a height. The works of
fiction that will live are not the creations of men who
have blasphemed the human heart, but of men who,
like Anatole France, have risen above the literary ten-
dencies of their generation, never doubting humanity,
and keeping their pages irreproachably pure. In the
art of Anatole France there is no sensuousness: his
study is altogether of the nobler emotions. What the
pessimistic coarseness of self-called "Naturalism" has
proven itself totally unable to feel, he paints for us
truthfully, simply, and touchingly,—the charm of age,
in all its gentleness, lovableness, and indulgent wisdom. The dear old man who talks about his books to
his cat, who has remained for fifty years true to the
memory of the girl he could not win, and who, in spite
of his world-wide reputation for scholarship, finds himself so totally helpless in all business matters, and so
completely at the mercy of his own generous impulses,
—may be, indeed, as the most detestable Mademoiselle
Préfère observes, "a child"; but his childishness is
only the delightful freshness of a pure and simple
heart which could never become aged. His artless
surprise at the malevolence of evil minds, his toler-
ations of juvenile impertinence, his beautiful comprehension of the value of life and the sweetness of youth,

his self-disparagements and delightful compunctions
of conscience, his absolute unselfishness and incapacity
to nourish a resentment, his fine gentle irony which
never wounds and always amuses : these, and many
other traits, combine to make him one of the most
intensely living figures created in modern French
literature. It is quite impossible to imagine him as
unreal ; and, indeed, we feel to him as to some old
friend unexpectedly met with after years of absence,
whose face and voice are perfectly familiar, but whose
name will not be remembered until he repeats it himself. We might even imagine ourselves justified in
doubting the statement of M. Lemaître that Anatole
France was not an old bachelor, but a comparatively young man, and a married man, when he imagined Sylvestre Bonnard ;—we might, in short, refuse
to believe the book not strictly autobiographical,—
but for the reflection that its other personages live
with the same vividness for us as does the Member of the Institute. Thérèse, the grim old housekeeper, so simple and faithful ; Madame and Monsieur de Gabry, those delightful friends ; the glorious,
brutal, heroic Uncle Victor ; the perfectly lovable
Jeanne : these figures are not less sympathetic in
their several rôles.

But it is not because M. Anatole France has rare
power to create original characters, or to reflect for

us something of the more recondite literary life of Paris, that his charming story will live. It is because of his far rarer power to deal with what is older than any art, and withal more young, and incomparably more precious: the beauty of what is beautiful in human emotion. And that writer who touches the spring of generous tears by some simple story of gratitude, of natural kindness, of gentle self-sacrifice, is surely more entitled to our love than the sculptor who shapes for us a dream of merely animal grace, or the painter who images for us, however richly, the young bloom of that form which is only the husk of Being!

L. H.

CONTENTS.

"But it is not because M. Anatole France has rare power to create original characters, or to reflect for us something of the more recondite literary life of Paris, that his charming story will live. It is because of his far rarer power to deal with what is older than any art, and withal more young, and incomparably more precious: the beauty of what is beautiful in human emotion."

THE CRIME OF SYLVESTRE BONNARD

Part 1.—THE LOG.

December 24, 1849.

I HAD put on my slippers and my dressing-gown. I wiped away a tear with which the north wind blowing over the quay had obscured my vision. A bright fire was leaping in the chimney of my study. Ice-crystals, shaped like fern-leaves, were sprouting over the window-panes, and concealed from me the Seine with its bridges and the Louvre of the Valois.

I drew up my easy-chair to the hearth, and my *table-volante*, and took up so much of my place by the fire as Hamilcar deigned to allow me. Hamilcar was lying in front of the andirons, curled up on a cushion, with his nose between his paws. His thick fine fur rose and fell with his regular breathing. At my coming, he slowly slipped a glance of his agate eyes at me from between his half-opened lids, which he closed again almost at once, thinking to himself, "It is nothing; it is only my friend."

"Hamilcar," I said to him, as I stretched my legs—

1

"Hamilcar, somnolent Prince of the City of Books—
thou guardian nocturnal! Like that Divine Cat who
combated the impious in Heliopolis—in the night of
the great combat—thou dost defend from vile nibblers
those books which the old savant acquired at the cost
of his slender savings and indefatigable zeal. Sleep,
Hamilcar, softly as a sultana, in this library, that shel-
ters thy military virtues; for verily in thy person are
united the formidable aspect of a Tartar warrior and
the slumbrous grace of a woman of the Orient. Sleep,
thou heroic and voluptuous Hamilcar, while awaiting
that moonlight hour in which the mice will come forth
to dance before the 'Acta Sanctorum' of the learned
Bollandists!"

The beginning of this discourse pleased Hamilcar,
who accompanied it with a throat-sound like the song
of a kettle on the fire. But as my voice waxed louder,
Hamilcar notified me by lowering his ears and by
wrinkling the striped skin of his brow that it was bad
taste on my part to so declaim.

"This old-book man," evidently thought Hamilcar,
"talks to no purpose at all, while our housekeeper
never utters a word which is not full of good sense,
full of signification—containing either the announcement of a meal or the promise of a whipping. One
knows what she says. But this old man puts together
a lot of sounds signifying nothing."

So thought Hamilcar to himself. Leaving him to
his reflections, I opened a book, which I began to read

with interest; for it was a catalogue of manuscripts.
I do not know any reading more easy, more fascinat-
ing, more delightful than that of a catalogue. The
one which I was reading—edited in 1824 by Mr.
Thompson, librarian to Sir Thomas Raleigh—sins, it
is true, by excess of brevity, and does not offer that
character of exactitude which the archivists of my
own generation were the first to introduce into works
upon diplomatics and paleography. It leaves a good
deal to be desired and to be divined. This is perhaps
why I find myself aware, while reading it, of a state
of mind which in a nature more imaginative than
mine might be called reverie. I had allowed myself
to drift away thus gently upon the current of my
thoughts, when my housekeeper announced, in a tone
of ill-humor, that Monsieur Coccoz desired to speak
with me.

In fact, some one had slipped into the library after
her. He was a little man—a poor little man of puny
appearance, wearing a thin jacket. He approached
me with a number of little bows and smiles. But he
was very pale, and, although still young and alert, he
looked ill. I thought, as I looked at him, of a wounded squirrel. He carried under his arm a green *toilette*,
which he put upon a chair; then unfastening the four
corners of the *toilette*, he uncovered a heap of little
yellow books.

"Monsieur," he then said to me, "I have not the
honor to be known to you. I am a book-agent, Mon-

sieur. I represent the leading houses of the capital, and in the hope that you will kindly honor me with your confidence, I take the liberty to offer you a few novelties."

Kind gods! just gods! such novelties as the homunculus Coccoz showed me! The first volume that he put in my hand was "L'Histoire de la Tour de Nesle," with the amours of Marguerite de Bourgogne and the Captain Buridan.

"It is a historical book," he said to me, with a smile—"a book of real history."

"In that case," I replied, "it must be very tiresome; for all the historical books which contain no lies are extremely tedious. I write some authentic ones myself; and if you were unlucky enough to carry a copy of any of them from door to door you would run the risk of keeping it all your life in that green-baize of yours, without ever finding even a cook foolish enough to buy it from you."

"Certainly, Monsieur," the little man answered, out of pure good-nature.

And, all smiling again, he offered me the "Amours d'Héloïse et d'Abeilard;" but I made him understand that, at my age, I had no use for love-stories.

Still smiling, he proposed me the "Règle des Jeux de la Société" — piquet, bésigue, écarté, whist, dice, draughts, and chess.

"Alas!" I said to him, "if you want to make me remember the rules of bésigue, give me back my old

friend Bignan, with whom I used to play cards every
evening before the Five Academies solemnly escorted
him to the cemetery ; or else bring down to the frivolous level of human amusements the grave intelligence of Hamilcar, whom you see on that cushion,
for he is the sole companion of my evenings."

The little man's smile became vague and uneasy.

"Here," he said, "is a new collection of society
amusements—jokes and puns—with a recipe for changing a red rose to a white rose."

I told him that I had fallen out with roses for a long
time, and that, as to jokes, I was satisfied with those
which I unconsciously permitted myself to make in
the course of my scientific labors.

The homunculus offered me his last book, with his
last smile.   He said to me :

"Here is the 'Clef de Songes'—the 'Key of
Dreams'—with the explanation of any dreams that
anybody can have ; dreams of gold, dreams of robbers,
dreams of death, dreams of falling from the top of a
tower. . . . It is exhaustive."

I had taken hold of the tongs, and, brandishing
them energetically, I replied to my commercial visitor :

"Yes, my friend ; but those dreams and a thousand
others, joyous or tragic, are all summed up in one—
the Dream of Life ; is your little yellow book able to
give me the key to that ?"

"Yes, Monsieur," answered the homunculus ; "the

book is complete, and is not dear—one franc twenty-five centimes, Monsieur."

I called my housekeeper—for there is no bell in my room—and said to her:

"Thérèse, Monsieur Coccoz—whom I am going to ask you to show out—has a book here which might interest you: the 'Key of Dreams.' I will be very glad to buy it for you."

My housekeeper responded:

"Monsieur, when one has not even time to dream awake, one has still less time to dream asleep. Thank God, my days are just enough for my work and my work for my days, and I am able to say every night, 'Lord, bless Thou the rest which I am going to take.' I never dream, either on my feet or in bed; and I never mistake my eider-down coverlet for a devil, like my cousin did; and, if you will allow me to give my opinion about it, I think you have books enough here now. Monsieur has thousands and thousands of books, which simply turn his head; and as for me, I have just two, which are quite enough for all my wants and purposes—my Catholic prayer-book and my 'Cuisinière Bourgeoise.'"

And with these words my housekeeper helped the little man to fasten up his stock again within the green *toilette*.

The homunculus Coccoz had ceased to smile. His relaxed features took such an expression of suffering that I felt sorry to have made fun of so unhappy a

man. I called him back, and told him that I had
caught a glimpse of a copy of the "Histoire d'Estelle
et de Némorin," which he had among his books; that
I was very fond of shepherds and shepherdesses, and
that I would be quite willing to purchase, at a reasonable price, the story of those two perfect lovers.

"I will sell you that book for one franc twenty-five
centimes, Monsieur," replied Coccoz, whose face at once
beamed with joy. "It is historical; and you will be
pleased with it. I know now just what suits you. I
see that you are a *connoisseur*. To-morrow I will bring
you the 'Crimes des Papes.' It is a good book. I
will bring you the *édition d'amateur*, with colored
plates."

I begged him not to do anything of the sort, and
sent him away happy. When the green *toilette* and
the agent had disappeared in the shadow of the corridor I asked my housekeeper whence this little man
had dropped upon us.

"Dropped is the word," she answered; "he dropped
on us from the roof, Monsieur, where he lives with his
wife."

"You say he has a wife, Thérèse? That is marvellous! women are very strange creatures! This one
must be a very unfortunate little woman."

"I don't really know what she is," answered Thérèse: "but every morning I see her trailing a silk
dress covered with grease-spots over the stairs. She
makes soft eyes at people. And, in the name of com-

mon-sense! does it become a woman that has been received here out of charity to make eyes and to wear dresses like that? For they allowed the couple to occupy the attic during the time the roof was being repaired, in consideration of the fact that the husband is sick and the wife in an interesting condition. The concierge even says that the pains came on her this morning, and that she is now confined. They must have been very badly off for a child!"

"Thérèse," I replied, "they had no need of a child, doubtless. But Nature had decided they should bring one into the world; Nature made them fall into her snare. One must have exceptional prudence to defeat Nature's schemes. Let us be sorry for them, and not blame them! As for silk dresses, there is no young woman who does not like them. The daughters of Eve adore adornment. You yourself, Thérèse—who are so serious and sensible—what a fuss you make when you have no white apron to wait at table in! But, tell me, have they got everything necessary in their attic?"

"How could they have it, Monsieur?" my housekeeper made answer. "The husband, whom you have just seen, used to be a jewelry-peddler—at least, so the concierge tells me—and nobody knows why he stopped selling watches. You have just seen that he is now selling almanacs. That is no way to make an honest living, and I never will believe that God's blessing can come to an almanac-peddler. Between our selves, the wife looks to me for all the world like a good-for-nothing—a *Marie-couche-toi-là*. I think she would be just as capable of bringing up a child as I would be of playing the guitar. Nobody seems to know where they came from; but I am sure they must have come by Misery's coach from the country of *Sans-souci*.

"Wherever they have come from, Thérèse, they are unfortunate; and their attic is cold."

"*Pardi!*—the roof is broken in several places, and the rain comes in by streams. They have neither furniture nor clothing. _ don't think cabinet-makers and weavers work much for Christians of that sect!"

"That is very sad, Thérèse; a Christian woman much less well provided for than this pagan, Hamilcar here!—what does she have to say?"

"Monsieur, I never speak to those people; I don't know what she says or what she sings. But she sings all day long; I hear her from the stairway whenever I am going out or coming in."

"Well! the heir of the Coccoz family will be able to say, like the Egg in the village riddle: '*Ma mère me fit en chantant.*' * The like happened in the case of Henry IV. When Jeanne d'Albret felt herself about to be confined she began to sing an old Béarnaise canticle:

---

* "My mother sang when she brought me into the world."

> "'Notre-Dame du bout du pont,
>   Venez à mon aide en cette heure!
>   Priez le Dieu du ciel
>   Qu'il me délivre vite,
>   Qu'il me donne un garçon!'

"It is certainly unreasonable to bring little unfortunates into the world. But the thing is done every day, my dear Thérèse, and all the philosophers on earth will never be able to reform the silly custom. Madame Coccoz has followed it, and she sings. That is creditable, at all events! But, tell me, Thérèse, have you not put on the soup to boil to-day?"

"Yes, Monsieur; and it is time for me to go and skim it."

"Good! but don't forget, Thérèse, to take a good bowl of soup out of the pot and carry it to Madame Coccoz, our Attic neighbor."

My housekeeper was on the point of leaving the room when I added, just in time:

"Thérèse, before you do anything else, please call your friend the porter, and tell him to take a good bundle of wood out of our stock and carry it up to the attic of those Coccoz folks. See, above all, that he puts a first-class log in the lot—a real Christmas log. As for the homunculus, if he comes back again, do not allow either himself or any of his yellow books to come in here."

Having taken all these little precautions with the refined egotism of an old bachelor, I returned to my catalogue again.

With what surprise, with what emotion, with what anxiety did I therein discover the following mention, which I cannot even now copy without feeling my hand tremble:

"*LA LÉGENDE DORÉE DE JACQUES DE GÊNES* (*Jacques de Voragine*);—*traduction française, petit in*-4.

"This MS. of the fourteenth century contains, besides the tolerably complete translation of the celebrated work of Jacques de Voragine, 1. The Legends of Saints Ferréol, Ferrution, Germain, Vincent, and Droctoveus; 2. A poem *On the Miraculous Burial of Monsieur Saint-Germain of Auxerre*. This translation, as well as the legends and the poem, are due to the Clerk Alexander.

"This MS. is written upon vellum. It contains a great number of illuminated letters, and two finely executed miniatures, in a rather imperfect state of conservation:— one represents the Purification of the Virgin, and the other the Coronation of Proserpine."

What a discovery! Perspiration moistened my forehead, and a veil seemed to come before my eyes. I trembled; I flushed; and, without being able to speak, I felt a sudden impulse to cry out at the top of my voice.

What a treasure! For more than forty years I had been making a special study of the history of Christian Gaul, and particularly of that glorious Abbey of Saint-Germain-des-Prés, whence issued forth those King-Monks who founded our national dynasty. Now, despite the culpable insufficiency of the description given, it was evident to me that the MS. of the Clerk Alexander must have come from the great Abbey. Everything proved this fact. All the legends added by the translator related to the pious foundation

of the Abbey by King Childebert. Then the legend
of Saint-Droctoveus was particularly significant; being the legend of the first abbot of my dear Abbey.
The poem in French verse on the burial of Saint-
Germain led me actually into the nave of that venerable basilica which was the *umbilicus* of Christian
Gaul.

The "Golden Legend" is in itself a vast and gracious work. Jacques de Voragine, Definitor of the
Order of Saint-Dominic, and Archbishop of Gênes,
collected in the thirteenth century the various legends
of Catholic saints, and formed so rich a compilation
that from all the monasteries and castles of the time
there arose the cry: "This is the 'Golden Legend.'"
The "Légende Dorée" was especially opulent in Roman
hagiography. Edited by an Italian monk, it reveals
its best merits in the treatment of matters relating to
the terrestrial domains of Saint Peter. Voragine can
only perceive the greater saints of the Occident as
through a cold mist. For this reason the Aquitanian
and Saxon translators of the good legend-writer were
careful to add to his recital the lives of their own
national saints.

I have read and collated a great many manuscripts
of the "Golden Legend." I know all those described
by my learned colleague, M. Paulin Paris, in his handsome catalogue of the MSS. of the Bibliothèque du
Roi. There were two among them which especially
drew my attention. One is of the fourteenth cen-

tury, and contains a translation of Jean Belet; the other, younger by a century, includes the version of Jacques Vignay. Both come from the Colbert collection, and were placed on the shelves of that glorious Colbertine library by the Librarian Baluze—whose name I can never pronounce without uncovering my head; for even in the century of the giants of erudition, Baluze astounds by his greatness. I know also a very curious codex of the Bigot collection; I know seventy-four printed editions of the work, commencing with the venerable ancestor of all—the Gothic of Strasburg, begun in 1471, and finished in 1475. But no one of those MSS., no one of those editions, contains the legends of Saints Ferréol, Ferrution, Germain, Vincent, and Droctoveus; no one bears the name of the Clerk Alexander; no one, in fine, came from the Abbey of Saint-Germain-des-Prés. Compared with the MS. described by Mr. Thompson, they are only as straw to gold. I have seen with my eyes, I have touched with my fingers, an incontrovertible testimony to the existence of this document. But the document itself—what has become of it? Sir Thomas Raleigh went to end his days by the shores of the Lake of Como, whither he carried with him a part of his literary wealth. Where did the books go after the death of that aristocratic collector? Where could the manuscript of the Clerk Alexander have gone?

"And why," I asked myself, " why should I have

learned that this precious book exists, if I am never to possess it—never even to see it? I would go to seek it in the burning heart of Africa, or in the icy regions of the Pole if I knew it were there. But I do not know where it is. I do not know if it be guarded in a triple-locked iron case by some jealous bibliomaniac. I do not know if it be growing mouldy in the attic of some ignoramus. I shudder at the thought that perhaps its torn-out leaves may have been used to cover the pickle-jars of some house-keeper."

August 30, 1850.

THE heavy heat compelled me to walk slowly. I kept close to the walls of the north quays; and, in the lukewarm shade, the shops of the dealers in old books, engravings, and antiquated furniture drew my eyes and appealed to my fancy. Rummaging and idling among these, I hastily enjoyed some verses spiritedly thrown off by a poet of the Pleiad. I examined an elegant Masquerade by Watteau. I felt, with my eye, the weight of a two-handed sword, a steel *gorgerin*, a morion. What a thick helmet! What a ponderous breastplate—*Seigneur!* A giant's garb? No—the carapace of an insect. The men of those days were cuirassed like beetles; their weakness was within them. To-day, on the contrary, our strength is interior, and our armed souls dwell in feeble bodies.

. . . Here is a pastel-portrait of a lady of the old
time — the face, vague like a shadow, smiles; and a
hand, gloved with an openwork mitten, retains upon
her satiny knees a lap-dog, with a ribbon about its
neck. That picture fills me with a sort of charming
melancholy. Let those who have no half-effaced pas-
tels in their own hearts laugh at me! Like the horse
that scents the stable, I hasten my pace as I near
my lodgings. There it is — that great human hive,
in which I have a cell, for the purpose of therein
distilling the somewhat acrid honey of erudition. I
climb the stairs with slow effort. Only a few steps
more, and I shall be at my own door. But I divine,
rather than see, a robe descending with a sound of
rustling silk. I stop, and press myself against the
balustrade to make room. The lady who is coming
down is bareheaded; she is young; she sings; her
eyes and teeth gleam in the shadow, for she laughs
with lips and eyes at the same time. She is certainly a neighbor, and a very familiar one. She holds
in her arms a pretty child, a little boy—quite naked,
like the son of a goddess; he has a medal hung round
his neck by a little silver chain. I see him sucking
his thumbs and looking at me with those big eyes
so newly opened on this old universe. The mother
simultaneously looks at me in a sly, mysterious way;
she stops—I think blushes a little—and holds out the
little creature to me. The baby has a pretty wrinkle
between wrist and arm, a pretty wrinkle about his

neck, and all over him, from head to foot, the dain-
tiest dimples laugh in his rosy flesh.

The mamma shows him to me with pride.

"Monsieur," she says, "don't you think he is very
pretty—my little boy?"

She takes one tiny hand, lifts it to the child's own
lips, and, drawing out the darling pink fingers again
towards me, says,

"Baby, throw the gentleman a kiss."

Then, folding the little being in her arms, she flees
away with the agility of a cat, and is lost to sight in
a corridor which, judging by the odor, must lead to
some kitchen.

I enter my own quarters.

"Thérèse, who can that young mother be whom I
saw bareheaded in the stairway just now, with a
pretty little boy?"

And Thérèse replies that it was Madame Coccoz.

I stare up at the ceiling, as if trying to obtain some
further illumination. Thérèse then recalls to me the
little book-peddler who tried to sell me almanacs last
year, while his wife was being confined.

"And Coccoz himself?" I asked.

I was answered that I would never see him again.
The poor little man had been laid away under ground,
without my knowledge, and, indeed, with the knowledge of very few people, only a short time after the
happy delivery of Madame Coccoz. I learned that his
wife had been able to console herself. I did likewise.

"But, Thérèse," I asked, "has Madame Coccoz got everything she needs in that attic of hers?"

"You would be a great dupe, Monsieur," replied my housekeeper, "if you should bother yourself about that creature. They gave her notice to quit the attic when the roof was repaired. But she stays there yet—in spite of the proprietor, the agent, the concierge, and the bailiffs. I think she has bewitched every one of them. She will leave that attic when she pleases, Monsieur; but she is going to leave in her own carriage. Let me tell you that!"

Thérèse reflected for a moment; and then uttered these words:

"A pretty face is a curse from Heaven."

"Then I ought to thank Heaven for having spared me that curse. But here! put my hat and cane away. I am going to amuse myself with a few pages of Moréri. If I can trust my old fox-nose, we are going to have a nicely flavored pullet for dinner. Look after that estimable fowl, my girl, and spare your neighbors, so that you and your old master may be spared by them in turn."

Having thus spoken, I proceeded to follow out the tufted ramifications of a princely genealogy.

—

May 7, 1851.

I HAVE passed the winter according to the ideal of the sages, *in angello cum libello;* and now the swal-

2

lows of the Quai Malaquais find me on their return
about as when they left me. He who lives little,
changes little; and it is scarcely living at all to use
up one's days over old texts.

Yet I feel myself to-day a little more deeply im-
pregnated than ever before with that vague melancholy which life distils. The economy of my intelligence (I dare scarcely confess it to myself!) has remained disturbed ever since that momentous hour in
which the existence of the manuscript of the Clerk
Alexander was first revealed to me.

It is strange that I should have lost my rest simply
on account of a few old sheets of parchment; but it
is unquestionably true. The poor man who has no
desires possesses the greatest of riches; he possesses
himself. The rich man who desires something is only
a wretched slave. I am just such a slave. The sweet-
est pleasures—those of converse with some one of a
delicate and well-balanced mind, or dining out with a
friend—are insufficient to enable me to forget the
manuscript which I know that I want, and have been
wanting from the moment I knew of its existence.
I feel the want of it by day and by night: I feel the
want of it in all my joys and pains; I feel the want
of it while at work or asleep.

I recall my desires as a child. How well I can now
comprehend the intense wishes of my early years!

I can see once more, with astonishing vividness, a
certain doll which, when I was eight years old, used

to be displayed in the window of an ugly little shop of the Rue de la Seine. I cannot tell how it happened that this doll attracted me. I was very proud of being a boy; I despised little girls; and I longed impatiently for the day (which, alas! has come) when a strong white beard should bristle on my chin. I played at being a soldier; and, under the pretext of obtaining forage for my rocking-horse, I used to make sad havoc among the plants my poor mother used to keep on her window-sill. Manly amusements those, I should say! And, nevertheless, I was consumed with longing for a doll. Characters like Hercules have such weaknesses occasionally. Was the one I had fallen in love with at all beautiful? No. I can see her now. She had a splotch of vermilion on either cheek, short soft arms, horrible wooden hands, and long sprawling legs. Her flowered petticoat was fastened at the waist with two pins. Even now I can see the black heads of those two pins. It was a decidedly vulgar doll—smelt of the *faubourg*. I remember perfectly well that, even child as I was then, before I had put on my first pair of trousers, I was quite conscious in my own way that this doll lacked grace and style—that she was gross, that she was coarse. But I loved her in spite of that; I loved her just for that; I loved her only; I wanted her. My soldiers and my drums had become as nothing in my eyes. I ceased to stick sprigs of heliotrope and veronica into the mouth of my rocking-horse. That

doll was all the world to me. I invented ruses worthy
of a savage to oblige Virginie, my nurse, to take me
by the little shop in the Rue de la Seine. I would
press my nose against the window until my nurse had
to take my arm and drag me away. "Monsieur Sylvestre, it is late, and your mamma will scold you."
Monsieur Sylvestre in those days made very little of
either scoldings or whippings. But his nurse lifted
him up like a feather, and Monsieur Sylvestre yielded
to force. In after-years, with age, he degenerated,
and sometimes yielded to fear. But at that time he
used to fear nothing.

I was unhappy. An unreasoning but irresistible
shame prevented me from telling my mother about
the object of my love. Thence all my sufferings.
For many days that doll, incessantly present in fancy,
danced before my eyes, stared at me fixedly, opened
her arms to me, assuming in my imagination a sort
of life which made her appear at once mysterious and
weird, and thereby all the more charming and desir-
able.

Finally, one day—a day I shall never forget—my
nurse took me to see my uncle, Captain Victor, who
had invited me to breakfast. I admired my uncle a
great deal, as much because he had fired the last
French cartridge at Waterloo, as because he used to
make with his own hands, at my mother's table, certain *chapons-à-l'ail*, which he afterwards put into the
chicory-salad. I thought that was very fine! My

Uncle Victor also inspired me with much respect by his frogged coat, and still more by his way of turning the whole house upside down from the moment he came into it. Even now I cannot tell just how he managed it, but I can affirm that whenever my Uncle Victor found himself in any assembly of twenty persons, it was impossible to see or to hear anybody but him. My excellent father, I have reason to believe, never shared my admiration for Uncle Victor, who used to sicken him with his pipe, gave him great thumps in the back by way of friendliness, and accused him of lacking energy. My mother, though always showing a sister's indulgence to the captain, sometimes advised him to fondle the brandy-bottle a little less frequently. But I had no part either in these repugnances or these reproaches, and Uncle Victor inspired me with the purest enthusiasm. It was therefore with a feeling of pride that I entered into the little lodging-house where he lived, in the Rue Guénégaud. The entire breakfast, served on a small table close to the fire-place, consisted of pork meats and confectionery.

The Captain stuffed me with cakes and pure wine. He told me of numberless injustices to which he had been a victim. He complained particularly of the Bourbons; and as he neglected to tell me who the Bourbons were, I got the idea—I can't tell how—that the Bourbons were horse-dealers established at Waterloo. The Captain, who never interrupted his talk ex cept for the purpose of pouring out wine, furthermore made charges against a number of *morveux*, of *jean-fesses*, and "good-for-nothings" whom I did not know anything about, but whom I hated from the bottom of my heart. At dessert I thought I heard the Captain say my father was a man who could be led anywhere by the nose; but I am not quite sure that I understood him. I had a buzzing in my ears; and it seemed to me that the table was dancing.

My uncle put on his frogged coat, took his *chapeau tromblon*, and we descended to the street, which seemed to me singularly changed. It looked to me as if I had not been in it before for ever so long a time. Nevertheless, when we came to the Rue de la Seine, the idea of my doll suddenly returned to my mind and excited me in an extraordinary way. My head was on fire. I resolved upon a desperate expedient. We were passing before the window. She was there, behind the glass — with her red cheeks, and her flowered petticoat, and her long legs.

"Uncle," I said, with a great effort, "will you buy that doll for me?"

And I waited.

"Buy a doll for a boy—*sacrebleu!*" cried my uncle, in a voice of thunder. "Do you wish to dishonor yourself? And it is that old Mag there that you want! Well, I must compliment you, my young fellow! If you grow up with such tastes as that, you will never have any pleasure in life; and your com-

rades will call you a precious ninny. If you asked me
for a sword or a gun, my boy, I would buy them for
you with the last silver crown of my pension. But to
buy a doll for you—a thousand thunders!—to disgrace
you! Never in the world! Why, if I were ever to
see you playing with a puppet rigged out like that,
Monsieur, my sister's son, I would disown you for my
nephew!"

On hearing these words, I felt my heart so wrung
that nothing but pride—a diabolic pride—kept me
from crying.

My uncle, suddenly calming down, returned to his
ideas about the Bourbons; but I, still smarting from
the blow of his indignation, felt an unspeakable shame.
My resolve was quickly made. I promised myself
never to disgrace myself—I firmly and forever re-
nounced that red-cheeked doll.

I felt that day, for the first time, the austere sweetness of sacrifice.

Captain, though it be true that all your life you
swore like a pagan, smoked like a beadle, and drank
like a bell-ringer, be your memory nevertheless honored—not merely because you were a brave soldier,
but also because you revealed to your little nephew in
petticoats the sentiment of heroism! Pride and lazi-
ness had made you almost insupportable, O my Uncle
Victor!—but a great heart used to beat under those
frogs upon your coat. You always used to wear, I
now remember, a rose in your button-hole. That rose

which you allowed, as I now have reason to believe. the shop-girls to pluck for you—that large, open-hearted flower, scattering its petals to all the winds, was the symbol of your glorious youth. You despised neither absinthe nor tobacco; but you despised life. Neither delicacy nor common-sense could have been learned from you, Captain; but you taught me, even at an age when my nurse had to wipe my nose, a lesson of honor and self-abnegation that I will never forget.

You have now been sleeping for many years in the Cemetery of Mont-Parnasse, under a plain slab bearing this epitaph :

CI-GIT

ARISTIDE VICTOR MALDENT,

CAPITAINE D'INFANTERIE,

CHEVALIER DE LA LEGION D'HONNEUR.

But such, Captain, was not the inscription devised by yourself to be placed above those old bones of yours —knocked about so long on fields of battle and in haunts of pleasure. Among your papers was found this proud and bitter epitaph, which, despite your last will, none could have ventured to put upon your tomb :

CI-GIT

UN BRIGAND DE LA LOIRE.

" Thérèse, we will get a wreath of immortelles to-morrow, and lay them on the tomb of the ' Brigand of the Loire.' " . . .

But Thérèse is not here. And how, indeed, could

she be near me, seeing that I am at the *rond-point* of the Champs-Élysées? There, at the termination of the avenue, the Arc de Triomphe, which bears under its vaults the names of Uncle Victor's companions-in-arms, opens its giant gate against the sky. The trees of the avenue are unfolding to the sun of spring their first leaves, still all pale and chilly. Beside me the carriages keep rolling by to the Bois de Boulogne. Unconsciously I have wandered into this fashionable avenue on my promenade, and halted, quite stupidly, in front of a booth stocked with gingerbread and decanters of liquorice-water, each topped by a lemon. A miserable little boy, covered with rags, which expose his chapped skin, stares with widely opened eyes at those sumptuous sweets which are not for such as he. With the shamelessness of innocence he betrays his longing. His round, fixed eyes contemplate a certain gingerbread man of lofty stature. It is a general, and it looks a little like Uncle Victor I take it, I pay for it, and present it to the little pauper, who dares not extend his hand to receive it—for, by reason of precocious experience, he cannot believe in luck; he looks at me, in the same way that certain big dogs do, with the air of one saying, " You are cruel to make fun of me like that!"

" Come, little stupid," I say to him, in that rough tone I am accustomed to use, " take it—take it, and eat it; for you, happier than I was at your age, you can satisfy your tastes without disgracing yourself." . . .

And you, Uncle Victor—you, whose manly figure has
been recalled to me by that gingerbread general, come,
glorious Shadow, help me to forget my new doll. We
remain forever children, and are always running after
new toys.

Same day.

In the oddest way that Coccoz family has become
associated in my mind with the Clerk Alexander.

"Thérèse," I said, as I threw myself into my easy-
chair, "tell me if the little Coccoz is well, and whether
he has got his first teeth yet—and bring me my slippers."

"He ought to have them by this time, Monsieur,"
replied Thérèse; "but I never saw them. The very
first fine day of spring the mother disappeared with
the child, leaving furniture and clothes and everything
behind her. They found thirty-eight empty pomade-
pots in the attic. It exceeds all belief! She had visitors latterly; and you may be quite sure she is not now
in a convent of nuns. The niece of the concierge says
she saw her driving about in a carriage on the boulevards. I always told you she would end badly."

"Thérèse," I replied, "that young woman has not
ended either badly or well as yet. Wait until the
term of her life is over to judge her. And be careful
not to talk too much with that concierge. It seemed
to me—though I only saw her for a moment on the
stairs—that Madame Coccoz was very fond of her

child. For that mother's-love, at least, she deserves credit."

"As far as that goes, Monsieur, certainly the little one never wanted for anything. In all the Quarter one could not have found a child better kept, or better nourished, or more petted and coddled. Every God's-day she puts a clean bib on him, and sings to him to make him laugh from morning till night."

"Thérèse, a poet has said, 'That child whose mother has never smiled upon him is worthy neither of the table of the gods nor of the couch of the goddesses.'"

July 8, 1852.

HAVING been informed that the Chapel of the Virgin at Saint-Germain-des-Prés was being repaved, I entered the church with the hope of discovering some old inscriptions, possibly exposed by the labors of the workmen. I was not disappointed. The architect kindly showed me a stone which he had just had raised up against the wall. I knelt down to look at the inscription engraved upon that stone; and then, half aloud, I read in the shadow of the old apsis these words, which made my heart leap:

"*Cy-gist Alexandre, moyne de cette église, qui fist mettre en argent le menton de Saint-Vincent et de Saint-Amant et le pié des Innocens; qui toujours en son vivant fut preud 'homme et vayllant. Priez pour l'âme de lui.*"

I wiped gently away with my handkerchief the dust covering that burial-stone; I could have kissed it.

"It is he! it is Alexander!" I cried out; and from the height of the vaults the name fell back upon me with a clang, as if broken.

The silent severity of the beadle, whom I saw advancing towards me, made me ashamed of my enthusiasm; and I fled between the two holy-water sprinklers with which two rival "*rats d'église*" seemed desirous of barring my way.

At all events it was certainly my own Alexander! there could be no more doubt possible; the translator of the "Golden Legend," the author of the lives of Saints Germain, Vincent, Ferréol, Ferrution, and Droctoveus was, just as I had supposed, a monk of Saint-Germain-des-Prés. And what a good monk, too—pious and generous! He had a silver chin, a silver head, and a silver foot made, that certain precious remains should be covered with an incorruptible envelope! But will I never be able to know his work? or is this new discovery only destined to increase my regrets?

––––

August 20, 1859.

"I, that please some, try all; both joy and terror
  Of good and bad; that make and unfold error—
  Now take upon me, in the name of Time
  To use my wings. Impute it not a crime
  To me or my swift passage, that I slide
  O'er years."

Who speaks thus? 'Tis an old man whom I know too well. It is Time.

Shakespeare, after having terminated the third act of the "Winter's Tale," pauses in order to leave time for little Perdita to grow up in wisdom and in beauty; and when he raises the curtain again he evokes the ancient Scythe-bearer upon the stage to render account to the audience of those many long days which have weighed down upon the head of the jealous Leontes.

Like Shakespeare in his play, I have left in this diary of mine a long interval to oblivion; and after the fashion of the poet, I make Time himself intervene to explain the omission of ten whole years. Ten whole years, indeed, have passed since I wrote one single line in this diary; and now that I take up the pen again, I have not the pleasure, alas! to describe a Perdita "now grown in grace." Youth and beauty are the faithful companions of poets; but those charming phantoms scarcely visit the rest of us, even for the space of a season. We do not know how to retain them with us. If the fair shade of some Perdita should ever, through some inconceivable whim, take a notion to traverse my brain, she would hurt herself horribly against heaps of dog-eared parchments. Happy the poets!—their white hairs never scare away the hovering shades of Helens, Francescas, Juliets, Julias, and Dorotheas! But the nose alone of Sylvestre Bonnard would put to flight the whole swarm of love's heroines.

Yet I, like others, have felt beauty; I have known

that mysterious charm which Nature has lent to animate form; and the clay which lives has given to me that shudder of delight which makes the lover and the poet. But I have never known either how to love or how to sing. Now, in my memory—all encumbered as it is with the rubbish of old texts—I can discern again, like a miniature forgotten in some attic, a certain bright young face, with violet eyes. . . . Why, Bonnard, my friend, what an old fool you are becoming! Read that catalogue which a Florentine bookseller sent you this very morning. It is a catalogue of Manuscripts; and he promises you a description of several famous ones, long preserved by the collectors of Italy and Sicily. There is something better suited to you, something more in keeping with your present appearance.

I read; I cry out! Hamilcar, who has assumed with the approach of age an air of gravity that intimidates me, looks at me reproachfully, and seems to ask me whether there is any rest in this world, since he cannot enjoy it beside me, who am old also like himself.

In the sudden joy of my discovery, I need a confidant; and it is to the sceptic Hamilcar that I address myself with all the effusion of a happy man.

"No, Hamilcar! no," I said to him; "there is no rest in this world, and the quietude you long for is incompatible with the duties of life. And you say that we are old, indeed! Listen to what I read in this catalogue, and then tell me whether this is a time to be reposing·

**"'*LA LÉGENDE DORÉE DE JACQUES DE VORAGINE;—*
traduction française du quatorzième siècle, par le Clerc Ale-
xandre.

"'Superb MS., ornamented with two miniatures, wonderfully executed,
and in a perfect state of conservation:—one representing the Purification
of the Virgin, the other the Coronation of Proserpine.

"'At the termination of the "Légende Dorée" are the Legends of Saints
Ferréol, Ferrution, Germain, and Droctoveus (xxviij pp.), and the Miraculous Sepulture of Monsieur Saint-Germain d'Auxerre (xij pp.).

"'This rare manuscript, which formed part of the collection of Sir
Thomas Raleigh, is now in the private study of Signor Micael-Angelo
Polizzi, ot Girgenti.'

"You hear that, Hamilcar? The manuscript of the
Clerk Alexander is in Sicily, at the house of Micael-
Angelo Polizzi. Heaven grant he may be a friend of
learned men! I am going to write to him!"

Which I did forthwith. In my letter I requested
Signor Polizzi to allow me to examine the manuscript
of Clerk Alexander, stating on what grounds I ventured to consider myself worthy of so great a favor.
I offered at the same time to put at his disposal several
unpublished texts in my own possession, not devoid of
interest. I begged him to favor me with a prompt
reply, and below my signature I wrote down all my
honorific titles.

"Monsieur! Monsieur! where are you running like
that?" cried Thérèse, quite alarmed, coming down the
stairs in pursuit of me, four steps at a time, with my
hat in her hand.

"I am going to post a letter, Thérèse."

"*Seigneur-Dieu!* is that a way to run out in the
street, bareheaded, like a crazy man?"

"I am crazy, I know, Thérèse. But who is not? Give me my hat, quick!"

"And your gloves, Monsieur! and your umbrella!"

I had reached the bottom of the stairs, but still heard her protesting and lamenting.

October 10, 1859.

I AWAITED Signor Polizzi's reply with ill-contained impatience. I could not even remain quiet; I would make sudden nervous gestures—open books and violently close them again. One day I happened to upset a book with my elbow—a volume of Moréri. Hamilcar, who was washing himself, suddenly stopped, and looked angrily at me, with his paw over his ear. Was this the tumultuous existence he must expect under my roof? Had there not been a tacit understanding between us that we should live a peaceful life? I had broken the covenant.

"My poor dear comrade," I made answer, "I am the victim of a violent passion, which agitates and masters me. The passions are enemies of peace and quiet, I acknowledge; but without them there would be no arts or industries in the world. Everybody would sleep naked on a manure-heap; and you would not be able, Hamilcar, to repose all day on a silken cushion, in the City of Books."

I expatiated no further to Hamilcar on the theory of the passions, however, because my housekeeper brought me a letter. It bore the postmark of Naples, and read as follows:

"MOST ILLUSTRIOUS SIR,—I do indeed possess that incomparable manuscript of the 'Golden Legend' which could not escape your keen observation. All-important reasons, however, forbid me, imperiously, tyrannically, to let the manuscript go out of my possession for a single day, for even a single minute. It will be a joy and pride for me to have you examine it in my humble home at Girgenti, which will be embellished and illuminated by your presence. It is with the most anxious expectation of your visit that I presume to sign myself, Seigneur Academician,

"Your humble and devoted servant,

"MICAEL-ANGELO POLIZZI,

"Wine-merchant and Archæologist at Girgenti, Sicily."

Well, then! I will go to Sicily:

"*Extremum hunc, Arethusa, mihi concede laborem.*"

———

October 25, 1859.

MY resolve had been taken and my preparations made; it only remained for me to notify my house-keeper. I must acknowledge it was a long time before I could make up my mind to tell her I was going away. I feared her remonstrances, her railleries, her objurgations, her tears. "She is a good, kind girl," I said to myself; "she is attached to me; she will want to prevent me from going; and the Lord knows that when she has her mind set upon anything, gestures and cries cost her no effort. In this instance she will be sure to call the concierge, the scrubber, the mattress-

3

maker, and the seven sons of the fruit-seller; they will all kneel down in a circle around me; they will begin to cry, and then they will look so ugly that I shall be obliged to yield, so as not to have the pain of seeing them any more."

Such were the awful images, the sick dreams, which fear marshalled before my imagination. Yes, fear— "fecund Fear," as the poet says—gave birth to these monstrosities in my brain. For—I may as well make the confession in these private pages—I am afraid of my housekeeper. I am aware that she knows I am weak; and this fact alone is sufficient to dispel all my courage in any contest with her. Contests are of frequent occurrence; and I invariably succumb.

But for all that, I had to announce my departure to Thérèse. She came into the library with an armful of wood to make a little fire—"*une flambée*," she said. For the mornings are chilly. I watched her out of the corner of my eye while she crouched down at the hearth, with her head in the opening of the fire-place. I do not know how I then found the courage to speak, but I did so without much hesitation. I got up, and, walking up and down the room, observed in a careless tone, with that swaggering manner characteristic of cowards,

" By the way, Thérèse, I am going to Sicily."

Having thus spoken, I awaited the consequence with great anxiety. Thérèse did not reply. Her head and her vast cap remained buried in the fire-place; and nothing in her person, which I closely watched, betrayed the least emotion. She poked some paper under the wood, and blew up the fire. That was all!

Finally I saw her face again;—it was calm—so calm that it made me vexed. "Surely," I thought to myself, "this old maid has no heart. She lets me go away without saying so much as '*Ah!*' Can the absence of her old master really affect her so little?"

"Well, then go, Monsieur," she answered, at last, "only be back here by six o'clock! There is a dish for dinner to-day which will not wait for anybody."

Naples, November 10, 1859.

"*Co tra calle vive, magna, e lave a faccia.*"

I understand, my friend—for three centimes I can eat, drink, and wash my face, all by means of one of those slices of watermelon you display there on a little table. But Occidental prejudices would prevent me from enjoying that simple pleasure freely and frankly. And how could I suck a watermelon? I have enough to do merely to keep on my feet in this crowd. What a luminous, noisy night in the Strada di Porto? Mountains of fruit tower up in the shops, illuminated by multi-colored lanterns. Upon charcoal furnaces lighted in the open air water boils and steams, and ragouts are singing in frying-pans. The smell of fried fish and hot meats tickles my nose and makes me sneeze. At this moment I find that my handkerchief has left the pocket of my frock-coat. I am pushed, lifted up, and turned about in every direction by the gayest, the most talkative, the most animated, and the most adroit populace possible to imagine; and suddenly a young woman of the people, while I am admiring her magnificent hair, with a single shock of her powerful elastic shoulder, pushes me staggering three paces back at least, without injury, into the arms of a maccaroni-eater, who receives me with a smile.

I am in Naples. How I ever managed to arrive here, with a few mutilated and shapeless remains of baggage, I cannot tell, because I am no longer myself. I have been travelling in a condition of perpetual fright; and I think that I must have looked awhile ago in this bright city like an owl bewildered by sunshine. To-night it is much worse! Wishing to obtain a glimpse of popular manners, I went to the Strada di Porto, where I now am. All about me animated throngs of people crowd and press before the eating-places; and I float like a waif among these living surges, which, even while they submerge you, still caress. For this Neapolitan people has, in its very vivacity, something indescribably gentle and polite. I am not roughly jostled, I am merely swayed about; and I think that by dint of thus rocking me to and fro, these good folks want to lull me asleep on my feet. I admire, as I tread the lava pavements of the *strada*, those porters and fishermen who move by me chatting, singing, smoking, gesticulating, quarrelling, and embracing each other the next moment with astonishing versatility of mood. They live through all their senses at the same time; and, being philosophers without knowing it, keep the measure of their desires in accordance with the brevity of life. I approach a much-patronized tavern, and see inscribed above the entrance this quatrain in Neapolitan patois:

> *" Amice, alliegre magnammo e bevimmo*
> *Nfin che n'ce stace noglio a la lucerna :*
> *Chi sa s'a l'autro munno n'ce vedimmo ?*
> *Chi sa s'a l'autro munno n'ce taverna ?"* *

Even such counsels was Horace wont to give to his friends. You received them, Posthumus; you heard them also, Leuconoë, perverse beauty who wished to know the secrets of the future. That future is now the past, and we know it well. Of a truth you were foolish to worry yourselves about so small a matter; and your friend showed his good sense when he told you to take life wisely and to filter your Greek wines— *"Sapias, vina liques."* Even thus the sight of a fair land under a spotless sky urges to the pursuit of quiet pleasures. But there are souls forever harassed by some sublime discontent; those are the noblest. You were of such, Leuconoë; and I, visiting for the first time, in my declining years, that city where your beauty was famed of old, I salute with deep respect your

---

* " Friends, let us merrily eat and drink as long as oil remains in the lamp. Who knows if we shall meet again in the other world ? Who knows if in the other world there be a tavern ?"

melancholy memory.   Those souls of kin to your own
who appeared in the age of Christianity were souls of
saints ; and the " Golden Legend " is full of the miracles
they wrought.   Your friend Horace left a less noble
posterity, and I see one of his descendants in the person
of that tavern poet, who at this moment is serving out
wine in cups under the epicurean motto of his sign.

And yet life decides in favor of friend Flaccus, and
his philosophy is the only one which adapts itself to
the course of events.   There is a fellow leaning against
that trellis-work covered with vine-leaves, and eating
an ice, while watching the stars.   He would not stoop
even to pick up the old manuscript I am going to seek
with so much trouble and fatigue.   And in truth man
is made rather to eat ices than to pore over old texts.

I continued to wander about among the drinkers
and the singers.   There were lovers biting into beautiful fruit, each with an arm about the other's waist.
Man must be naturally bad ; for all this strange joy
only evoked in me a feeling of uttermost despondency.
That thronging populace displayed such artless delight in the simple act of living, that all the shynesses
begotten by my old habits as an author awoke and
intensified into something like fright.   Furthermore, I
found myself much discouraged by my inability to
understand a word of all the storm of chatter about
me.   It was a humiliating experience for a philologist.
Thus I had begun to feel quite sulky, when I was
startled to hear some one just behind me observe :

"Dimitri, that old man is certainly a Frenchman. He looks so bewildered that I really feel sorry for him. Shall I speak to him? . . . He has such a good-natured look, with that round back of his—do you not think so, Dimitri?"

It was said in French by a woman's voice. For the moment it was disagreeable to hear myself spoken of as an old man. Is a man old at sixty-two? Only the other day, on the Pont des Arts, my colleague Perrot d'Avrignac complimented me on my youthful appearance; and I should think him a better authority about one's age than that young chatterbox who has taken it on herself to make remarks about my back. My back is round, she says. Ah! ah! I had some suspicion myself to that effect, but I am not going now to believe it at all, since it is the opinion of a giddy-headed young woman. Certainly I will not turn my head round to see who it was that spoke; but I am sure it was a pretty woman. Why? Because she talks like a capricious person and like a spoiled child. Ugly women may be naturally quite as capricious as pretty ones; but as they are never petted and spoiled, and as no allowances are made for them, they soon find themselves obliged either to suppress their whims or to hide them. On the other hand, the pretty women can be just as fantastical as they please. My neighbor is evidently one of the latter. . . . But, after all, coming to think it over, she really did nothing worse than to express, in her own way, a kindly thought about me, for which I ought to feel grateful.

These reflections—including the last and decisive one—passed through my mind in less than a second; and if I have taken a whole minute to tell them, it is only because I am a bad writer, which failing is characteristic of most philologists. In less than a second, therefore, after the voice had ceased, I did turn round, and saw a pretty little woman—a sprightly brunette.

"Madame," I said, with a bow, "excuse my involuntary indiscretion. I could not help overhearing what you have just said. You would like to be of service to a poor old man. And the wish, Madame, has already been fulfilled—the mere sound of a French voice has given me such pleasure that I must thank you."

I bowed again, and turned to go away; but my foot slipped upon a melon-rind, and I would certainly have embraced the Parthenopean soil had not the young lady put out her hand and caught me.

There is a force in circumstances—even in the very smallest circumstances — against which resistance is vain. I resigned myself to remain the *protégé* of the fair unknown.

"It is late," she said; "do you not wish to go back to your hotel, which must be quite close to ours—unless it be the same one?"

"Madame," I replied, "I do not know what time it is, because somebody has stolen my watch; but I think, as you say, that it must be time to retire; and I will be very glad to regain my hotel in the company of such courteous compatriots."

So saying, I bowed once more to the young lady, and also saluted her companion, a silent colossus with a gentle and melancholy face.

After having gone a little way with them, I learned, among other matters, that my new acquaintances were the Prince and Princess Trépof, and that they were making a trip round the world for the purpose of finding match-boxes, of which they were making a collection.

We proceeded along a narrow, tortuous *vicoletto*, lighted only by a single lamp burning in the niche of a Madonna. The purity and transparency of the air gave a celestial softness and clearness to the very darkness itself; and one could find one's way without difficulty under such a limpid night. But in a little while we began to pass through a " venella," or, in Neapolitan parlance, a *sottoportico*, which led under so many archways and so many far-projecting balconies that no gleam of light from the sky could reach us. My young guide had made us take this route as a short cut, she assured us; but I think she did so quite as much simply in order to show that she felt at home in Naples, and knew the city thoroughly. Indeed, she needed to know it very thoroughly to venture by night into that labryinth of subterranean alleys and flights of steps. If ever any man showed absolute docility in allowing himself to be guided, that man was myself. Dante never followed the steps of Beatrice with more confidence than I felt in following those of Princess Trépof.

The lady appeared to find some pleasure in my conversation, for she invited me to take a carriage-drive with her on the morrow to visit the grotto of Posilippo and the tomb of Virgil. She declared she had seen me somewhere before; but she could not remember if it had been at Stockholm or at Canton. In the former event I was a very celebrated professor of geology; in the latter, a provision-merchant whose courtesy and kindness had been much appreciated. One thing certain was that she had seen my back somewhere before.

"Excuse me," she added; "we are continually travelling, my husband and I, to collect match-boxes and to change our *ennui* by changing country. Perhaps it would be more reasonable to content ourselves with a single variety of *ennui*. But we have made all our preparations and arrangements for travelling: all our plans have been laid out in advance, and it gives us no trouble, whereas it would be very troublesome for us to stop anywhere in particular. I tell you all this so that you may not be surprised if my recollections have become a little mixed up. But from the moment I first saw you at a distance this evening, I felt —in fact I knew—that I had seen you before. Now the question is, 'Where was it that I saw you?' You are not, then, either the geologist or the provision-merchant?"

"No, Madame," I replied, "I am neither the one nor the other; and I am sorry for it—since you have had reason to esteem them. There is really nothing about me worthy of your interest. I have spent all my life poring over books, and I have never travelled: you might have known that from my bewilderment, which excited your compassion. I am a member of the Institute."

" You are a member of the Institute ! How nice ! Will you not write something for me in my album ? Do you know Chinese ? I would like so much to have you write something in Chinese or Persian in my album. I will introduce you to my friend, Miss Fergusson, who travels everywhere to see all the famous people in the world. She will be delighted ! . . . Dimitri, did you hear that ?—this gentleman is a member of the Institute, and he has passed all his life over books."

The prince nodded approval.

" Monsieur," I said, trying to engage him in our conversation, " it is true that something can be learned from books ; but a great deal more can be learned by travelling, and I regret that I have not been able to go round the world like you. I have lived in the same house for thirty years, and I scarcely ever go out."

" Lived in the same house for thirty years !" cried Madame Trépof ; is it possible ?"

" Yes, Madame," I answered. " But you must know the house is situated on the bank of the Seine, and in the very handsomest and most famous part of the world. From my window I can see the Tuileries and the Louvre, the Pont-Neuf, the towers of Notre-Dame, the turrets of the Palais de Justice, and the spire of the Sainte-Chapelle. All those stones speak to me; they tell me stories about the days of Saint-Louis, of the Valois, of Henri IV., and of Louis XIV. I understand them, and I love them all. It is only a very small corner of the world, but honestly, Madame, where is there a more glorious spot?"

At this moment we found ourselves upon a public square—a *largo* steeped in the soft glow of the night. Madame Trépof looked at me in an uneasy manner; her lifted eyebrows almost touched the black curls about her forehead.

"Where do you live, then?" she demanded, brusquely.

"On the Quai Malaquais, Madame, and my name is Bonnard. It is not a name very widely known, but I am contented if my friends do not forget it."

This revelation, unimportant as it was, produced an extraordinary effect upon Madame Trépof. She immediately turned her back upon me and caught her husband's arm.

"Come, Dimitri!" she exclaimed, "do walk a little faster. I am horribly tired, and you will not hurry yourself in the least. We shall never get home. . . . As for you, monsieur, your way lies over there!"

She made a vague gesture in the direction of some dark *vicolo*, pushed her husband the opposite way, and called to me, without even turning her head,

"Adieu, Monsieur! We shall not go to Posilippo to-morrow, nor the day after, either. I have a frightful headache! Dimitri, you are unendurable! Will you not walk faster?"

I remained for the moment stupefied, vainly trying to think what I could have done to offend Madame Trépof. I had also lost my way, and seemed doomed to wander about all night. In order to ask my way, I would have to see somebody; and it did not seem likely that I should find a single human being who could understand me. In my despair I entered a street at random—a street, or rather a horrible alley that had the look of a murderous place. It proved so in fact, for I had not been two minutes in it before I saw two men fighting with knives. They were attacking each other even more fiercely with their tongues than with their weapons; and I concluded from the nature of the abuse they were showering upon each other that it was a love affair. I prudently made my way into a side alley while those two good fellows were still much too busy with their own affairs to think about mine. I wandered hopelessly about for a while, and at last sat down, completely discouraged, on a stone bench, inwardly cursing the strange caprices of Madame Trépof.

"How are you, Signor? Are you back from San Carlo? Did you hear the diva sing? It is only at Naples you can hear singing like hers."

I looked up, and recognized my host. I had seated

myself with my back to the façade of my hotel, un-der the window of my own room.

Monte-Allegro, November 30, 1859.

WE were all resting—myself, my guides, and their mules—on the road from Sciacca to Girgenti, at a tavern in the miserable village of Monte-Allegro, whose inhabitants, consumed by the *mal' aria*, con-tinually shiver in the sun. But nevertheless they are Greeks, and their gayety triumphs over all circum-stances. A few gather about the tavern, full of smil-ing curiosity. One good story would have sufficed, had I known how to tell it to them, to make them forget all the woes of life. They had all a look of intelligence; and their women, although tanned and faded, wore their long black cloaks with much grace.

Before me I could see old ruins whitened by the sea-wind—ruins about which no grass ever grows. The dismal melancholy of deserts prevails over this arid land, whose cracked surface can barely nourish a few shrivelled mimosas, cacti, and dwarf palms. Twenty yards away, along the course of a ravine, stones were gleaming whitely like a long line of scat-tered bones. They told me that was the bed of a stream.

I had been about fifteen days in Sicily. On com-ing into the Bay of Palermo—which opens between the two mighty naked masses of the Pelligrino and

the Catalfano, and extends inward along the " Golden
Conch"—the view inspired me with such admiration
that I resolved to travel a little in this island, so en-
nobled by historic memories, and rendered so beautiful by the outlines of its hills, which reveal the principles of Greek art. Old pilgrim though I was, grown
hoary in the Gothic Occident—I dared to venture upon
that classic soil; and, securing a guide, I went from
Palermo to Trapani, from Trapani to Sélinonte, from
Sélinonte to Sciacca — which I left this morning to
go to Girgenti, where I am to find the MS. of Clerk
Alexander. The beautiful things I have seen are still
so vivid in my mind that I feel the task of writing
them would be a useless fatigue. Why spoil my
pleasure-trip by collecting notes? Lovers who love
truly do not write down their happiness

Wholly absorbed by the melancholy of the present
and the poetry of the past, my thoughts peopled with
beautiful shapes, and my eyes ever gratified by the
pure and harmonious lines of the landscape, I was
resting in the tavern at Monte Allegro, sipping a
glass of heavy, fiery wine, when I saw two persons
enter the waiting-room, whom, after a moment's hesitation, I recognized as the Prince and Princess Trépof.

This time I saw the princess in the light—and what
a light! He who has known that of Sicily can better
comprehend the words of Sophocles: " *O holy light!*
. . . *Eye of the Golden Day!*" Madame Trépof,
dressed in brown-holland and wearing a broad-brimmed

straw hat, appeared to me a very pretty woman of about twenty-eight. Her eyes were luminous as a child's; but her slightly plump chin indicated the age of plenitude. She is, I must confess it, quite an attractive person. She is supple and changeful; her mood is like water itself—and, thank Heaven! I am no navigator. I thought I discerned in her manner a sort of ill-humor, which I attributed presently, by reason of some observations she uttered at random, to the fact that she had met no brigands upon her route.

"Such things only happen to us!" she exclaimed, with a gesture of discouragement.

She called for a glass of iced water, which the land. lord presented to her with a gesture that recalled to me those scenes of funeral offerings painted upon Greek vases.

I was in no hurry to introduce myself to a lady who had so abruptly dropped my acquaintance in the public square at Naples; but she perceived me in my corner, and her frown notified me very plainly that our accidental meeting was disagreeable to her.

After she had sipped her ice-water for a few moments — whether because her whim had suddenly changed, or because my loneliness aroused her pity, I did not know—she walked directly to me.

"Good-day, Monsieur Bonnard," she said. "How do you do? What strange chance enables us to meet again in this frightful country?"

"This country is not frightful, Madame," I replied. Beauty is so great and so august a quality that centuries of barbarism cannot efface it so completely that adorable vestiges of it will not always remain. The majesty of the antique Ceres still overshadows these arid valleys; and that Greek Muse who made Arethusa and Mænalus ring with her divine accents, still sings for my ears upon the barren mountain and in the place of the dried-up spring. Yes, Madame, when our globe, no longer inhabited, shall, like the moon, roll a wan corpse through space, the soil which bears the ruins of Sélimonte will still keep the seal of beauty in the midst of universal death; and then, then, at least there will be no frivolous mouth to blaspheme the grandeur of these solitudes."

I knew well enough that my words were beyond the comprehension of the pretty little empty-head which heard them. But an old fellow like myself who has worn out his life over books does not know how to adapt his tone to circumstances. Besides, I wished to give Madame Trépof a lesson in politeness. She received it with so much submission, and with such an air of comprehension, that I hastened to add, as good-naturedly as possible,

"As to whether the chance which has enabled me to meet you again be lucky or unlucky, I cannot decide the question until I am sure that my presence be not disagreeable to you. You appeared to become weary of my company very suddenly at Naples the other day. I can only attribute that misfortune to my naturally unpleasant manner—since, on that occasion, I had had the honor of meeting you for the first time in my life."

These words seemed to cause her inexplicable joy. She smiled upon me in the most gracious, mischievous way, and said very earnestly, holding out her hand, which I touched with my lips,

"Monsieur Bonnard, do not refuse to accept a seat in my carriage. You can chat with me on the way about antiquity, and that will amuse me ever so much."

"My dear," exclaimed the prince, "you can do just as you please; but you ought to remember that one is horribly cramped in that carriage of yours; and I fear you are only offering Monsieur Bonnard the chance of getting a frightful attack of lumbago."

Madame Trépof simply shook her head by way of explaining that such considerations had no weight with her whatever; then she untied her hat. The darkness of her black curls descended over her eyes, and bathed them in velvety shadow. She remained a little while quite motionless, and her face assumed a surprising expression of reverie. But all of a sudden she darted at some oranges which the tavern-keeper had brought in a basket, and began to throw them, one by one, into a fold of her dress.

"These will be nice on the road," she said. "We are going just where you are going—to Girgenti. I must tell you all about it. You know that my husband is making a collection of match-boxes. We bought thirteen hundred match-boxes at Marseilles. But we heard there was a factory of them at Girgenti. According to what we were told, it is a very small factory, and its products—which are very ugly—never go outside the city and its suburbs. So we are going to Girgenti just to buy match-boxes. Dimitri has been a collector of all sorts of things; but the only kind of collection which can now interest him is a collection of match-boxes. He has already got five thousand two hundred and fourteen different kinds. Some of them gave us frightful trouble to find. For instance, we knew that at Naples boxes were once made with the portraits of Mazzini and Garibaldi on them; and that the police had seized the plates from which the portraits were printed, and put the manufacturer in jail. Well, by dint of searching and inquiring for ever so long a while, we found one of those boxes at last for sale at one hundred francs, instead of two sous. It was not really too dear at that price; but we were denounced for buying it. We were taken for conspirators. All our baggage was searched; they could not find the box, because I had hidden it so well; but they found my jewels, and carried them off. They have them still. The incident made quite a sensation, and we were going to get arrested. But the king was displeased about it, and he ordered them to leave us alone. Up to

that time, I used to think it was very stupid to collect match-boxes; but when I found that there were
risks of losing liberty, and perhaps even life, by doing
it, I began to feel a taste for it. Now I am an absolute fanatic on the subject. We are going to Sweden
next summer to complete our series. . . . Are we not,
Dimitri?"

I felt—must I confess it?—a thorough sympathy
with these intrepid collectors. No doubt I would
rather have found Monsieur and Madame Trépof engaged in collecting antique marbles or painted vases
in Sicily. I should have liked to have found them interested in the ruins of Syracuse, or the poetical tra-
ditions of the Eryx. But at all events, they were
making some sort of a collection—they belonged to
the great confraternity—and I could not possibly
make fun of them without making fun of myself.
Besides, Madame Trépof had spoken of her collection
with such an odd mingling of irony and enthusiasm
that I could not help finding the idea a very good one.

We were getting ready to leave the tavern, when
we noticed some people coming down-stairs from the
upper room, carrying carbines under their dark cloaks.
To me they had the look of thorough bandits; and
after they were gone I told Monsieur Trépof my
opinion of them. He answered me, very quietly, that
he also thought they were regular bandits; and the
guides begged us to apply for an escort of gendarmes,
but Madame Trépof besought us not to do anything

of the kind. She declared that we must not "spoil her journey."

Then, turning her persuasive eyes upon me, she asked,

"Do you not believe, Monsieur Bonnard, that there is nothing in life worth having except sensations?"

"Why, certainly, Madame," I answered; "but then we must take into consideration the nature of the sensations themselves. Those which a noble memory or a grand spectacle creates within us certainly represent what is best in human life; but those merely resulting from the menace of danger seem to me sensations which one should be very careful to avoid as much as possible. For example, would you think it a very pleasant thing, Madame, while travelling over the mountains at midnight, to find the muzzle of a carbine suddenly pressed against your forehead?"

"Oh, no!" she replied; "the comic-operas have made carbines absolutely ridiculous, and it would be a great misfortune to any young woman to find herself in danger from an absurd weapon. But it would be quite different with a knife—a very cold and very bright knife-blade, which makes a cold shudder go right through one's heart."

She shuddered even as she spoke; closed her eyes, and threw her head back. Then she resumed:

"People like you are so happy! You can interest yourselves in all sorts of things!"

She gave a sidelong look at her husband, who was

talking with the innkeeper. Then she leaned towards me, and murmured very low:

"You see, Dimitri and I, we are both suffering from *ennui!* We have still the match-boxes. But at last one gets tired even of match-boxes. Besides, our collection will soon be complete. And then what are we going to do?"

"Oh, Madame!" I exclaimed, touched by the moral unhappiness of this pretty person, "if you only had a son, then you would know what to do. You would then learn the purpose of your life, and your thoughts would become at once more serious and yet more cheerful."

"But I have a son," she replied. "He is a big boy; he is eleven years old, and he suffers from *ennui* like the rest of us. Yes, my George has *ennui,* too; he is tired of everything. It is very wretched."

She glanced again towards her husband, who was superintending the harnessing of the mules on the road outside—testing the condition of girths and straps. Then she asked me whether there had been many changes on the Quai Malaquais during the past ten years. She declared she never visited that neighborhood because it was too far away.

"Too far from Monte-Allegro?" I queried.

"Why, no!" she replied. "Too far from the Avenue des Champs-Élysées, where we live."

And she murmured over again, as if talking to herself, "Too far!—too far!" in a tone of reverie which

I could not possibly account for. All at once she smiled again, and said to me,

"I like you, Monsieur Bonnard!—I like you very, very much!"

The mules had been harnessed. The young woman hastily picked up a few oranges which had rolled off her lap; rose up; looked at me, and burst out laughing.

"Oh!" she exclaimed, "how I should like to see you grappling with the brigands! You would say such extraordinary things to them! . . . Please take my hat, and hold my umbrella for me, Monsieur Bonnard."

"What a strange little mind!" I thought to myself, as I followed her. "It could only have been in a moment of inexcusable thoughtlessness that Nature gave a child to such a giddy little woman!"

———

Girgenti. Same day.

HER manners had shocked me. I left her to arrange herself in her *lettica*, and I made myself as comfortable as I could in my own. These vehicles, which have no wheels, are carried by two mules—one before and one behind. This kind of litter, or chaise, is of ancient origin. I had often seen representations of similar ones in the French MSS. of the fourteenth century. I had no idea then that one of those vehicles would be at a future day placed at my own disposal. We must never be too sure of anything.

For three hours the mules sounded their little bells, and thumped the calcined ground with their hoofs. On either hand there slowly defiled by us the barren monstrous shapes of a nature totally African.

Half-way we made a halt to allow our animals to recover breath.

Madame Trépof came to me on the road, took my arm, and drew me a little away from the party. Then, very suddenly, she said to me in a tone of voice I had never heard before:

"Do not think that I am a wicked woman. My George knows that I am a good mother."

We walked side by side for a moment in silence. She looked up, and I saw that she was crying.

"Madame," I said to her, "look at this soil which has been burned and cracked by five long months of fiery heat. A little white lily has sprung up from it."

And I pointed with my cane to the frail stalk, tipped by a double blossom.

"Your heart," I said, "however arid it be, bears also its white lily; and that is reason enough why I do not believe that you are what you say—a wicked woman."

"Yes, yes, yes!" she cried, with the obstinacy of a child—"I am a wicked woman. But I am ashamed to appear so before you who are so good—so very, very good."

"You do not know anything at all about it," I said to her.

"I know it! I know all about you, Monsieur Bonnard!" she declared, with a smile.

And she jumped back into her *lettica*.

———

Girgenti, November 30, 1859.

I awoke the following morning in the House of Gellias. Gellias was a rich citizen of ancient Agrigentum. He was equally celebrated for his generosity and for his wealth; and he endowed his native city with a great number of free inns. Gellias has been dead for thirteen hundred years; and today there is no more gratuitous hospitality among civilized peoples. But the name of Gellias has become that of a hotel in which, by reason of fatigue, I was able to obtain one good night's sleep.

The modern Girgenti lifts its high, narrow, solid streets, dominated by a sombre Spanish cathedral, upon the site of the acropolis of the antique Agrigentum. I can see from my windows, half-way on the hillside towards the sea, the white range of temples partially destroyed. The ruins alone have some aspect of coolness. All the rest is arid. Water and life have forsaken Agrigentum. Water—the divine Nestis of the Agrigentine Empedocles—is so necessary to animated beings that nothing can live far from the rivers and the springs. But the port of Girgenti, situated at a distance of three kilometres from the city, has a great commerce. "And it is in this dismal city," I said to myself, "upon this precipitous rock, that the manuscript of Clerk Alexander is to be found!" I asked my way to the house of Signor Michael-Angelo Polizzi, and proceeded thither.

I found Signor Polizzi, dressed all in white from head to feet, busy cooking sausages in a frying-pan. At the sight of me, he let go the handle of the frying-pan, threw up his arms in the air, and uttered shrieks of enthusiasm. He was a little man whose pimply features, aquiline nose, round eyes, and projecting chin formed a very expressive physiognomy.

He called me "Excellence," said he was going to mark that day with a white stone, and made me sit down. The hall in which we were represented the union of kitchen, reception-room, bedchamber, studio, and wine-cellar. There were charcoal furnaces visible, a bed, paintings, an easel, bottles, strings of onions, and a magnificent lustre of colored glass pendants. I glanced at the paintings on the wall.

"The arts! the arts!" cried Signor Polizzi, throwing up his arms again to heaven—"the arts! What dignity! what consolation! Excellence, I am a painter!"

And he showed me an unfinished Saint-Francis, which indeed could very well remain unfinished forever without any loss to religion or to art. Next he showed me some old paintings of a better style, but apparently restored after a decidedly reckless manner.

"I repair," he said—"I repair old paintings. Oh, the Old Masters! What genius! what soul!"

"Why, then," I said to him, "you must be a painter, an archæologist, and a wine-merchant all in one?"

"At your service, Excellence," he answered. "I have a *zucco* here at this very moment—a *zucco* of which every single drop is a pearl of fire. I want your Lordship to taste of it."

"I esteem the wines of Sicily," I responded; "but it was not for the sake of your flagons that I came to see you, Signor Polizzi."

He: "Then you have come to see me about paintings. You are an amateur. It is an immense delight for me to receive amateurs. I am going to show you the *chef-d'œuvre* of Monrealese; yes, Excellence, his *chef-d'œuvre!* An Adoration of Shepherds! It is the pearl of the whole Sicilian school!"

I: "Later on I will be glad to see the *chef-d'œuvre*, but let us first talk about the business which brings me here."

His little quick bright eyes watched my face curiously; and I perceived, with anguish, that he had not the least suspicion of the purpose of my visit.

A cold sweat broke out over my forehead; and in the bewilderment of my anxiety I stammered out something to this effect:

"I have come from Paris expressly to look at a manuscript of the 'Légende Dorée,' which you informed me was in your possession."

At these words he threw up his arms, opened his

mouth and eyes to the widest possible extent, and betrayed every sign of extreme nervousness.

"Oh! the manuscript of the 'Golden Legend!' A pearl, Excellence! a ruby, a diamond! Two miniatures so perfect that they give one the feeling of glimpses of Paradise! What suavity! Those colors ravished from the corollas of flowers make a honey for the eyes! Even a Sicilian could have done no better!"

"Let you see it!" cried Polizzi. "But how can I, either my anxiety or my hope.

"Let you see it!" cried Polizzi. "But how can I, Excellence? I have not got it any more! I have not got it!"

And he seemed determined to tear out his hair. He might indeed have pulled every hair in his head out of his hide before I should have tried to prevent him. But he stopped of his own accord, before he had done himself any grevious harm.

"What!" I cried out in anger—"what! you make me come all the way from Paris to Girgenti, by promising to show me a manuscript, and now, when I come, you tell me you have not got it! It is simply infamous, Monsieur! I shall leave your conduct to be judged by all honest men!"

Anybody who could have seen me at that moment would have been able to form a good idea of the aspect of a furious sheep.

"It is infamous! it is infamous!" I repeated, waving my arms, which trembled from anger.

Then Michael-Angelo Polizzi let himself fall into a chair in the attitude of a dying hero. I saw his eyes fill with tears, and his hair—until then flamboyant and erect upon his head—fall down in limp disorder over his brow.

"I am a father, Excellence! I am a father!" he groaned, wringing his hands.

He continued, sobbing:

"My son Rafael—the son of my poor wife, for whose death I have been mourning fifteen years—Rafael, Excellence, wanted to settle in Paris; he hired a shop in the Rue Lafitte for the sale of curiosities. I gave him everything precious which I had—I gave him my finest majolicas; my most beautiful Urbino ware; my masterpieces of art: what paintings, Signor! Even now they dazzle me when I see them only in imagination! And all of them signed! Finally, I gave him the manuscript of the 'Golden Legend!' I would have given him my flesh and my blood! An only son, Signor! the son of my poor saintly wife!"

"So," I said, "while I—relying upon your written word, Monsieur—was travelling to the very heart of Sicily to find the manuscript of the Clerk Alexander, the same manuscript was actually exposed for sale in a window in Rue Lafitte, only fifteen hundred yards from my house?"

"Yes, it was there! that is positively true!" exclaimed Signor Polizzi, suddenly growing calm again; "and it is there still—at least I hope it is, Excellence."

He took a card from a shelf as he spoke, and offered it to me, saying,

"Here is the address of my son. Make it known to your friends, and you will oblige me. Faïence and enamelled wares; hangings; pictures. He has a complete stock of objects of art—all at the fairest possible prices—and everything authentic, I can vouch for it, upon my honor! Go and see him. He will show you the manuscript of the 'Golden Legend.' Two miniatures miraculously fresh in color!"

I was feeble enough to take the card he held out to me.

The fellow was taking further advantage of my weakness to make me circulate the name of Rafael Polizzi among the societies of learning!

My hand was already on the door-knob, when the Sicilian caught me by the arm; he had a look as of sudden inspiration.

"Ah! Excellence!" he cried, "what a city is this city of ours! It gave birth to Empedocles! Empedocles! What a great man! what a great citizen! What audacity of thought! what virtue; what soul! At the port over there is a statue of Empedocles, before which I bare my head each time that I pass by! When Rafael, my son, was going away to found an establishment of antiquities in the Rue Lafitte, at Paris, I took him to the port, and there, at the foot of that statue of Empedocles, I bestowed upon him my paternal benediction! 'Always remember Empedocles!' I said to him.

Ah! Signor, what our unhappy country needs to-day is a new Empedocles! Would you not like me to show you the way to his statue, Excellence? I will be your guide among the ruins here. I will show you the temple of Castor and Pollux, the temple of the Olympian Jupiter, the temple of the Lucinian Juno, the antique well, the tomb of Théron, and the Gate of Gold! All the professional guides are asses; but we—we shall make excavations, if you are willing—and we shall discover treasures! I know the science of discovering hidden treasures—the secret art of finding their whereabouts—a gift from Heaven!"

I succeeded in tearing myself away from his grasp. But he ran after me again, stopped me at the foot of the stairs, and said in my ear,

"Listen, Excellence. I will conduct you about the city; I will introduce you to some Girgentines! What a race! what types! what forms! Sicilian girls, Signor!—the antique beauty itself!"

"Go to the devil!" I cried, at last, in anger, and rushed into the street, leaving him still writhing in the loftiness of his enthusiasm.

When I had got out of his sight, I sank down upon a stone, and began to think, with my face in my hands.

"And it was for this," I said to myself—"it was to hear such propositions as this that I came to Sicily!" That Polizzi is simply a scoundrel, and his son another; and they made a plan together to ruin me." But what was their scheme? I could not unravel it

Meanwhile, it may be imagined how discouraged and humiliated I felt.

A merry burst of laughter caused me to turn my head, and I saw Madame Trépof running in advance of her husband, and holding up something which I could not distinguish clearly.

She sat down beside me, and showed me—laughing more merrily all the while—an abominable little paste board box, on which was printed a red-and-blue face, which the inscription declared to be the face of Empedocles.

" Yes, Madam," I said, " but that abominable Polizzi, to whom I advise you not to send Monsieur Trépot, has made me fall out forever with Empedocles; and this portrait is not at all of a nature to make me feel more kindly to the ancient philosopher."

" Oh !" declared Madame Trépof, " it is ugly, but it is rare ! These boxes are not exported at all ; you can buy them only where they are made. Dimitri has six others just like this in his pocket. We got them so as to exchange with other collectors. You understand ? At nine o'clock this morning we were at the factory. You see we did not waste our time."

" So I certainly perceive, Madame," I replied, bitterly ; " but I have lost mine."

I then saw that she was naturally a good-hearted woman. All her merriment vanished.

" Poor Monsieur Bonnard ! poor Monsieur Bonnard !" she murmured.

And, taking my hand in hers, she added:

"Tell me about your troubles."

I told her about them. My story was long; but she was evidently touched by it, for she asked me quite a number of circumstantial questions, which I took for proof of friendly interest. She wanted to know the exact title of the manuscript, its shape, its appearance, and its age; she asked me for the address of Signor Rafael Polizzi.

And I gave it to her; thus doing (O destiny!) precisely what the abominable Polizzi had told me to do.

It is sometimes difficult to check one's self. I recommenced my plaints and my imprecations. But this time Madame Trépof only burst out laughing.

"Why do you laugh?" I asked her.

"Because I am a wicked woman," she answered.

And she fled away, leaving me all disheartened on my stone.

Paris, December 8, 1859.

My unpacked trunks still encumbered the hall. I was seated at a table covered with all those good things which the land of France produces for the delectation of *gourmets.* I was eating a *paté de Chartres,* which is alone sufficient to make one love one's country. Thérèse, standing before me with her hands joined over her white apron, was looking at me with benignity, with anxiety, and with pity. Hamilcar was rubbing himself against my legs, wild with delight.

These words of an old poet came back to my memory:

"Happy is he who, like Ulysses, hath made a goodly journey"

. . . "Well," I thought to myself, "I travelled to no purpose; I have come back with empty hands; but, like Ulysses, I made a goodly journey."

And having taken my last sip of coffee, I asked Thérèse for my hat and cane, which she gave me not without dire suspicions: she feared I might be going upon another journey. But I reassured her by telling her to have dinner ready at six o'clock.

It had always been a keen pleasure for me to breathe the air in those Parisian streets whose every paving-slab and every stone I love devotedly. But I had an end in view, and I took my way straight to the Rue Lafitte. I was not long in finding the establishment of Signor Rafael Polizzi. It was distinguishable by a great display of old paintings which, although all bearing the signature of some illustrious artist, had a certain family air of resemblance that might have suggested some touching idea about the fraternity of genius, had it not still more forcibly suggested the professional tricks of Polizzi Sr. Enriched by these doubtful works of art, the shop was further rendered attractive by various petty curiosities:poniards, drinking-vessels, goblets, *figulines*, brass *gaudrons*, and Hispano-Arabian wares of metallic lustre.

Upon a Portuguese arm-chair, decorated with an escutcheon, lay a copy of the "Heures" of Simon Vostre, open at the page which has an astrological figure upon it; and an old Vitruvius, placed upon a quaint chest, displayed its masterly engravings of caryatides and telamones. This apparent disorder which only masked cunning arrangement, this factitious hazard which had placed the best objects in the most favorable light, would have increased my distrust of the place, but that the distrust which the mere name of Polizzi had already inspired could not have been increased by any circumstances—being already infinite.

Signor Rafael, who sat there as the presiding genius of all these vague and incongruous shapes, impressed me as a phlegmatic young man, with a sort of English character. He betrayed no sign whatever of those transcendent faculties displayed by his father in the arts of mimicry and declamation.

I told him what I had come for; he opened a cabinet and drew from it a manuscript, which he placed on a table that I might examine it at my leisure.

Never in my life did I experience such an emotion —except, indeed, during some brief months of my youth, months whose memories, though I should live a hundred years, would remain as fresh at my last hour as in the first day they came to me.

It was, indeed, the very manuscript described by the librarian of Sir Thomas Raleigh; it was, indeed, the

manuscript of the Clerk Alexander which I saw, which
I touched! The work of Voragine himself had been
perceptibly abridged; but that made little difference
to me. All the inestimable additions of the monk of
Saint-Germain-des-Prés were there. That was the
main point! I tried to read the Legend of Saint Droctoveus; but I could not—all the lines of the page quivered before my eyes, and there was a sound in my ears
like the noise of a windmill in the country at night.
Nevertheless, I was able to see that the manuscript
offered every evidence of indubitable authenticity.
The two drawings of the Purification of the Virgin
and the Coronation of Proserpine were meagre in de-
sign and vulgar in violence of coloring. Considerably
damaged in 1824, as attested by the catalogue of Sir
Thomas, they had obtained during the interval a new
aspect of freshness. But this miracle did not surprise
me at all. And, besides, what did I care about the two
miniatures? The legends and the poem of Alexander
—those alone formed the treasure I desired. My
eyes devoured as much of it as they had the power
to absorb.

I affected indifference while asking Signor Polizzi
the price of the manuscript; and, while awaiting his
reply, I offered up a secret prayer that the price might
not exceed the amount of ready money at my disposal
—already much diminished by the cost of my expen-
sive voyage. Signor Polizzi, however, informed me
that he was not at liberty to dispose of the article, in-

asmuch as it did not belong to him, and was to be sold at auction shortly, at the Hôtel des Ventes, with a number of other MSS. and several *incunabula*.

This was a severe blow to me. I tried to preserve my calmness, notwithstanding, and replied somewhat to this effect:

"You surprise me, Monsieur! Your father, whom I talked with recently at Girgenti, told me positively the manuscript was yours. You cannot now attempt to make me discredit your father's word."

"I *did* own the manuscript, indeed," answered Signor Rafael with absolute frankness; "but I do not own it any longer. I sold that manuscript—the remarkable interest of which you have not failed to perceive—to an amateur whom I am forbidden to name, and who, for reasons which I am not at liberty to mention, finds himself obliged to sell his collection. I am honored with the confidence of my customer, and was commissioned by him to draw up the catalogue and manage the sale, which takes place the 24th of December. Now, if you will be kind enough to give me your address, I will have the pleasure of sending you the catalogue, which is already in press. You will find the 'Légende Dorée' described in it as 'No. 42.'"

I gave my address, and left the shop.

The polite gravity of the son impressed me quite as disagreeably as the impudent buffoonery of the father. I hated, from the bottom of my heart, the tricks of the vile hagglers! It was perfectly evident that the two rascals had a secret understanding, and had only devised this auction-sale, with the aid of a professional appraiser, to force the bidding on the manuscript I wanted so much up to an outrageous figure. I was completely at their mercy. There is one evil in all passionate desires, even the noblest—namely, that they leave us subject to the will of others, and in so far dependent. This reflection made me suffer cruelly; but it did not conquer my longing to own the work of Clerk Alexander. While I was thus meditating, I heard a coachman swear. And I discovered it was I whom he was swearing at only when I felt the pole of a carriage poke me in the ribs. I started aside, barely in time to save myself from being run over; and whom did I perceive through the windows of the *coupé?* Madame Trépof, being taken by two beautiful horses, and a coachman all wrapped up in furs like a Russian *boyard,* into the very street I had just left. She did not notice me; she was laughing to herself with that artless grace of expression which still preserved for her, at thirty years, all the charm of her early youth.

"Well, well!" I said to myself, "she is laughing! I suppose she must have just found another match-box."

And I made my way back to the Ponts, feeling very miserable.

Nature, eternally indifferent, neither hastened nor

hurried the twenty-fourth day of December. I went
to the Hôtel Bullion, and took my place in *Salle* No
4. immediately below the high desk at which the auc
tioneer Bouloze and the expert Polizzi were to sit. I
saw the hall gradually fill with familiar faces. I shook
hands with several old booksellers of the quays; but
that prudence which any large interest inspires in even
the most self-assured caused me to keep silence in re
gard to the reason of my unaccustomed presence in the
halls of the Hôtel Bullion. On the other hand, I ques
tioned those gentlemen closely about the purpose of
their attendance at the auction-sale; and I had the
satisfaction of finding them all interested about mat
ters in no wise related to my affair.

Little by little the hall became thronged with inter
ested or merely curious spectators; and, after half an
hour's delay, the auctioneer, with his ivory hammer
the clerk with his bundle of memorandum-papers, and
the crier, carrying his collection-box fixed to the end
of a pole, all took their places on the platform in the
most solemn business manner. The hall-boys ranged
themselves at the foot of the desk. The presiding offi
cer having declared the sale open, a partial hush fol
lowed.

A commonplace lot of *Preces piæ*, with miniatures,
were first sold off at mediocre prices. Needless to say
the illuminations of these books were in perfect con
dition!

The lowness of the bids gave courage to the gather

ing of second-hand booksellers present, who began to mingle with us, and became familiar. The dealers in old brass and *bric-à-brac* pressed forward in their turn, waiting for the doors of an adjoining room to be opened; and the voice of the auctioneer was drowned by the jests of the *Auvergnats*.

A magnificent codex of the "Guerre des Juifs" revived attention. It was long disputed for. "Five thousand francs! five thousand!" called the crier, while the *bric-à-brac* dealers remained silent with admiration. Then seven or eight antiphonaries brought us back again to low prices. A fat old woman, in loose gown and bare-headed—a dealer in secondhand goods—encouraged by the size of the books and the low prices bidden, had one of the antiphonaries knocked down to her for thirty francs.

At last the expert Polizzi announced No. 42: "The 'Golden Legend;' French MS.; inedited; two superb miniatures. Started with a bid of three thousand francs."

"Three thousand! three thousand bid!" yelled the crier.

"Three thousand!" dryly repeated the auctioneer.

There was a buzzing in my head, and, as through a cloud, I saw a host of curious faces all turning towards the manuscript, which a boy was carrying open through the audience.

"Three thousand and fifty!" I said.

I was frightened by the sound of my own voice, and

further confused by seeing, or thinking that I saw, all eyes turned upon me.

"Three thousand and fifty on the right!" called the crier, taking up my bid.

"Three thousand one hundred!" responded Signor Polizzi.

Then began a heroic duel between the expert and myself.

"Three thousand five hundred!"

"Six hundred!"

"Seven hundred!"

"Four thousand!"

"Four thousand five hundred."

Then, by a sudden bold stroke, Signor Polizzi raised the bid at once to six thousand.

Six thousand francs was all the money I could dispose of. It represented the possible. I risked the impossible.

"Six thousand one hundred!"

Alas! even the impossible did not suffice.

"Six thousand five hundred!" replied Signor Polizzi, with calm.

I bowed my head and sat there stupefied, unable to answer either yes or no to the crier, who called to me:

"Six thousand five hundred, by me—not by you on the right there!—it is my bid—no mistake! Six thousand five hundred!"

"Perfectly understood!" declared the auctioneer. "Six thousand five hundred. Perfectly clear; perfectly plain. . . . Any more bids? The last bid is six thousand five hundred francs!"

A solemn silence prevailed. Suddenly I felt as if my head had burst open. It was the hammer of the ministerial officer, who, with a loud blow on the platform, adjudged No. 42 irrevocably to Signor Polizzi. Forthwith the pen of the clerk, coursing over the *papier-timbré*, registered that great fact in a single line.

I was absolutely prostrated, and I felt the utmost need of rest and quiet. Nevertheless, I did not leave my seat. My powers of reflection slowly returned. Hope is tenacious. I had one more hope. It occurred to me that the new owner of the "Légende Dorée" might be some intelligent and liberal bibliophile who would allow me to examine the MS., and perhaps even to publish the more important parts. And, with this idea, as soon as the sale was over I approached the expert as he was leaving the platform.

"Monsieur," I asked him, "did you buy in No. 42 on your own account, or on commission?"

"On commission. I was instructed not to let it go at any price."

"Can you tell me the name of the purchaser?"

"Monsieur, I regret that I cannot serve you in that respect. I have been strictly forbidden to mention the name."

I went home in despair.

December 30, 1859.

"Thérèse! don't you hear the bell! Somebody has been ringing at the door for the last quarter of an hour!"

Thérèse does not answer. She is chattering down-stairs with the concierge, for sure. So that is the way you observe your old master's birthday? You desert me even on the eve of Saint-Sylvestre! Alas! if I am to hear any kind wishes to-day, they must come up from the ground; for all who love me have long been buried. I really don't know what I am still living for. There is the bell again! . . . I get up slowly from my seat at the fire, with my shoulders still bent from stooping over it, and go to the door myself. Who do I see at the threshold? It is not a dripping Love, and I am not an old Anacreon; but it is a very pretty little boy of about ten years old. He is alone; he raises his face to look at me. His cheeks are blushing; but his little pert nose gives one an idea of mischievous pleasantry. He has feathers in his cap, and a great lace-ruff on his jacket. The pretty little fellow! He holds in both arms a bundle as big as himself, and asks me if I am Monsieur Sylvestre Bonnard. I tell him yes; he gives me the bundle, tells me his mamma sent it to me, and then he runs down-stairs.

I go down a few steps; I lean over the balustrade, and see the little cap whirling down the spiral of the stairway like a feather in the wind. "Good-by, my little boy !" I should have liked so much to question him. But what, after all, could I have asked? it is not polite to question children. Besides, the package itself will probably give me more information than the messenger could.

It is a very big bundle, but not very heavy. I take it into my library, and there untie the ribbons and unfasten the paper wrappings; and I see—what? a log! a first-class log! a real Christmas log, but so light that I know it must be hollow. Then I find that it is indeed composed of two separate pieces, opening on hinges, and fastened with hooks. I slip the hooks back, and find myself inundated with violets! Violets! they pour over my table, over my knees, over the carpet. They tumble into my vest, into my sleeves. I am all perfumed with them.

"Thérèse! Thérèse! fill me some vases with water, and bring them here, quick! Here are violets sent to us I know not from what country nor by what hand; but it must be from a perfumed country, and by a very gracious hand. . . . Do you hear me, old crow?"

I have put all the violets on my table—now completely covered by the odorous mass. But there is still something in the log . . . a book—a manuscript. It is . . . I cannot believe it, and yet I cannot doubt it.

. . It is the "Légende Dorée"!—it is the manuscript of the Clerk Alexander! Here is the "Purification of the Virgin" and the "Coronation of Proserpine;"—here is the legend of Saint Droctoveus. I contemplate this voilet-perfumed relic. I turn the leaves of it—between which the dark rich blossoms have slipped in here and there; and, right opposite the legend of Saint-Cecilia, I find a card bearing this name:

"Princess Trépof."

Princess Trépof!—you who laughed and wept by turns so sweetly under the fair sky of Agrigentum!—you, whom a cross old man believed to be only a foolish little woman!—to-day I am convinced of your rare and beautiful folly; and the old fellow whom you now overwhelm with happiness will go to kiss your hand, and give you back, in another form, this precious manuscript, of which both he and science owe you an exact and sumptuous publication!

Thérèse entered my study just at that moment; she seemed to be very much excited.

"Monsieur!" she cried, "guess whom I saw just now in a carriage, with a coat-of-arms painted on it, that was stopping before the door?"

"*Parbleu!*—Madame Trépof," I exclaimed.

"I don't know anything about any Madame Trépof," answered my housekeeper. "The woman I saw just now was dressed like a duchess, and had a little boy with her, with lace-frills all along the seams of his clothes. And it was that same little Madame Coccoz you once sent a log to, when she was confined here about eleven years ago. I recognized her at once."

"What!" I exclaimed, "you mean to say it was Madame Coccoz, the widow of the almanac-peddler?"

"Herself, Monsieur! The carriage-door was open for a minute to let her little boy, who had just come from I don't know where, get in. She hasn't changed scarcely at all. Well, why should those women change?—they never worry themselves about anything. Only the Coccoz woman looks a little fatter than she used to be. And the idea of a woman that was taken in here out of pure charity coming to show off her velvets and diamonds in a carriage with a crest painted on it! Isn't it shameful!"

"Thérèse!" I cried, in a terrible voice, "if you ever speak to me again about that lady except in terms of the deepest respect, you and I will fall out! ... Bring me the Sèvres vases to put those violets in, which now give the City of Books a charm it never had before."

While Thérèse went off with a sigh to get the Sèvres vases, I continued to contemplate those beautiful scattered violets, whose odor spread all about me like the perfume of some sweet presence, some charming soul; and I asked myself how it had been possible for me never to recognize Madame Coccoz in the person of the Princess Trépof. But that vision of the young widow, showing me her little child on the stairs, had been a very rapid one. I had much more reason to reproach myself for having passed by a gracious and lovely soul without knowing it.

"Bonnard," I said to myself, "thou knowest how to decipher old texts; but thou dost not know how to read in the Book of Life. That giddy little Madame Trépof, whom thou once believed to possess no more soul than a bird, has expended, in pure gratitude, more zeal and finer tact than thou didst ever show for anybody's sake. Right royally hath she repaid thee for the log-fire of her churching-day!

"Thérèse! Awhile ago you were a magpie; now you are becoming a tortoise! Come and give some water to these Parmese violets."

I.

THE FAIRY.

WHEN I left the train at the Melun station, night had already spread its peace over the silent country. The soil, heated through all the long day by a strong sun—by a *"gros soleil,"* as the harvesters of the Val de Vire say—still exhaled a warm heavy smell. Lush dense odors of grass passed over the level of the fields. I brushed away the dust of the railroad car, and joyfully inhaled the pure air. My travelling-bag —filled by my housekeeper with linen and various small toilet articles, *munditis,* seemed so light in my hand that I swung it about just as a schoolboy swings his strapped package of rudimentary books when the class is let out.

Would to Heaven that I were again a little urchin at school! But it is fully fifty years since my good dead mother made me some *tartines* of bread and preserves, and placed them in a basket of which she slipped the handle over my arm, and then led me, thus prepared, to the school kept by Monsier Douloir, at a corner of the Passage du Commerce well known to the sparrows, between a court and a garden. The enormous Monsier Douloir smiled upon us genially and patted my cheek to show, no doubt, the affectionate interest which my first appearance had inspired. But when my mother had passed out of the court, startling the sparrows as she went, Monsieur Douloir ceased to smile—he showed no more affectionate interest; he appeared, on the contrary, to consider me as a very troublesome little fellow. I discovered, later on, that he entertained the same feelings towards all his pupils. He distributed whacks of his ferule with an agility no one could have expected on the part of so corpulent a person. But his first aspect of tender interest invariably reappeared when he spoke to any of our mothers in our presence; and always at such times, while warmly praising our remarkable aptitudes, he would cast down upon us a look of intense affection. Still, those were happy days which I passed on the benches of Monsieur Douloir with my little playfellows, who, like myself, cried and laughed by turns with all their might, from morning till evening.

After a whole half-century these souvenirs float up again, fresh and bright as ever, to the surface of memory, under this starry sky, whose face has in no wise changed since then, and whose serene and immutable lights will doubtless see many other schoolboys such as I was slowly turn into gray-headed savants, afflicted with catarrh.

Stars, who have shone down upon each wise or foolish head among all my forgotten ancestors, it is under your soft light that I now feel stir within me a certain poignant regret! I would that I could have a son who might be able to see you when I shall see you no more. How I should love him! Ah! such a son would—what am I saying?—why, he would be now just twenty years old if you had only been willing, Clémentine—you whose cheeks used to look so ruddy under your pink hood! But you married that young bank clerk, Noël Alexandre, who made so many millions afterwards! I never met you again after your marriage, Clémentine, but I can see you now, with your bright curls and your pink hood.

A looking-glass! a looking-glass! a looking-glass! Really, I would be curious to see what I look like now, with my white hair, sighing Clémentine's name to the stars! Still, it is not right to end with sterile irony the thought begun in the spirit of faith and love. No, Clémentine, if your name came to my lips by chance this beautiful night, be it forever blessed, your dear name! and may you ever, as a happy mother, a happy grandmother, enjoy to the very end of life with your rich husband the utmost degree of that happiness which you had the right to believe you could not win with the poor young scholar who loved you! If—though I cannot even now imagine it—if your beautiful hair has become white, Clémentine, bear worthily the bundle of keys confided to you by Noël Alex-

andre, and impart to your grandchildren the knowledge of all domestic virtues!

The beautiful Night! She rules, with such noble
repose, over men and animals alike, kindly loosed by
her from the yoke of daily toil; and even I feel her
beneficent influence, although my habits of sixty years
have so changed me that I can feel most things only
through the signs which represent them. My world
is wholly formed of words—so much of a philologist
I have become! Each one dreams the dream of life
in his own way. I have dreamed it in my library; and
when the hour shall come in which I must leave this
world, may it please God to take me from my ladder
—from before my shelves of books! . . .

"Well, well! it is really himself, *pardieu!* How
are you, Monsieur Sylvestre Bonnard? And where
have you been travelling to all this time, over the
country, while I was waiting for you at the station
with my cabriolet? You escaped me when the train
came in, and I was driving back, quite disappointed, to
Lusance. Give me your valise, and get up here beside me in the carriage. Why, do you know it is fully
seven kilometres from here to the château?"

Who addresses me thus, at the very top of his voice,
from the height of his cabriolet? Monsieur Paul de
Gabry, nephew and heir of Monsieur Honoré de Ga-
bry, peer of France in 1842, who recently died at
Monaco. And it was precisely to Monsieur Paul de
Gabry's house that I was going with that valise of

mine, so carefully strapped by my housekeeper. This
excellent young man has just inherited, conjointly with
his two brothers-in-law. the property of his uncle, who,
belonging to a very ancient family of distinguished
lawyers, had accumulated in his château at Lusance a
library rich in MSS., some dating back to the fourteenth century. It was for the purpose of making an
inventory and a catalogue of these MSS. that I had
come to Lusance at the urgent request of Monsieur
Paul de Gabry, whose father, a perfect gentleman and
distinguished bibliophile, had maintained the most
pleasant relations with me during his lifetime. To
tell the truth, Monsieur Paul has not inherited the fine
tastes of his father. Monsieur Paul likes sporting : he
is a great authority on horses and dogs ; and I much
fear that of all the sciences capable of satisfying or of
duping the inexhaustible curiosity of mankind, those
of the stable and the dog-kennel are the only ones
thoroughly mastered by him.

I cannot say I was surprised to meet him, since we
had made a rendezvous ; but I acknowledge that I
had become so preoccupied with my own thoughts
that I had forgotten all about the Château de Lusance
and its inhabitants, and that the voice of the gentleman calling out to me as I started to follow the
country road winding away before me—"*un bon ru-
ban de queue*," as they say — had given me quite a
start.

I fear my face must have betrayed my incongruous

distraction by a certain stupid expression which it is apt to assume in most of my social transactions. My valise was pulled up into the carriage, and I followed my valise. My host pleased me by his straightforward simplicity.

"I don't know anything myself about your old parchments," he said; "but I think you will find some folks to talk to at the house. Besides the curé, who writes books himself, and the doctor, who is a very good fellow—although a radical—you will meet somebody able to keep you company. I mean my wife. She is not a very learned woman, but there are few things which she can't divine pretty well. Then I count upon being able to keep you with us long enough to make you acquainted with Mademoiselle Jeanne, who has the fingers of a magician and the soul of an angel."

"And is this delightfully gifted young lady one of your family?" I asked.

"Not at all," replied Monsieur Paul.

"Then she is just a friend of yours?" I persisted, rather stupidly.

"She has lost both her father and mother," answered Monsieur de Gabry, keeping his eyes fixed upon the ears of his horse, whose hoofs rang loudly over the road blue-tinted by the moonshine. "Her father managed to get us into some very serious trouble; and we did not get off with a fright either!"

Then he shook his head, and changed the subject.

He gave me due warning of the ruinous condition in which I would find the château and the park; they had been absolutely deserted for thirty-two years.

I learned from him that Monsieur Honoré de Gabry, his uncle, had been on very bad terms with some poachers, whom he used to shoot at like rabbits. One of them, a vindictive peasant, who had received a whole charge of shot in his face, lay in wait for the Seigneur one evening behind the trees of the mall, and very nearly succeeded in killing him, for the ball took off the tip of his ear.

"My uncle," Monsieur Paul continued, "tried to discover who had fired the shot; but he could not see any one, and he walked back slowly to the house. The day after he called his steward, and ordered him to close up the manor and the park, and allow no living soul to enter. He expressly forbade that anything should be touched, or looked after, or any reparations made on the estate during his absence. He added, between his teeth, that he would return at Easter, or Trinity Sunday, as they say in the song; and, just as the song has it, Trinity Sunday passed without a sign of him. He died last year at Monaco; my brother-in-law and myself were the first to enter the château after it had been abandoned for thirty-two years. We found a chestnut-tree growing in the middle of the parlor. As for the park, it was useless trying to visit it, because there were no more paths, no alleys."

My companion ceased to speak; and only the regular hoof-beat of the trotting horse, and the chirping of insects in the grass, broke the silence. On either hand, the sheaves standing in the fields took, in the vague moonlight, the appearance of tall white women kneeling down; and I abandoned myself awhile to those wonderful childish fancies which the charm of night always suggests. After driving under the heavy shadows of the mall, we turned to the right and rolled up a lordly avenue, at the end of which the chateau suddenly rose into view—a black mass, with turrets *en poivrière.* We followed a sort of causeway, which gave access to the court-of-honor, and which, passing over a moat full of running water, doubtless replaced a long-vanished drawbridge. The loss of that drawbridge must have been, I think, the first of various humiliations to which the warlike manor had been subjected ere being reduced to that pacific aspect with which it received me. The stars reflected themselves with marvellous clearness in the dark water. Monsieur Paul, like a courteous host, escorted me to my chamber in the very top of the building, at the end of a long corridor; and then, excusing himself for not presenting me at once to his wife by reason of the lateness of the hour, bade me good-night.

My apartment, painted in white, and hung with chintz, seemed to keep some traces of the elegant gallantry of the eighteenth century. A heap of still-glowing ashes—which testified to the pains taken to dispel humidity — filled the fireplace, whose marble mantelpiece supported a bust of Marie Antoinette in *biscuit*.   Attached to the frame of the tarnished and discolored mirror, two brass hooks, that had once doubtless served the ladies of old-fashioned days to hang their *chatelaines* on, seemed to offer a very opportune means of suspending my watch, which I took care to wind up beforehand ; for, contrary to the opinion of the Thelemites, I hold that man is only master of time, which is Life itself, when he has divided it into hours, minutes, and seconds—that is to say, into parts proportioned to the brevity of human existence.

And I thought to myself that life really seems short to us only because we measure it irrationally by our own mad hopes.   We have all of us, like the old man in the fable, a new wing to add to our building. I want, for example, before I die, to finish my " History of the Abbots of Saint-Germain-des-Prés."   The time God allots to each one of us is like a precious tissue which we embroider as we best know how.   I had begun my woof with all sorts of philological illustrations. . . . So my thoughts wandered on ; and at last, as I bound my *foulard* about my head, the notion of Time led me back to the past ; and for the second time within the same round of the dial I thought of you, Clémentine—to bless you again in your posterity, if you have any, before blowing out my candle and falling asleep amidst the chanting of the frogs.

II.

During breakfast I had many opportunities to appreciate the good taste, tact, and intelligence of Madame de Gabry, who told me that the château had its ghosts, and was especially haunted by the "Lady-with-three-wrinkles-in-her-back," a poisoner during her lifetime, and thereafter a Soul-in-pain. I could never describe how much wit and animation she gave to this old nurse's tale. We took our coffee on the terrace, whose balusters, clasped and forcibly torn away from their stone coping by a vigorous growth of ivy, remained suspended in the grasp of the amorous plant like bewildered Athenian women in the arms of ravishing Centaurs.

The château, shaped something like a four-wheeled wagon, with a turret at each of the four angles, had lost all original character by reason of repeated remodellings. It was merely a fine spacious building, nothing more. It did not appear to me to have suffered much damage during its abandonment of thirty-two years. But when Madame de Gabry conducted me into the great salon of the ground-floor, I saw that the planking was bulged in and out, the plinths rotten, the wainscotings split apart, the paintings of the piers turned black and hanging more than half out of their settings. A chestnut-tree, after forcing up the planks of the floor, had grown tall under the ceiling, and was reaching out its large-leaved branches towards the glassless windows.

This spectacle was not devoid of charm; but I could not look at it without anxiety, as I remembered that the rich library of Monsieur Honoré de Gabry, in an adjoining apartment, must have been exposed for the same length of time to the same forces of decay. Yet, as I looked at the young chestnut-tree in the salon, I could not but admire the magnificent vigor of Nature, and that resistless power which forces every germ to develop into life. On the other hand I felt saddened to think that, whatever effort we scholars may make to preserve dead things from passing away, we are laboring painfully in vain. Whatever has lived becomes the necessary food of new existences. And the Arab who builds himself a hut out of the marble fragments of a Palmyra temple is really more of a philosopher than all the guardians of museums at London, Munich, or Paris.

August 11.

ALL day long I have been classifying MSS. . . . The sun came in through the lofty uncurtained windows; and, during my reading, often very interesting, I could hear the languid bumble-bees bump heavily against the windows, and the flies, intoxicated with light and heat, making their wings hum in circles round my head. So loud became their humming about three o'clock that I looked up from the document I was reading—a document containing very precious materials for the history of Melun in the thirteenth century — to watch the concentric movements of those tiny creatures. "*Bestions*," Lafontaine calls them: he found this form of the word in the old popular speech, whence also the term, *tapisserie-à-bestions*, applied to figured tapestry. I was compelled to confess that the effect of heat upon the wings of a fly is totally different from that it exerts upon the brain of a paleographical archivist; for I found it very difficult to think, and a rather pleasant languor weighing upon me, from which I could rouse myself only by a very determined effort. The dinner-bell then startled me in the midst of my labors; and I had barely time to put on my new dress-coat, so as to make a respectable appearance before Madame de Gabry.

The repast, generously served, seemed to prolong itself for my benefit. I am more than a fair judge of wine; and my hostess, who discovered my knowledge in this regard, was friendly enough to open a certain bottle of Château-Margaux in my honor. With deep respect I drank of this famous and knightly old wine, which comes from the slopes of Bordeaux, and of which the flavor and exhilarating power are beyond all praise. The ardor of it spread gently through my veins, and filled me with an almost juvenile animation. Seated beside Madame de Gabry on the terrace, under the gloaming which gave a charming melancholy to the park, and lent to every object an air of mystery, I took pleasure in communicating my impres

sions of the scene to my hostess. I discoursed with
a vivacity quite remarkable on the part of a man
so devoid of imagination as I am. I described to her
spontaneously, without quoting from any old texts,
the caressing melancholy of the evening, and the beauty of that natal earth which feeds us, not only with
bread and wine, but also with ideas, sentiments, beliefs,
and which will at last take us all back to her maternal breast again, like so many tired little children at
the close of a long day.

"Monsieur," said the kind lady, "you see these old
towers, those trees, that sky; is it not quite natural
that the personages of the popular tales and folk-
songs should have been evoked by such scenes? Why,
over there is the very path which Little Red Riding-
hood followed when she went to the woods to pick
nuts. Across this changeful and always vapory sky
the fairy chariots used to roll; and the north tower
might have sheltered under its pointed roof that same
old spinning woman whose distaff pricked the Sleeping Beauty in the Wood."

I continued to muse upon her pretty fancies, while
Monsieur Paul related to me, as he puffed a very
strong cigar, the history of some suit he had brought
against the commune about a water-right. Madame
de Gabry, feeling the chill night-air, began to shiver
under the shawl her husband had wrapped about her,
and left us to go to her room. I then decided, instead
of going to my own, to return to the library and con-

tinue my examination of the manuscripts. In spite
of the protests of Monsieur Paul, I entered what I
may call, in old-fashioned phrase, "the book-room,"
and started to work by the light of a lamp.

After having read fifteen pages, evidently written
by some ignorant and careless scribe, for I could
scarcely discern their meaning, I plunged my hand
into the pocket of my coat to get my snuff-box; but
this movement, usually so natural and almost instinc-
tive, this time cost me some effort and even fatigue.
Nevertheless, I got out the silver box, and took from it
a pinch of the odorous powder, which, somehow or
other, I managed to spill all over my shirt-bosom under my baffled nose. I am sure my nose must have
expressed its disappointment, for it is a very expressive nose. More than once it betrayed my secret
thoughts, and especially upon a certain occasion at
the public library of Coutances, where I discovered,
right in front of my colleague Brioux, the "Cartulary
of Notre-Dame-des-Anges."

What a delight! My little eyes remained as dull
and expressionless as ever behind my spectacles. But
at the mere sight of my thick pug-nose, which quivered with joy and pride, Brioux knew that I had found
something. He noted the volume I was looking at,
observed the place where I put it back, pounced upon
it as soon as I turned my back, copied it secretly, and
published it in haste, for the sake of playing me a
trick. But his edition swarms with errors, and I had

the satisfaction of afterwards criticising some of the gross blunders he made.

But to come back to the point at which I left off: I began to suspect that I was getting very sleepy indeed. I was looking at a chart of which the interest may be divined from the fact that it contained mention of a hutch sold to Jehan d'Estonville, priest, in 1312. But although, even then, I could recognize the importance of the document, I did not give it that attention it so strongly invited. My eyes would keep turning, against my will, towards a certain corner of the table where there was nothing whatever interesting to a learned mind. There was only a big German book there, bound in pigskin, with brass studs on the sides, and very thick cording upon the back. It was a fine copy of a compilation which has little to recommend it except the wood engravings it contains, and which is well known as the "Cosmography of Munster." This volume, with its covers slightly open, was placed upon edge, with the back upwards.

I could not say for how long I had been staring causelessly at the sixteenth-century folio, when my eyes were captivated by a sight so extraordinary that even a person as devoid of imagination as I could not but have been greatly astonished by it.

I perceived, all of a sudden, without having noticed her coming into the room, a little creature seated on the back of the book, with one knee bent and one leg hanging down—somewhat in the attitude of the amazons of Hyde Park or the Bois de Boulogne on horseback. She was so small that her swinging foot did not reach the table, over which the trail of her dress extended in a serpentine line. But her face and figure were those of an adult. The fulness of her corsage and the roundness of her waist could leave no doubt of that, even for an old *savant* like myself. I will venture to add that she was very handsome, with a proud mien; for my iconographic studies have long accustomed me to recognize at once the perfection of a type and the character of a physiognomy. The countenance of this lady who had seated herself inopportunely on the back of a " Cosmography of Munster " expressed a mingling of haughtiness and mischievousness. She had the air of a queen, but a capricious queen; and I judged, from the mere expression of her eyes, that she was accustomed to wield great authority somewhere, in a very whimsical manner. Her mouth was imperious and mocking, and those blue eyes of hers seemed to laugh in a disquieting way under her finely arched black eyebrows. I have always heard that black eyebrows are very becoming to blondes; and this lady was very blonde. On the whole, the impression she gave me was one of greatness.

It may seem odd to say that a person who was no taller than a wine-bottle, and who might have been hidden in my coat pocket—but that it would have been very disrespectful to put her in it—gave me precisely an idea of greatness. But in the fine proportions of the lady seated upon the "Cosmography of Munster" there was such a proud elegance, such a harmonious majesty, and she maintained an attitude at once so easy and so noble, that she really seemed to me a very great person. Although my ink-bottle, which she examined with an expression of such mockery as appeared to indicate that she knew in advance every word that could ever come out of it at the end of my pen, was for her a deep basin in which she would have blackened her gold-clocked pink stockings up to the garter, I can assure you that she was great, and imposing even in her sprightliness.

Her costume, worthy of her face, was extremely magnificent; it consisted of a robe of gold-and-silver brocade, and a mantle of nacarat velvet, lined with vair. Her head-dress was a sort of *hennin*, with two high points; and pearls of splendid lustre made it bright and luminous as a crescent moon. Her little white hand held a wand. That wand drew my attention very strongly, because my archæological studies had taught me to recognize with certainty every sign by which the notable personages of legend and of history are distinguished. This knowledge came to my aid during various very queer conjectures with which I was laboring. I examined the wand, and saw that it appeared to have been cut from a branch of hazel.

" Then it is a fairy's wand," I said to myself;—" consequently the lady who carries it is a fairy."

Happy at thus discovering what sort of a person was before me, I tried to collect my mind sufficiently to make her a graceful compliment. It would have given me much satisfaction, I confess, if I could have talked to her about the part taken by her people, not less in the life of the Saxon and Germanic races, than in that of the Latin Occident. Such a dissertation, it appeared to me, would have been an ingenious method of thanking the lady for having thus appeared to an old scholar, contrary to the invariable custom of her kindred, who never show themselves but to innocent children or ignorant village-folk.

Because one happens to be a fairy, one is none the less a woman, I said to myself ; and since Madame Récamier, according to what I heard J. J. Ampère say, used to blush with pleasure when the little chimney-sweeps opened their eyes as wide as they could to look at her, surely the supernatural lady seated upon the " Cosmography of Munster " might feel flattered to hear an erudite man discourse learnedly about her, as about a medal, a seal, a fibula, or a token. But such an undertaking, which would have cost my timidity a great deal, became totally out of the question when I observed the Lady of the Cosmography suddenly take from an alms-purse hanging at her girdle the very smallest nuts I had ever seen, crack the shells between her teeth, and throw them at my nose,

while she nibbled the kernels with the gravity of a
suckling child.

At this conjuncture, I did what the dignity of science
demanded of me—I remained silent. But the nutshells caused such a painful tickling that I put up my
hand to my nose, and found, to my great surprise, that
my spectacles were straddling the very end of it—so
that I was actually looking at the lady, not through
my spectacles, but over them. This was incomprehensible, because my eyes, worn out over old texts,
cannot ordinarily distinguish anything without glasses
—could not tell a melon from a decanter, though the
two were placed close up to my nose.

That nose of mine, remarkable for its size, its shape,
and its coloration, legitimately attracted the attention
of the fairy ; for she seized my goose-quill pen, which
was sticking up from the ink-bottle like a plume, and
she began to pass the feather-end of that pen over my
nose. I had had more than once, in company, occasion
to suffer cheerfully from the innocent mischief of
young ladies, who made me join their games, and
would offer me their cheeks to kiss through the back
of a chair, or invite me to blow out a candle which
they would lift suddenly above the range of my breath.
But until that moment no person of the fair sex had
ever subjected me to such a whimsical piece of famil-
iarity as that of tickling my nose with my own feather
pen. Happily I remembered the maxim of my late
grandfather, who was accustomed to say that every-

thing was permissible on the part of ladies, and that whatever they do to us is to be regarded as a grace and a favor. Therefore, as a grace and a favor I received the nutshells and the titillations with my own pen, and I tried to smile. Much more!—I even found speech.

"Madame," I said, with dignified politeness, "you accord the honor of a visit not to a silly child, nor to a boor, but to a bibliophile who is very happy to make your acquaintance, and who knows that long ago you used to make elf-knots in the manes of mares at the crib, drink the milk from the skimming-pails, slip *graines-à-gratter* down the backs of our great-grand-mothers, make the hearth sputter in the faces of the old folks, and, in short, fill the house with disorder and gayety. You can also boast of giving the nicest frights in the world to lovers who stayed out in the woods too late of evenings. But I thought you had vanished out of existence at least three centuries ago. Can it really be, Madame, that you are still to be seen in this age of railroads and telegraphs? My concierge, who used to be a nurse in her young days, does not know your story; and my little boy-neighbor, whose nose is still wiped for him by his *bonne*, declares that you do not exist."

"What do you yourself think about it?" she cried, in an argentine voice, straightening up her royal little figure in a very haughty fashion, and whipping the back of the "Cosmography of Munster" as though it were a hippogriffe.

"I don't really know," I answered, rubbing my eyes. This reply, indicating a deeply scientific scepticism, had the most deplorable effect upor my questioner.

"Monsieur Sylvestre Bonnard," she said to me, "you are nothing but an old pedant. I always suspected as much. The smallest little ragamuffin who goes along the road with his shirt-tail sticking out through a hole in his pantaloons knows more about me than all the old spectacled folks in your Institutes and your Academies. To know is nothing at all; to imagine is everything. Nothing exists except that which is imagined. I am imaginary. That is to exist, I should certainly think! I am dreamed of, and I appear. Everything is only dream; and as nobody ever dreams about you, Sylvestre Bonnard, it is *you* who do not exist. I charm the world; I am everywhere—on a moonbeam, in the trembling of a hidden spring, in the moving of leaves that murmur, in the white vapors that rise each morning from the hollow meadow, in the thickets of pink brier—everywhere! . . . I am seen; I am loved. There are sighs uttered, weird thrills of pleasure felt by those who follow the light print of my feet, as I make the dead leaves whisper. I make the little children smile; I give wit to the dullest-minded nurses. Leaning above the cradles, I play, I comfort, I lull to sleep—and you doubt whether I exist! Sylvestre Bonnard, your warm coat covers the hide of an ass!"

She ceased speaking: her delicate nostrils swelled

with indignation; and while I admired, despite my vexation, the heroic anger of this little person, she pushed my pen about in the ink-bottle, backward and forward, like an oar, and then suddenly threw it at my nose, point first.

I rubbed my face, and felt it all covered with ink. She had disappeared. My lamp was extinguished. A ray of moonlight streamed down through a window and descended upon the "Cosmography of Munster." A strong cool wind, which had arisen very suddenly without my knowledge, was blowing my papers, pens, and wafers about. My table was all stained with ink. I had left my window open during the storm. What an imprudence!

III.

I WROTE to my housekeeper, as I promised, that I was safe and sound. But I took good care not to tell her that I had caught cold from going to sleep in the library at night with the window open; for the good woman would have been as unsparing in her remonstrances to me as parliaments to kings. "At your age, Monsieur," she would have been sure to say, "one ought to have more sense." She is simple enough to believe that sense grows with age. I seem to her an exception to this rule.

Not having any similar motive for concealing my

experiences from Madame de Gabry, I told her all about my vision, which she seemed to enjoy very much.

."Why, that was a charming dream of yours," she said; "and one must have real genius to dream such a dream."

"Then I am a real genius when I am asleep," I responded.

"When you dream," she replied; "and you are always dreaming."

I know that Madame de Gabry, in making this remark, only wished to please me; but that intention alone deserves my utmost gratitude, and it is therefore in a spirit of thankfulness and kindliest remembrance that I write down her words, which I will read over and over again until my dying day, and which will never be read by any one save myself.

I passed the next few days in completing the inventory of the manuscripts in the Lusance library. Certain confidential observations dropped by Monsieur Paul de Gabry, however, caused me some painful surprise, and made me decide to pursue the work after a different manner from that in which I had begun it. From those few words I learned that the fortune of Monsieur Honoré de Gabry, which had been badly managed for many years, and subsequently swept away to a large extent through the failure of a banker whose name I do not know, had been transmitted to the heirs of the old French nobleman only under the form of mortgaged real estate and irrecoverable assets.

Monsieur Paul, by agreement with his joint heirs, had decided to sell the library, and I was intrusted with the task of making arrangements to have the sale effected upon advantageous terms. But, totally ignorant as I was of all business methods and trade-customs, I thought it best to get the advice of a publisher who was one of my private friends. I wrote him at once to come and join me at Lusance; and while waiting for his arrival I took my hat and cane and made visits to the different churches of the diocese, in several of which I knew there were certain mortuary inscriptions to be found which had never been correctly copied.

So I left my hosts and departed on my pilgrimage. Exploring the churches and the cemeteries every day, visiting the parish priests and the village notaries, supping at the public inns with peddlers and cattle-dealers, sleeping at nights between sheets scented with lavender, I passed one whole week in the quiet but profound enjoyment of observing the living engaged in their various daily occupations even while I was thinking of the dead. As for the purpose of my researches, I made only a few mediocre discoveries, which caused me only a mediocre joy, and one therefore salubrious and not at all fatiguing. I copied a few interesting epitaphs; and I added to this little collection a few recipes for cooking country dishes, which a certain good priest kindly gave me.

With these riches. I returned to Lusance. and I

crossed the court-of-honor with such secret satisfaction as a *bourgeois* feels on entering his own home. This was the effect of the kindness of my hosts; and the impression I received on crossing their threshold proves, better than any reasoning could do, the excellence of their hospitality.

I entered the great parlor without meeting anybody; and the young chestnut-tree there spreading out its broad leaves seemed to me like an old friend. But the next thing which I saw—on the pier-table—caused me such a shock of surprise that I readjusted my glasses upon my nose with both hands at once, and then felt myself over so as to get at least some superficial proof of my own existence. In less than one second there thronged into my mind twenty different conjectures—the most rational of which was that I had suddenly become crazy. It seemed to me absolutely impossible that what I was looking at could exist; yet it was equally impossible for me not to see it as a thing actually existing. What caused my surprise was resting on the pier-table, above which rose a great dull speckled mirror.

I saw myself in that mirror; and I can say that I saw for once in my life the perfect image of stupefaction. But I made proper allowance for myself; I approved myself for being so stupefied by a really stupefying thing.

The object I was thus examining with a degree of astonishment that all my reasoning power failed to lessen, obtruded itself on my attention though quite motionless. The persistence and fixity of the phenomenon excluded any idea of hallucination. I am totally exempt from all nervous disorders capable of influencing the sense of sight. The cause of such visual disturbance is, I think, generally due to stomach trouble ; and, thank God! I have an excellent stomach. Moreover, visual illusions are accompanied with special abnormal conditions which impress the victims of hallucination themselves, and inspire them with a sort of terror. Now, I felt nothing of this kind; the object which I saw, although seemingly impossible in itself, appeared to me under all the natural conditions of reality. I observed that it had three dimensions, and colors, and that it cast a shadow. Ah! how I stared at it! The water came into my eyes so that I had to wipe the glasses of my spectacles.

Finally I found myself obliged to yield to the evidence, and to affirm that I had really before my eyes the Fairy, the very same Fairy I had been dreaming of in the library a few evenings before. It was she, it was her very self, I assure you! She had the same air of child-queen, the same proud supple poise ; she held the same hazel wand in her hand ; she still wore her double-peaked head-dress, and the trail of her long brocade robe undulated about her little feet. Same face, same figure. It was she indeed ; and to prevent any possible doubt of it, she was seated

on the back of a huge old-fashioned book strongly
resembling the "Cosmography of Munster." Her im-
mobility but half reassured me; I was really afraid
that she was going to take some more nuts out of her
alms-purse and throw the shells at my face.

I was standing there, waving my hands and gaping,
when the musical and laughing voice of Madame de
Gabry suddenly rang in my ears.

"So you are examining your fairy, Monsieur Bonnard!" said my hostess. "Well, do you think the
resemblance good?"

It was very quickly said; but even while hearing
it I had time to perceive that my fairy was a statuette
in colored wax, modelled with much taste and spirit by
some novice hand. But the phenomenon, even thus
reduced by a rational explanation, did not cease to
excite my surprise. How, and by whom, had the
Lady of the Cosmography been enabled to assume
plastic existence? That was what remained for me to
learn.

Turning towards Madame Gabry, I perceived that
she was not alone. A young girl dressed in black
was standing beside her. She had large intelligent
eyes, of a gray as sweet as that of the sky of the
Isle of France, and at once artless and characteristic
in their expression. At the extremities of her rather
thin arms were fidgeting uneasily two slender hands,
supple, but slightly red, as it becomes the hands of
young girls to be. Sheathed in her closely fitting

merino robe, she had the slim grace of a young tree;
and her large mouth bespoke frankness. I could not
describe how much the child pleased me at first sight!
She was not beautiful; but the three dimples of her
cheeks and chin seemed to laugh, and her whole person, which revealed the awkwardness of innocence,
had something in it indescribably good and sincere.

My gaze alternated from the statuette to the young
girl; and I saw her blush—so frankly and fully!—
the crimson passing over her face as by waves.

"Well," said my hostess, who had become sufficiently accustomed to my distracted moods to put the
same question to me twice, "is that the very same
lady who came in to see you through the window that
you left open? She was very saucy; but then you
were quite imprudent! Anyhow, do you recognize
her?"

"It is her very self," I replied; "I see her now on
that pier-table precisely as I saw her on the table in
the library."

"Then, if that be so," replied Madame de Gabry, "you
have to blame for it, in the first place, yourself, as a
man who, although devoid of all imagination, to use
your own words, knew how to depict your dream in
such vivid colors; in the second place, me, who was
able to remember and repeat faithfully all your dream;
and, lastly, Mademoiselle Jeanne, whom I now introduce to you, for she herself modelled that wax-figure
precisely according to my instructions."

Madame de Gabry had taken the young girl's hand as she spoke; but the latter had suddenly broken away from her, and was already running through the park with the speed of a bird.

"Little crazy creature!" Madame de Gabry cried after her. "How can one be so shy? Come back here to be scolded and kissed!"

But it was all of no avail; the frightened child disappeared among the shrubbery. Madame de Gabry seated herself in the only chair remaining in the dilapidated parlor.

"I should be much surprised," she said, "if my husband had not already spoken to you of Jeanne. She is a sweet child, and we both love her very much. Tell me the plain truth; what do you think of her statuette?"

I replied that the work was full of good taste and spirit, but that it showed some want of study and practice on the author's part; otherwise I had been extremely touched to think that those young fingers should have thus embroidered an old man's rough sketch of fancy, and figured so brilliantly the dreams of a dotard like myself.

"The reason I ask your opinion," replied Madame de Gabry, seriously, "is that Jeanne is a poor orphan. Do you think she could earn her living by modelling statuettes like this one?"

"As for that, no!" I replied; "and I think there is no reason to regret the fact. You say the girl is affectionate and sensitive; I can well believe you; I could believe it from her face alone. There are excitements in artist-life which impel generous hearts to act out of all rule and measure. This young creature is made to love; keep her for the domestic hearth. There only is real happiness."

"But she has no dowry!" replied Madame de Gabry.

Then, extending her hand to me, she continued:

"You are our friend; I can tell you everything. The father of this child was a banker, and one of our friends. He went into a colossal speculation, and it ruined him. He survived only a few months after his failure, in which, as Paul must have told you, three fourths of my uncle's fortune were lost, and more than half of our own.

"We had made his acquaintance at Monaco, during the winter we passed there at my uncle's house. He had an adventurous disposition, but such an engaging manner! He deceived himself before he ever deceived others. After all, it is in the ability to deceive one's self that the greatest talent is shown, is it not? Well, we were captured—my husband, my uncle, and I; and we risked much more than a reasonable amount in a very hazardous undertaking. But, bah! as Paul says, since we have no children we need not worry about it. Besides, we have the satisfaction of knowing that the friend in whom we trusted was an honest man. . . . You must know his name, it was so often in the papers and on public placards—Noël Alexandre. His wife was a very sweet person. I knew her only when she was already past her prime, with traces of having once been very pretty, and a taste for fashionable style and display which seemed quite becoming to her. She was naturally fond of social excitement; but she showed a great deal of courage and dignity after the death of her husband. She died a year after him, leaving Jeanne alone in the world."

"Clémentine!" I cried out.

And on thus learning what I had never even imagined—the mere idea of which would have set all the forces of my soul in revolt—upon hearing that Clémentine was no longer in this world, something like a great silence came within me; and the feeling which flooded my whole being was not a keen, strong pain, but a quiet and solemn sorrow. Yet I was conscious of some incomprehensible sense of alleviation, and my thought rose suddenly to heights before unknown.

"From wheresoever thou art at this moment, Clémentine," I said to myself, "look down upon this heart now indeed cooled by age, yet whose blood once boiled for thy sake, and say whether it is not reanimated by the mere thought of being able to love all that remains of thee on earth. Everything passes away since thou thyself hast passed away; but Life is immortal; it is that Life we must love in its forms eternally renewed. All the rest is child's play; and I myself, with all my books, am only like a child playing with marbles. The purpose of life—it is thou, Clémentine, who hast revealed it to me!".. .

Madame de Gabry aroused me from my thoughts by murmuring,

"The child is poor."

"The daughter of Clémentine is poor!" I exclaimed aloud; "how fortunate that it is so! I would not wish that any one but myself should provide for her and dower her! No! the daughter of Clémentine must not have her dowry from any one but me."

And, approaching Madame de Gabry as she rose from her chair, I took her right hand; I kissed that hand, and placed it on my arm, and said,

"You will conduct me to the grave of the widow of Noël Alexandre."

And I heard Madame de Gabry asking me,

"Why are you crying?"

IV.

THE LITTLE SAINT-GEORGE.

April 16.

Saint Droctoveus and the early abbots of Saint-Germain-des-Prés have been occupying me for the past forty years; but I do not know if I shall be able to write their history before I go to join them. It is already quite a long time since I became an old man. One day last year, on the Pont des Arts, one of my fellow-members at the Institute was lamenting before me over the *ennui* of becoming old.

"Still," Saint-Beuve replied to him, "it is the only way that has yet been found of living a long time."

I have tried this way, and I know just what it is worth. The trouble of it is not that one lasts too long, but that one sees all about him pass away— mother, wife, friends, children. Nature makes and unmakes all these divine treasures with gloomy indifference, and at last we find that we have not loved, we have only been embracing shadows. But how sweet some shadows are! If ever creature glided like a shadow through the life of a man, it was certainly that young girl whom I fell in love with when —incredible though it now seems—I was myself a youth.

A Christian sarcophagus from the catacombs of Rome bears a formula of imprecation, the whole terrible meaning of which I only learned with time. It says: "*Whatsoever impious man violates this sepulchre, may he die the last of his own people!*" In my capacity of archæologist, I have opened tombs and disturbed ashes in order to collect the shreds of apparel, metal ornaments, or gems that were mingled with those ashes. But I did it only through that scientific curiosity which does not exclude the feelings of reverence and of piety. May that malediction graven by some one of the first followers of the apostles upon a martyr's tomb never fall upon me! I

ought not to fear to survive my own people so long
as there are men in the world; for there are always
some whom one can love.

But the power of love itself weakens and gradually
becomes lost with age, like all the other energies of
man. Example proves it; and it is this which terrifies me. Am I sure that I have not myself already
suffered this great loss? I would surely have felt it,
but for the happy meeting which has rejuvenated me.
Poets speak of the Fountain of Youth: it does exist;
it gushes up from the earth at every step we take.
And one passes by without drinking of it!

The young girl I loved, married of her own choice
to a rival, passed, all gray-haired, into the eternal rest.
I have found her daughter—so that my life, which
before seemed to me without utility, now once more
finds a purpose and a reason for being.

To-day I "take the sun," as they say in Provence;
I take it on the terrace of the Luxembourg, at the
foot of the statue of Marguerite de Navarre. It is
a spring sun, intoxicating as young wine. I sit and
dream. My thoughts escape from my head like the
foam from a bottle of beer. They are light, and their
fizzing amuses me. I dream: such a pastime is certainly permissible to an old fellow who has published
thirty volumes of texts, and contributed to the *Jour-
nal des Savants* for twenty-six years. I have the
satisfaction of feeling that I performed my task as
well as it was possible for me to do, and that I util-

ized to their fullest extent those mediocre faculties with which Nature endowed me. My efforts were not all in vain, and I have contributed, in my own modest way, to that renaissance of historical labors which will remain the honor of this restless century. I shall certainly be counted among those ten or twelve who revealed to France her own literary antiquities. My publication of the poetical works of Gautier de Coincy inaugurated a judicious system and made a date. It is in the austere calm of old age that I decree to myself this deserved credit, and God, who sees my heart, knows whether pride or vanity have aught to do with this self-award of justice.

But I am tired; my eyes are dim; my hand trembles, and I see an image of myself in those old men of Homer, whose weakness excluded them from the battle, and who, seated upon the ramparts, lifted up their voices like crickets among the leaves.

So my thoughts were wandering when three young men seated themselves near me. I do not know whether each one of them had come in three boats, like the monkey of Lafontaine, but the three certainly displayed themselves over the space of twelve chairs. I took pleasure in watching them, not because they had anything very extraordinary about them, but because I discerned in them that brave joyous manner which is natural to youth. They were from the schools. I was less assured of it by the books they were carrying than by the character of their physiognomy. For all who busy themselves with the things of the mind can be at once recognized by an indescribable something which is common to all of them. I am very fond of young people; and these pleased me, in spite of a certain provoking wild manner which recalled to me my own college days with marvellous vividness. But they did not wear velvet doublets and long hair, as we used to do; they did not walk about, as we used to do, with a death's-head; they did not cry out, as we used to do, "Hell and malediction!" They were quite properly dressed, and neither their costume nor their language had anything suggestive of the Middle Ages. I must also add that they paid considerable attention to the women passing on the terrace, and expressed their admiration of some of them in very animated language. But their reflections, even on this subject, were not of a character to oblige me to flee from my seat. Besides, so long as youth is studious, I think it has a right to its gayeties.

One of them, having made some gallant pleasantry which I forget, the smallest and darkest of the three exclaimed, with a slight Gascon accent,

"What a thing to say! Only physiologists like us have any right to occupy ourselves about living matter. As for you, Gélis, who only live in the past— like all your fellow archivists and paleographers— you will do better to confine yourself to those stone women over there, who are your contemporaries."

And he pointed to the statues of the Ladies of Ancient France which towered up, all white, in a half-circle under the trees of the terrace. This joke, though in itself trifling, enabled me to know that the young man called Gélis was a student at the École des Chartes. From the conversation which followed I was able to learn that his neighbor, blond and wan almost to diaphaneity, taciturn and sarcastic, was Boulmier, a fellow-student. Gélis and the future doctor (I hope he will become one some day) discoursed together with much fantasy and spirit. In the midst of the loftiest speculations they would play upon words, and make jokes after the peculiar fashion of really witty persons—that is to say, in a style of enormous absurdity. I need hardly say, I suppose, that they only deigned to maintain the most monstrous kind of paradoxes. They employed all their powers of imagination to make themselves as ludicrous as possible, and all their powers of reasoning to assert the contrary of common-sense. All the better for them! I do not like to see young folks too rational.

The student of medicine, after glancing at the title of the book that Boulmier held in his hand, exclaimed,

" What!—you read Michelet—you ?"

" Yes," replied Boulmier, very gravely. " I like novels."

Gélis, who dominated both by his fine stature, imperious gestures, and ready wit, took the book, turned over a few pages rapidly, and said,

"Michelet always had a great propensity to emotional tenderness. He wept sweet tears over Maillard, that nice little man who introduced *la paperasserie* into the September massacres. But as emotional tenderness leads to fury, he becomes all at once furious against the victims. There was no help for it. It is the sentimentality of the age. The assassin is pitied, but the victim is considered quite unpardonable. In his later manner Michelet is more Michelet than ever before. There is no common-sense in it; it is simply wonderful! Neither art nor science, neither criticism nor narrative; only furies and fainting-spells and epileptic fits over matters which he never deigns to explain. Childish outcries—*envies de femme grosse!*— and a style, my friends!—not a single finished phrase! It is astounding!"

And he handed the book back to his comrade. "This is amusing madness," I thought to myself, "and not quite so devoid of common-sense as it appears. This young man, though only playing, has sharply touched the defect in the cuirass."

But the Provençal student declared that history was a thoroughly despicable exercise of rhetoric. According to him, the only true history was the natural history of man. Michelet was in the right path when he came in contact with the fistula of Louis XIV., but he fell back into the old rut almost immediately afterwards.

After this judicious expression of opinion, the young

physiologist went to join a party of passing friends. The two archivists, less well acquainted in the neighborhood of a garden so far from the Rue Paradis-aux-Marais, remained together, and began to chat about their studies. Gélis, who had completed his third class-year, was preparing a thesis on the subject of which he expatiated with youthful enthusiasm. Indeed, I thought the subject a very good one, particularly because I had recently thought myself called upon to treat a notable part of it. It was the *Monasti- cum Gallicanum.* The young erudite (I give him the name as a presage) wants to describe all the engravings made about 1690 for the work which Dom Michel Germain would have had printed but for the one irremediable hindrance which is rarely foreseen and never avoided. Dom Michel Germain left his manuscript complete, however, and in good order when he died. Will I be able to do as much with mine?—but that is not the present question. So far as I am able to understand, Monsieur Gélis intends to devote a brief archæological notice to each of the abbeys pictured by the humble engravers of Dom Michel Germain.

His friend asked him whether he was acquainted with all the manuscripts and printed documents relating to the subject. It was then that I pricked up my ears. They spoke at first of original sources; and I must confess they did so in a satisfactory manner, despite their innumerable and detestable puns. Then they began to speak about contemporary studies on the subject.

" Have you read," asked Boulmier, " the notice of
Courajod ?"

" Good !" I thought to myself.

" Yes," replied Gélis; " it is accurate."

" Have you read," said Boulmier, " the article by
Tamisey de Larroque in the ' Revue des Questions His-
toriques' ?"

" Good !" I thought to myself, for the second time.

" Yes," replied Gélis, " it is full of things.". . .

" Have you read," said Boulmier, " the ' Tableau des
Abbayes Bénédictines en 1600,' by Sylvestre Bonnard ?"

" Good !" I said to myself, for the third time.

" *Ma foi !* no !" replied Gélis. " Bonnard is an idiot !"

Turning my head, I perceived that the shadow had
reached the place where I was sitting. It was growing chilly, and I thought to myself what a fool I was
to have remained sitting there, at the risk of getting
the rheumatism, just to listen to the impertinence of
those two young fellows !

" Well ! well !" I said to myself as I got up. " Let
this prattling fledgling write his thesis, and sustain
it ! He will find my colleague Quicherat, or some
other professor at the school, to show him what an
ignoramus he is. I consider him neither more nor
less than a rascal; and really, now that I come to
think of it, what he said about Michelet awhile ago
was quite insufferable, outrageous ! To talk in that
way about an old master replete with genius ! It was
simply abominable !

April 17.

"Thérèse, give me my new hat, my best frock-coat, and my silver-headed cane."

But Thérèse is deaf as a sack of charcoal and slow as Justice. Years have made her so. The worst is that she thinks she can hear well and move about well; and, proud of her sixty years of upright domesticity, she serves her old master with the most vigilant despotism.

"What did I tell you?" . . . And now she will not give me my silver-headed cane, for fear that I might lose it! It is true that I often forget umbrellas and walking-sticks in the omnibuses and booksellers' shops. But I have a special reason for wanting to take out with me to-day my old cane with the engraved silver head representing Don Quixote charging a windmill, lance in rest, while Sancho Panza, with uplifted arms, vainly conjures him to stop. That cane is all that came to me from the heritage of my uncle, Captain Victor, who in his lifetime resembled Don Quixote much more than Sancho Panza, and who loved blows quite as much as most people fear them.

For thirty years I have been in the habit of carrying this cane upon all memorable or solemn visits which I make; and those two figures of knight and squire give me inspiration and counsel. I imagine I can hear them speak. Don Quixote says,

"Think well about great things; and know that

thought is the only reality in this world. Lift up Nature to thine own stature; and let the whole universe be for thee no more than the reflection of thine own heroic soul. Combat for honor's sake : that alone is worthy of a man ! and if it should fall to thee to receive wounds, shed thy blood as a beneficent dew, and smile."

And Sancho Panza says to me in his turn,

"Remain just what heaven made thee, comrade! Prefer the bread-crust which has become dry in thy wallet to all the partridges that roast in the kitchens of lords. Obey thy master, whether he be a wise man or a fool, and do not cumber thy brain with too many useless things. Fear blows; 'tis verily tempting God to seek after danger !"

But if the incomparable knight and his matchless squire are imaged only upon this cane of mine, they are realities to my inner conscience. Within every one of us there lives both a Don Quixote and a Sancho Panza to whom we hearken by turns; and though Sancho most persuades us, it is Don Quixote that we find ourselves obliged to admire. . . . But a truce to this dotage !—and let us go to see Madame de Gabry about some matters more important than the everyday details of life. . . .

—————

Same day.

I FOUND Madame de Gabry dressed in black, just buttoning her gloves.

"I am ready," she said.

Ready!—so I have always found her upon any occasion of doing a kindness.

After some compliments about the good health of her husband, who was taking a walk at the time, we descended the stairs and got into the carriage.

I do not know what secret influence I feared to dissipate by breaking silence, but we followed the great deserted drives without speaking, looking at the crosses, the monumental columns, and the mortuary wreaths awaiting sad purchasers.

The vehicle at last halted at the extreme verge of the land of the living, before the gate upon which words of hope are graven.

"Follow me," said Madame de Gabry, whose tall stature I noticed then for the first time. She first walked down an alley of cypresses, and then took a very narrow path contrived between the tombs. Finally, halting before a plain slab, she said to me,

"It is here."

And she knelt down. I could not help noticing the beautiful easy manner in which this Christian woman fell upon her knees, leaving the folds of her robe to spread themselves at random about her. I had never before seen any lady kneel down with such frankness and such forgetfulness of self, except two fair Polish exiles, one evening long ago, in a deserted church in Paris.

This image passed like a flash; and I saw only the

sloping stone on which was graven the name of Clémentine. What I then felt was something so deep and vague that only the sound of some rich music could convey any idea of it. I seemed to hear instruments of celestial sweetness make harmony in my old heart. With the solemn accords of a funeral chant there seemed to mingle the subdued melody of a song of love; for my soul blended into one feeling the grave sadness of the present with the familiar graces of the past.

I cannot tell whether we had remained a long time at the tomb of Clémentine before Madame de Garby arose. We passed through the cemetery again without speaking to each other. Only when we found ourselves among the living once more did I feel able to speak.

"While following you there," I said to Madame de Gabry, "I could not help thinking of those angels with whom we are said to meet on the mysterious confines of life and death. That tomb you led me to, of which I knew nothing—as I know nothing, or scarcely anything, concerning her whom it covers—brought back to me emotions which were unique in my life, and which seem in the dulness of that life like some light gleaming upon a dark road. The light recedes farther and farther away as the journey lengthens; I have now almost reached the bottom of the last slope; and, nevertheless, each time I turn to look back I see the glow as bright as ever.

"You, Madame, who knew Clémentine as a wife and mother after her hair had become gray, you cannot imagine her as I see her still; a young fair girl, all pink and white. Since you have been so kind as to be my guide, dear Madame, I ought to tell you what feelings were awakened in me by the sight of that grave to which you led me. Memories throng back upon me. I feel myself like some old gnarled and mossy oak which awakens a nestling world of birds by the shaking of its branches. Unfortunately the song my birds sing is old as the world, and can amuse no one but myself."

"Tell me your souvenirs," said Madame de Gabry. "I cannot read your books, because they are written only for scholars; but I like very much to have you talk to me, because you know how to give interest to the most ordinary things in life. And talk to me just as you would talk to an old woman. This morning I found three gray threads in my hair."

"Let them come without regret, Madame," I replied. "Time deals gently only with those who take it gently. And when in some years more you will have a silvery fringe under your black fillet, you will be reclothed with a new beauty, less vivid but more touching than the first; and you will find your husband admiring your gray tresses as much as he did that black curl which you gave him when about to be married, and which he preserves in a locket as a thing sacred. . . . These boulevards are broad and very quiet. We can talk at our ease as we walk along. I will tell you, to begin with, how I first made the acquaintance of Clémentine's father. But you must not expect anything extraordinary, or anything even remarkable; you would be greatly deceived.

"Monsieur de Lessay used to live in the second story of an old house in the Avenue de l'Observatoire, having a stuccoed front, ornamented with antique busts, and a large unkept garden attached to it. That façade and that garden were the first images my child-eyes perceived; and they will be the last, no doubt, which I shall still see through my closed eyelids when the Inevitable Day comes. For it was in that house that I was born; it was in that garden I first learned, while playing, to feel and know some particles of this old universe. Magical hours!— sacred hours!—when the soul, all fresh from the making, first discovers the world, which for its sake seems to assume such caressing brightness, such mysterious charm! And that, Madame, is indeed because the universe itself is only the reflection of our soul.

"My mother was a being very happily constituted. She rose with the sun, like the birds; and she herself resembled the birds by her domestic industry, by her maternal instinct, by her perpetual desire to sing, and by a sort of brusque grace, which I could feel the charm of very well even as a child. She was the soul of the house, which she filled with her systematic and joyous activity. My father was just as slow as she was brisk. I can recall very well that placid face of his, over which at times an ironical smile used to flit. He was fatigued with active life; and he loved his fatigue. Seated beside the fire in his big arm-chair, he used to read from morning till night; and it is from him that I inherit my love of books. I have in my library a Mably and a Raynal, which he annotated with his own hand from beginning to end. But it was utterly useless attempting to interest him in anything practical whatever. When my mother would try, by all kinds of gracious little ruses, to lure him out of his retirement, he would simply shake his head with that inexorable gentleness which is the force of weak characters. He used in this way to greatly worry the poor woman, who could not enter at all into his own sphere of meditative wisdom, and could understand nothing of life except its daily duties and the merry labor of each hour. She thought him sick, and feared he was going to become still more so. But his apathy had a different cause.

"My father, entering the Naval Office under Monsieur Decrès, in 1801, gave early proof of high administrative talent. There was a great deal of activity in the marine department in those times; and in 1805 my father was appointed chief of the Second Administrative Division. That same year, the Emperor, whose attention had been called to him by the Minister, ordered him to make a report upon the organization of the English navy. This work, which reflected

a profoundly liberal and philosophic spirit, of which
the editor himself was unconscious, was only finished
in 1807—about eighteen months after the defeat of
Admiral Villeneuve at Trafalgar. Napoleon, who,
from that disastrous day, never wanted to hear the
word ship mentioned in his presence, angrily glanced
over a few pages of the memoir, and then threw it
into the fire, vociferating, 'Words!—words! I said
once before that I hated ideologists.' My father was
told afterwards that the Emperor's anger was so intense at the moment that he stamped the manuscript
down into the fire with his boot-heels. At all events,
it was his habit, when very much irritated, to poke
down the fire with his feet until he had scorched his
boot-soles. My father never fully recovered from this
disgrace; and the fruitlessness of all his efforts towards reform was certainly the cause of the apathy
which came upon him at a later day. Nevertheless,
Napoleon, after his return from Elba, sent for him,
and ordered him to prepare some liberal and patriotic
bulletins and proclamations for the fleet. After Waterloo, my father, whom the event had rather saddened than surprised, retired into private life, and was
not interfered with — except that it was generally
averred of him that he was a Jacobin, a *buveur-de-
sang*—one of those men with whom no one could af-
ford to be on intimate terms. My mother's eldest
brother, Victor Maldent, an infantry captain—retired
on half-pay in 1814, and disbanded in 1815—aggravat-

ed by his bad attitude the situation in which the fall
of the Empire had placed my father. Captain Victor
used to shout in the *cafés* and the public balls that
the Bourbons had sold France to the Cossacks. He
used to show everybody a tricolored cockade hidden
in the lining of his hat; and carried with much osten-
tation a walking-stick the handle of which had been
so carved that the shadow thrown by it made the sil-
houette of the Emperor.

"Unless you have seen certain lithographs by Char-
let, Madame, you could form no idea of the physiognomy of my Uncle Victor, when he used to stride
about the garden of the Tuileries with a fiercely elegant manner of his own—buttoned up in his frogged
coat, with his cross-of-honor upon his breast, and a
bouquet of violets in his button-hole.

"Idleness and intemperance greatly intensified the
vulgar recklessness of his political passions. He used
to insult people whom he happened to see reading the
Quotidienne, or the *Drapeau Blanc*, and compel them
to fight with him. In this way he had the pain and
the shame of wounding a boy of sixteen in a duel.
In short, my Uncle Victor was the very reverse of a
well-educated person; and as he came to breakfast
and dine at our house every blessed day in the year,
his bad reputation became attached to our family.
My poor father suffered cruelly from some of his
guest's pranks; but being very good-natured, he never
made any remarks, and continued to give the free-

dom of his house to the captain, who only despised him for it.

" All this which I have told you, Madame, was explained to me afterwards. But at the time in question, my uncle the captain filled me with the very enthusiasm of admiration, and I promised myself to try to become some day as like him as possible. So one fine morning, in order to begin the likeness, I put my arms akimbo, and swore like a trooper. My excellent mother at once gave me such a box on the ear that I remained half stupefied for some little while before I could even burst out crying. I can still see the old arm-chair, covered with yellow Utrecht velvet, behind which I wept innumerable tears that day.

" I was a very little fellow then. One morning my father, lifting me upon his knees, as he was in the habit of doing, smiled at me with that slightly ironical smile which gave a certain piquancy to his perpetual gentleness of manner. As I sat on his knee, playing with his long white hair, he told me something which I did not understand very well, but which interested me very much, for the simple reason that it was mysterious to me. I think, but am not quite sure, that he related to me that morning the story of the little King of Yvetot, according to ·˙ song. All of a sudden we heard a great report; and the windows rattled. My father slipped me down gently on the floor at his feet; he threw up his trembling arms, with a strange gesture; his face became all inert and

9

white, and his eyes seemed enormous. He tried to speak, but his teeth were chattering. At last he murmured, "They have shot him!" I did not know what he meant, and felt only a vague terror. I knew afterwards, however, that he was speaking of Marshal Ney, who fell on the 7th of December, 1815, under the wall enclosing a vacant lot beside our house.

"About that time I used often to meet on the stairway an old man (or, perhaps, not exactly an old man) with little black eyes which flashed with extraordinary vivacity, and an impassive swarthy face. He did not seem to me alive—or at least he did not seem to me alive in the same way that other men were alive. I had once seen, at the residence of Monsieur Denon, where my father had taken me with him on a visit, a mummy brought from Egypt; and I believed in good faith that Monsieur Denon's mummy used to get up when no one was looking, leave its gilded case, put on a brown coat and powdered wig, and become transformed into Monsieur de Lessay. And even to-day, dear Madame, while I reject that opinion as being without foundation, I must confess that Monsieur de Lessay bore a very strong resemblance to Monsieur Denon's mummy. The fact is enough to explain why this person inspired me with fantastic terror.

"In reality, Monsieur de Lessay was a small gentleman and a great philosopher. As a disciple of Mably and Rousseau, he flattered himself on being a man without any prejudices; and this pretension itself is a very great prejudice.

" He professed to hate fanaticism, yet was himself a fanatic on the topic of toleration. I am telling you, Madame, about a character belonging to an age that is past. I fear I will not be able to make you understand, and I am sure I will not be able to interest you. It was so long ago! But I will abridge as much as possible : besides, I did not promise you anything interesting ; and you could not have expected to hear of remarkable adventures in the life of Sylvestre Bonnard."

Madame de Gabry encouraged me to proceed, and I resumed :

"Monsieur de Lessay was brusque with men and courteous to ladies. He used to kiss the hand of my mother, whom the customs of the Republic and the Empire had not habituated to such gallantry. In him, I touched the age of Louis XVI. Monsieur de Lessay was a geographer ; and nobody, I believe, ever showed more pride than he in occupying himself with the face of the earth. Under the Old Régime he had attempted philosophical agriculture, and thus squandered his estates to the very last acre. When he had ceased to own one square foot of ground, he took possession of the whole globe, and prepared an extraordinary number of maps, based upon the narratives of travellers. But as he had been mentally nourished with the very marrow of the " Encyclopédie," he was not satisfied with merely parking off human beings within so many degrees, minutes, and seconds of latitude and longitude. He also occupied himself, alas! with the question of their happiness. It is worthy of remark, Madame, that those who have given themselves the most concern about the happiness of peoples have made their neighbors very miserable. Monsieur de Lessay, who was more of a geometrician than D'Alembert, and more of a philosopher than Jean Jacques, was also more of a royalist than Louis XVIII. But his love for the King was as nothing to his hate for the Emperor. He had joined the conspiracy of Georges against the First Consul; but in the framing of the indictment he was not included among the inculpated parties, having been either ignored or despised, and this injury he never could forgive Bonaparte, whom he called the Ogre of Corsica, and to whom he used to say he would never have confided even the command of a regiment, so pitiful a soldier he judged him to be.

"In 1820, Monsieur de Lessay, who had then been a widower for many years, married again, at the age of sixty, a very young woman, whom he pitilessly kept at work preparing maps for him, and who gave him a daughter some years after their marriage, and died in childbed. My mother had nursed her during her brief illness, and had taken care of the child. The name of that child was Clémentine.

"It was from the time of that birth and that death that the relations between our family and Monsieur de

Lessay began. In the meanwhile I had been growing dull as I began to leave my true childhood behind me. I had lost the charming power of being able to see and feel; and things no longer caused me those delicious surprises which form the enchantment of the more tender age. For the same reason, perhaps, I have no distinct remembrance of the period following the birth of Clémentine; I only know that a few months afterwards I had a misfortune, the mere thought of which still wrings my heart. I lost my mother. A great silence, a great coldness, and a great darkness seemed all at once to fill the house.

"I fell into a sort of torpor. My father sent me to the *lycée*, but I could only arouse myself from my lethargy with the greatest effort.

"Still, I was not altogether a dullard, and my professors were able to teach me almost everything they wanted, namely, a little Greek and a great deal of Latin. My acquaintances were confined to the ancients. I learned to esteem Miltiades, and to admire Themistocles. I became familiar with Quintus Fabius, as far, at least, as it was possible to become familiar with so great a Consul. Proud of these lofty acquaintances, I scarcely ever condescended to notice little Clémentine and her old father, who, in any event, went away to Normandy one fine morning without my having deigned to give a moment's thought to their possible return.

They came back, however, Madame, they came back!

Influences of Heaven, forces of nature, all ye mysterious powers which vouchsafe to man the ability to love, you know how I again beheld Clémentine! They re-entered our melancholy home. Monsieur de Lessay no longer wore a wig. Bald, with a few gray locks about his ruddy temples, he had all the aspect of robust old age. But that divine being whom I saw all resplendent, as she leaned upon his arm — she whose presence illuminated the old faded parlor—she was not an apparition! It was Clémentine herself! I am speaking the simple truth: her violet eyes seemed to me in that moment supernatural, and even to-day I cannot imagine how those two living jewels could have endured the fatigues of life, or become subjected to the corruption of death.

" She betrayed a little shyness in greeting my father, whom she did not remember. Her complexion was slightly pink, and her half-open lips smiled with that smile which makes one think of the Infinite—perhaps because it betrays no particular thought, and expresses only the joy of living and the bliss of being beautiful. Under a pink hood her face shone like a gem in an open casket; she wore a cashmere scarf over a robe of white muslin plaited at the waist, from beneath which protruded the tip of a little Morocco shoe. . . . Oh! you must not make fun of me, dear Madame, that was the fashion of the time; and I do not know whether our new fashions have nearly so much simplicity, brightness, and decorous grace.

"Monsieur de Lessay informed us that, in consequence of having undertaken the publication of a historical atlas, he had come back to live in Paris, and that he would be pleased to occupy his former room, if it was still vacant. My father asked Mademoiselle de Lessay whether she was pleased to visit the capital. She appeared to be, for her smile blossomed out in reply. She smiled at the windows that looked out upon the green and luminous garden; she smiled at the bronze Marius seated among the ruins of Carthage above the dial of the clock; she smiled at the old yellow-velveted arm-chairs, and at the poor student who was afraid to lift his eyes to look at her. From that day—how I loved her!

"But here we are already at the Rue de Sèvres, and in a little while we shall be in sight of your windows. I am a very bad story-teller; and if I were —by some impossible chance—to take it into my head to compose a novel, I know I should never succeed. I have been drawing out to tiresome length a narrative which I must finish briefly; for there is a certain delicacy, a certain grace of soul, which an old man could not help offending by any complacent expatiation upon the sentiments of even the purest love. Let us take a short turn on this boulevard, lined with convents; and my recital will be easily finished within the distance separating us from that little spire you see over there. . . .

"Monsieur de Lessay, on finding that I had graduated at the École des Chartes, judged me worthy to assist him in preparing his historical atlas. The plan was to illustrate, by a series of maps, what the old philosopher termed the Vicissitudes of Empires from the time of Noah down to that of Charlemagne. Monsieur de Lessay had stored up in his head all the errors of the eighteenth century in regard to antiquity. I belonged, so far as my historical studies were concerned, to the new school; and I was just at that age when one does not know how to dissemble. The manner in which the old man understood, or, rather, misunderstood, the epoch of the Barbarians,—his obstinate determination to find in remote antiquity only ambitious princes, hypocritical and avaricious prelates, virtuous citizens, poet-philosophers, and other personages who never existed outside of the novels of Marmontel,—made me dreadfully unhappy, and at first used to excite me into attempts at argument,—rational enough, but perfectly useless and sometimes dangerous, for Monsieur de Lessay was very irascible, and Clémentine was very beautiful. Between her and him I passed many hours of torment and of delight. I was in love; I was a coward, and I granted to him all that he demanded of me in regard to the political and historical aspect which the Earth—that was at a later day to bear Clémentine—presented in the time of Abraham, of Menes, and of Deucalion.

"As fast as we drew our maps Mademoiselle de Lessay tinted them in water-colors. Bending over the table, she held the brush lightly between two fingers; the shadow of her eyelashes descended upon her cheeks, and bathed her half-closed eyes in a delicious penumbra. Sometimes she would lift her head, and I would see her lips pout. There was so much expression in her beauty that she could not breathe without seeming to sigh; and her most ordinary poses used to throw me into the deepest ecstasies of admiration. Whenever I gazed at her I fully agreed with Monsieur de Lessay that Jupiter had once reigned as a despot-king over the mountainous regions of Thessaly, and that Orpheus had committed the imprudence of leaving the teaching of philosophy to the clergy. I am not now quite sure whether I was a coward or a hero when I accorded all this to the obstinate old man.

"Mademoiselle de Lessay, I must acknowledge, paid very little attention to me. But this indifference seemed to me so just and so natural that I never even dreamed of thinking I had a right to complain about it; it made me unhappy, but without my knowing that I was unhappy at the time. I was hopeful;—we had then only got as far as the First Assyrian Empire.

"Monsieur de Lessay came every evening to take coffee with my father. I do not know how they became such friends; for it would have been difficult to find two characters more oppositely constituted. My father was a man who admired very few things, but was capable of excusing a great many. Still, as he grew older, he evinced more and more dislike of every thing in the shape of exaggeration. He clothed his ideas with a thousand delicate shades of expression, and never pronounced an opinion without all sorts of reservations. These conversational habits, natural to a finely trained mind, used to greatly irritate the dry, terse old aristocrat, who was never in the least disarmed by the moderation of an adversary—quite the contrary! I always foresaw one danger. That danger was Bonaparte. My father had not himself retained any particular affection for his memory; but, having worked under his direction, he did not like to hear him abused, especially in favor of the Bourbons, against whom he had serious reason to feel resentment. Monsieur de Lessay, more of a Voltairean and a Legitimist than ever, now traced back to Bonaparte the origin of every social, political, and religious evil. Such being the situation, the idea of Uncle Victor made me feel particularly uneasy. This terrible uncle had become absolutely insufferable now that his sister was no longer there to calm him down. The harp of David was broken, and Saul was wholly delivered over to the spirit of madness. The fall of Charles X. had increased the audacity of the old Napoleonic veteran, who uttered all imaginable bravadoes. He no longer frequented our house, which had become too silent for him. But sometimes, at the dinner-hour, we would see him suddenly make his appearance, all covered with flowers, like a mausoleum. Ordinarily he would sit down to table with an oath, growled out from the very bottom of his chest, and brag, between every two mouthfuls, of his good fortune with the ladies as a *vieux brave.* Then, when the dinner was over, he would fold up his napkin in the shape of a bishop's mitre, gulp down half a decanter of brandy, and rush away with the hurried air of a man terrified at the mere idea of remaining for any length of time, without drinking, in conversation with an old philosopher and a young scholar. I felt perfectly sure that, if ever he and Monsieur de Lessay should come together, all would be lost. But that day came, madame!

"The captain was almost hidden by flowers that day, and seemed so much like a monument commemorating the glories of the Empire that one would have liked to pass a garland of immortelles over each of his arms. He was in an extraordinarily good humor; and the first person to profit by that good humor was our cook — for he put his arm round her waist while she was placing the roast on the table.

"After dinner he pushed away the decanter presented to him, observing that he was going to burn some brandy in his coffee later on. I asked him tremblingly whether he would not prefer to have his coffee at once. He was very suspicious, and not at all dull of comprehension—my Uncle Victor. My precipitation seemed to him in very bad taste; for he looked at me in a peculiar way, and said.

"'Patience! my nephew. It isn't the business of the baby of the regiment to sound the retreat! Devil take it! You must be in a great hurry, Master Pedant, to see if I've got spurs on my boots!'

"It was evident the captain had divined that I wanted him to go. And I knew him well enough to be sure that he was going to stay. He stayed. The least circumstances of that evening remain impressed on my memory. My uncle was extremely jovial. The mere idea of being in somebody's way was enough to keep him in good humor. He told us, in regular barrack style, *ma foi!* a certain story about a monk, a trumpet, and five bottles of Chambertin, which must have been much enjoyed in garrison society, but which I would not venture to repeat to you, Madame, even if I could remember it. When we passed into the parlor, the captain called attention to the bad condition of our andirons, and learnedly discoursed on the merits of rottenstone as a brass-polisher. Not a word on the subject of politics. He was husbanding his forces. Eight o'clock sounded from the ruins of Carthage on the mantelpiece. It was Monsieur de Lessay's hour. A few moments later he entered the parlor with his daughter. The ordinary evening chat began. Clémentine sat down and began to work on some embroidery beside the lamp, whose shade left her pretty head in a soft shadow, and threw down upon her fingers a radiance that made them seem almost self-luminous. Monsieur de Lessay spoke of a comet announced by the astronomers, and developed some theories in relation to the subject, which however audacious, betrayed at least a certain degree of intellectual culture. My father, who knew a good deal about astronomy, advanced some sound ideas of his own, which he ended up with his eternal, ' But what do we know about it, after all?' In my turn I cited the opinion of our neighbor of the Observatory—the great Arago. My Uncle Victor declared that comets had a peculiar influence on the quality of wines, and related in support of this view a jolly tavern-story. I was so delighted with the turn the conversation had taken that I did all in my power to maintain it in the same groove, with the help of my most recent studies, by a long exposition of the chemical composition of those nebulous bodies which, although extending over a length of billions of leagues, could be contained in a small bottle. My father, a little surprised at my unusual eloquence, watched me with his peculiar, placid, ironical smile. But one cannot always remain in heaven. I spoke, as I looked at Clémentine, of a certain ' *comète*' of diamonds, which I had been admiring in a jeweler's window the evening before. It was a most unfortunate inspiration of mine.

"'Ah! my nephew,' cried Uncle Victor, 'that *comète* of yours was nothing to the one which the Empress Josephine wore in her hair when she came to Strasburg to distribute crosses to the army.'

"'That little Josephine was very fond of finery and display,' observed Monsieur de Lessay, between two sips of coffee. 'I do not blame her for it; she had good qualities, though rather frivolous in character. She was a Tascher, and she conferred a great honor on Bonaparte in marrying him. To say a Tascher does not, of course, mean a great deal; but to say a Bonaparte simply means nothing at all.'

"'What do you mean by that, Monsieur the Marquis?' demanded Captain Victor.

"'I am not a marquis,' dryly responded Monsieur de Lessay; 'and I mean simply that Bonaparte would have been very well suited had he married one of those cannibal women described by Captain Cook in his voyages—naked, tattooed, with a ring in her nose—devouring with delight putrefied human flesh.'

"I had foreseen it, and in my anguish (O pitiful human heart!) my first idea was about the remarkable exactness of my anticipations. I must say that the Captain's reply belonged to the sublime order. He put his arms akimbo, eyed Monsieur de Lessay contemptuously from head to foot, and said,

"'Napoleon, Monsieur the Vidame, had another spouse besides Josephine, another spouse besides Marie-Louise. That companion you know nothing of; but I have seen her, close to me. She wears a mantle of azure gemmed with stars; she is crowned with laurels; the Cross-of-Honor flames upon her breast. Her name is GLORY!'"

" Monsieur de Lessay set his cup on the mantle-piece, and quietly observed,

" ' Your Bonaparte was a blackguard !'

" My father rose up calmly, extended his arm, and said very softly to Monsieur de Lessay,

" 'Whatever the man was who died at St. Helena, I worked for ten years in his government, and my brother-in-law was three times wounded under his eagles. I beg of you, dear sir and friend, never to forget these facts in future.'

" What the sublime and burlesque insolence of the Captain could not do, the courteous remonstrance of my father effected immediately, throwing Monsieur de Lessay into a furious passion.

" ' I did forget,' he exclaimed, between his set teeth, livid in his rage, and fairly foaming at the mouth; 'the herring-cask always smells of herring, and when one has been in the service of rascals—'

" As he uttered the word, the Captain sprang at his throat; I am sure he would have strangled him upon the spot but for his daughter and me.

" My father, a little paler than his wont, stood there with his arms folded, and watched the scene with a look of inexpressible pity. What followed was still more lamentable—but why dwell further upon the folly of two old men. Finally I succeeded in separating them. Monsieur de Lessay made a sign to his daughter and left the the room. As she was following him, I ran out into the stairway after her.

"'Mademoiselle,' I said to her, wildly, taking her hand as I spoke, 'I love you! I love you!'

"For a moment she pressed my hand; her lips opened. What was it that she was going to say to me? But suddenly, lifting her eyes towards her father ascending the stairs, she drew her hand away, and made me a gesture of farewell.

"I never saw her again. Her father went to live in the neighborhood of the Pantheon, in an apartment which he had rented for the sale of his historical atlas. He died in it a few months afterwards of an apoplectic stroke. His daughter, I was told, retired to Caen to live with some aged relative. It was there that, later on, she married a bank-clerk, the same Noël Alexandre who became so rich and died so poor.

"As for me, Madame, I have lived alone, at peace with myself; my existence, equally exempt from great pains and great joys, has been tolerably happy. But for many years I could never see an empty chair beside my own of a winter's evening without feeling a sudden painful sinking at my heart. Last year I learned from you, who had known her, the story of her old age and death. I saw her daughter at your house. I have seen her; but I cannot yet say like the aged man of Scripture, '*And now, O Lord, let thy servant depart in peace!*' For if an old fellow like me can be of any use to anybody, I would wish, with your help, to devote my last energies and abilities to the care of this orphan."

I had uttered these last words in Madame de Gabry's own vestibule; and I was about to take leave of my kind guide when she said to me,

"My dear Monsieur, I cannot help you in this matter as much as I would like to do. Jeanne is an orphan and a minor. You cannot do anything for her without the authorization of her guardian."

"Ah!" I exclaimed, "I did not have the least idea in the world that Jeanne had a guardian!"

Madame de Gabry looked at me with visible surprise. She had not expected to find the old man quite so simple.

She resumed:

"The guardian of Jeanne Alexandre is Maître Mouche, notary at Levallois-Perret. I am afraid you will not be able to come to any understanding with him; for he is a very serious person."

"Why! good God!" I cried, "with what kind of people can you expect me to have any sort of understanding at my age, except serious persons."

She smiled with a sweet mischievousness—just like my father used to smile—and answered:

"With those who are like you—the innocent folks who wear their hearts on their sleeves. Monsieur Mouche is not exactly a man of that kind. He is cunning and light-fingered. But although I have very little liking for him, we will go together and see him, if you wish, and ask his permission to visit Jeanne, whom he has sent to a boarding-school at Les Ternes, where she is very unhappy."

10

We agreed at once upon a day; I kissed Madame de Gabry's hands, and we bid each other good-by.

From May 2 to May 5.

I HAVE seen him in his office, Maître Mouche, the guardian of Jeanne. Small, thin, and dry; his complexion looks as if it was made out of the dust of his pigeon-holes. He is a spectacled animal; for to imagine him without his spectacles would be impossible. I have heard him speak, this Maître Mouche; he has a voice like a tin rattle, and he uses choice phrases; but I would have been better pleased if he had not chosen his phrases so carefully. I have observed him, this Maître Mouche; he is very ceremonious, and watches his visitors slyly out of the corner of his eye.

Maître Mouche is quite pleased, he informs us; he is delighted to find we have taken such an interest in his ward. But he does not think we are placed in this world just to amuse ourselves. No: he does not believe it; and I am free to acknowledge that anybody in his company is likely to reach the same conclusion, so little is he capable of inspiring joyfulness. He fears that it would be giving his dear ward a false and pernicious idea of life to allow her too much enjoyment. It is for that reason that he requests Madame de Gabry not to invite the young girl to her house but at very long intervals.

We left the dusty notary and his dusty study with

a permit in due form (everything which issues from the office of Maître Mouche is in due form) to visit Mademoiselle Jeanne Alexandre on the first Thursday of each month at Mademoiselle Préfère's private school, Rue Demours, Aux Ternes.

The first Thursday in May I set out to pay a visit to Mademoiselle Préfère, whose establishment I discerned from afar off by a big sign, painted with blue letters. That blue tint was the first indication I received of Mademoiselle Préfère's character, which I was able to see more of later on. A scared-looking servant took my card, and abandoned me without one word of hope at the door of a chilly parlor, full of that stale odor peculiar to the dining-rooms of educational establishments. The floor of this parlor had been waxed with such pitiless energy, that I remained for a while in distress upon the threshold. But happily observing that little strips of woollen carpet had been scattered over the floor in front of each horse-hair chair, I succeeded, by cautiously stepping from one carpet-island to another, in reaching the angle of the mantlepiece, where I sat down quite out of breath.

Over the mantlepiece, in a large gilded frame, was a written document, entitled, in flamboyant Gothic lettering, *Tableau d'Honneur*, with a long array of names underneath, among which I did not have the pleasure of finding that of Jeanne Alexandre. After having read over several times the names of those girl-pupils who had thus made themselves honored in the eyes

of Mademoiselle Préfère, I began to feel uneasy at not
hearing any one coming. Mademoiselle Préfère would
certainly have succeeded in establishing the absolute
silence of the interstellar spaces throughout her peda-
gogical domains, had it not been that the sparrows
had chosen her yard to assemble in by legions, and
chirp at the top of their voices. It was a pleasure to
hear them. But there was no way of seeing them—
through the ground-glass windows. I had to content
myself with the sights of the parlor, decorated from
floor to ceiling, on all of its four walls, with drawings
executed by the pupils of the institution. There were
Vestals, flowers, thatched cottages, column-capitals,
and an enormous head of Tatius, King of the Sabines,
bearing the signature *Estelle Mouton.*

I had already passed some time in admiring the
energy with which Mademoiselle Mouton had deline-
ated the bushy eyebrows and the fierce gaze of the antique warrior, when a sound, faint like the rustling
of a dead leaf moved by the wind, caused me to turn
my head. It was not a dead leaf at all—it was Mademoiselle Préfère. With hands joined before her, she
came gliding over the mirror-polish of that wonderful
floor as the Saints of the "Golden Legend" were
wont to glide over the crystal surface of the waters.
But upon any other occasion, I am sure, Mademoiselle
Préfère would not have made me think in the least
about those virgins dear to mystical fancy. Her face
rather gave me the idea of a russet-apple preserved

for a whole winter in an attic by some economical housekeeper. Her shoulders were covered with a fringed pelerine, which had nothing at all remarkable about it, but which she wore as if it were a sacerdotal vestment, or the symbol of some high civic function.

I explained to her the purpose of my visit, and gave her my letter of introduction.

"Ah!—so you saw Monsieur Mouche!" she exclaimed. "Is his health *very* good? He is the most upright of men, the most—"

She did not finish the phrase, but raised her eyes to the ceiling. My own followed the direction of their gaze, and observed a little spiral of paper lace, suspended from the place of the chandelier, which was apparently destined, so far as I could discover, to attract the flies away from the gilded mirror-frames and the *Tableau d'honneur*.

"I have met Mademoiselle Jeanne Alexandre," I observed, "at the residence of Madame de Gabry, and had reason to appreciate the excellent character and quick intelligence of the young girl. As I used to know her parents very well, the friendship which I felt for them naturally inclines me to take an interest in her."

Mademoiselle Préfère, in lieu of making any reply, sighed profoundly, pressed her mysterious pelerine to her heart, and again contemplated the paper spiral.

At last she observed,

"Since you were once the friend of Monsieur and

Madame Alexandre, I hope and trust that, like Monsieur Mouche and myself, you deplore those crazy speculations which led them to ruin, and reduced their daughter to absolute poverty !"

I thought to myself, on hearing these words, how very wrong it is to be unlucky, and how unpardonable such an error on the part of those previously in a position worthy of envy.   Their fall at once avenges and flatters us ; and we are wholly pitiless.

After having answered, very frankly, that I knew nothing whatever about the history of the bank, I asked the schoolmistress if she was satisfied with Mademoiselle Alexandre.

" That child is indomitable !" cried Mademoiselle Préfère.

And she assumed an attitude of lofty resignation, to symbolize the difficult situation she was placed in by a pupil so hard to train.   Then, with more calmness of manner, she added :

" The young person is not unintelligent.   But she cannot resign herself to learn things by principles."

What a strange old maid this Mademoiselle Préfère is ! She walks without lifting her legs, and speaks without moving her lips ! Without, however, considering her peculiarities for more than a reasonable instant, I replied that principles were, no doubt, very excellent things, and that I could trust myself to her judgment in regard to their value; but that, after all, when one had learned something, it made very little difference what method had been followed in the learning of it.

Mademoiselle made a slow gesture of dissent. Thus, with a sigh, she declared,

" Ah, Monsieur ! those who do not understand educational methods are apt to have very false ideas on these subjects. I am certain they express their opinions with the best intentions in the world ; but they would do better, a great deal better, to leave all such questions to competent people."

I did not attempt to argue further ; and simply asked her whether I could see Mademoiselle Alexandre at once.

She looked at her pelerine, as if trying to read in the entanglement of its fringes, as in a conjuring-book, what sort of answer she ought to make ; then said,

" Mademoiselle Alexandre has a penance to perform, and a class-lesson to give ; but I should be very sorry to let you put yourself to the trouble of coming here all to no purpose. I am going to send for her. Only first allow me, Monsieur—as it is our custom— to put your name on the visitors' register."

She sat down at the table, opened a large copy-book, and, taking out Maître Mouche's letter again from under her pelerine, where she had placed it, looked at it, and began to write.

" ' Bonnard '—with a *d*, is it not ?" she asked. " Excuse me for being so particular ; but my opinion is

that proper names have an orthography. We have
dictation-lessons in proper names, Monsieur, at this
school—historical proper names, of course!"

After I had written down my name in a running
hand, she inquired whether she should not put down
after it my profession, title, quality — such as "retired merchant," "employé," "independent gentleman," or something else. There was a column in her
register expressly for that purpose.

"My goodness, Madame!" I said, "if you must absolutely fill that column of yours, put down 'Member
of the Institute.'"

It was still Mademoiselle Préfère's pelerine I saw
before me; but it was not Mademoiselle Préfère now
who wore it; it was a totally different person, oblig-
ing, gracious. caressing, radiant, happy. Her eyes
smiled; the little wrinkles of her face (there were a
vast number of them!) also smiled; her mouth smiled
likewise, but only on one side. I discovered afterwards
that was her best side. She spoke: her voice had
also changed with her manner; it was now sweet as
honey.

"You said, Monsieur, that our dear Jeanne was very
intelligent. I discovered the same thing myself, and
I am proud of being able to agree with you. This
young girl has really made me feel a great deal of
interest in her. She has what I call a happy disposition. . . . But excuse me for thus drawing upon your
valuable time."

She summoned the servant-girl, who looked much more hurried and scared than before, and who vanished with the order to go and tell Mademoiselle Alexandre that Monsieur Sylvestre Bonnard, Member of the Institute, was waiting to see her in the parlor.

Mademoiselle Préfère had barely time to confide to me that she had the most profound respect for all decisions of the Institute—whatever they might be—when Jeanne appeared, out of breath, red as a poppy, with her eyes very wide open, and her arms dangling helplessly at her sides—charming in her artless awkwardness.

"What a state you are in, my dear child!" murmured Mademoiselle Préfère, with maternal sweetness, as she arranged the girl's collar.

Jeanne certainly did present an odd aspect. Her hair combed back, and imperfectly held by a net from which loose curls were escaping; her slender arms, sheathed down to the elbows in lustring sleeves; her hands, which she did not seem to know what to do with, all red with chilblains; her dress, much too short, revealing that she had on stockings much too large for her, and shoes worn down at the heel; and a skipping-rope tied round her waist in lieu of a belt,—all combined to lend Mademoiselle Jeanne an appearance the reverse of presentable.

"Oh, you crazy girl!" sighed Mademoiselle Préfère, who now seemed no longer like a mother, but rather like an elder sister.

Then she suddenly left the room, gliding like a shadow over the polished floor.

I said to Jeanne,

"Sit down, Jeanne, and talk to me like you would to a friend. Are you not better satisfied here now than you were last year?"

She hesitated; then answered with a good-natured smile of resignation,

"Not much better."

I asked her to tell me about her school life. She began at once to enumerate all her different studies— piano, style, chronology of the Kings of France, sewing, drawing, catechism, deportment. . . . I could never remember them all! She still held in her hands, all unconsciously, the two ends of her skipping-rope, and she raised and lowered them regularly while making her enumeration. Then all at once she became conscious of what she was doing, blushed, stammered, and became so confused that I had to renounce my desire to know the full programme of study adopted in the Préfère Institution.

After having questioned Jeanne on various matters, and obtained only the vaguest answers, I perceived that her young mind was totally absorbed by the skipping-rope, and I entered bravely into that grave subject.

"So you have been skipping?" I said. "It is a very nice amusement, but one that you must not exert yourself too much at; for any excessive exercise of that

kind might seriously injure your health, and I should
be very much grieved about it, Jeanne—I should be
very much grieved, indeed!"

"You are very kind, Monsieur," the young girl said,
"to have come to see me and talk to me like this I
did not think about thanking you when I came in,
because I was too much surprised. Have you seen
Madame de Gabry? Please tell me something about
her, Monsieur"

"Madame de Gabry," I answered, "is very well.
I can only tell you about her, Jeanne, what an old
gardener once said of the lady of the castle, his mistress, when somebody anxiously inquired about her:
'Madame is in her road.' Yes, Madame de Gabry is
in her own road, and you know, Jeanne, what a good
road it is, and how steadily she can walk upon it. I
went out with her the other day, very, very far away
from the house; and we talked about you. We talked
about you, my child, at your mother's grave."

"I am very glad," said Jeanne.

And then, all at once, she began to cry.

I felt too much reverence for those generous tears
to attempt in any way to check the emotion that had
evoked them. But in a little while, as the girl wiped
her eyes, I asked her,

"Will you not tell me, Jeanne, why you were thinking so much about that skipping-rope a little while
ago?"

"Why, indeed I will, Monsieur. It was only because I had no right to come into the parlor with a skipping-rope. You know, of course, that I am past the age for playing at skipping. But when the servant said there was an old gentleman . . . oh! . . . I mean . . . that a gentleman was waiting for me in the parlor, I was making the little girls jump. Then I tied the rope round my waist in a hurry, so that it might not get lost. It was wrong. But I have not been in the habit of having many people come to see me. And Mademoiselle Préfère never lets us off if we commit any breach of deportment: so I know she is going to punish me, and I am very sorry about it." . .

"That is too bad, Jeanne!"

She became very grave, and said,

"Yes, Monsieur, it is too bad; because when I am punished myself, I have no more authority over the little girls."

I did not at once fully understand the nature of this unpleasantness; but Jeanne explained to me that, as she was charged by Mademoiselle Préfère with the duties of taking care of the youngest class, of washing and dressing the children, of teaching them how to behave, how to sew, how to say the alphabet, of showing them how to play, and, finally, of putting them to bed at the close of the day, she could not make herself obeyed by those turbulent little folks on the days she was condemned to wear a night-cap in the class-room, or to eat her meals standing up, from a plate turned upside down.

Having secretly admired the punishments devised by the Lady of the Enchanted Pelerine, I responded,

"Then, if I understand you rightly, Jeanne, you are at once a pupil here and a mistress? It is a condition of existence very common in the world. You are punished, and you punish?"

"Oh, Monsieur!" she exclaimed. "No! I never punish!"

"Then, I suspect," said I, "that your indulgence gets you many scoldings from Mademoiselle Préfère?"

She smiled, and winked.

Then I said to her that the troubles in which we often involve ourselves, by trying to act according to our conscience and to do the best we can, are never of the sort that totally dishearten and weary us, but are, on the contrary, wholesome trials. This sort of philosophy touched her very little. She even appeared totally unmoved by my moral exhortations. But was not this quite natural on her part?—and ought I not to have remembered that it is only those no longer innocent who can find pleasure in the systems of moralists? . . . I had at least good sense enough to cut short my sermonizing.

"Jeanne," I said, "you were asking a moment ago about Madame Gabry. Let us talk about that Fairy of yours. She was very prettily made. Do you do any modelling in wax now?"

"I have not a bit of wax," she exclaimed, wringing her hands—"no wax at all!"

"No wax!" I cried—"in a republic of busy bees?"
She laughed.

"And, then, you see, Monsieur, my *figurines*, as you call them, are not in Mademoiselle Préfère's programme. But I had begun to make a very small Saint-George for Madame de Gabry—a tiny little Saint-George, with a golden cuirass. Is not that right, Monsieur Bonnard—to give Saint-George a gold cuirass?"

"Quite right, Jeanne; but what became of it?"

"I am going to tell you. I kept it in my pocket because I had no other place to put it, and—and I sat down on it by mistake."

She drew out of her pocket a little wax figure, which had been squeezed out of all resemblance to human form, and of which the dislocated limbs were only attached to the body by their wire framework. At the sight of her hero thus marred, she was seized at once with compassion and gayety. The latter feeling obtained the mastery, and she burst into a clear laugh, which, however, stopped as suddenly as it had begun.

Mademoiselle Préfère stood at the parlor door, smiling.

"That dear child!" sighed the schoolmistress, in her tenderest tone. "I am afraid she will tire you. And, then, your time is so precious!"

I begged Mademoiselle Préfère to dismiss that illusion, and, rising to take my leave, I took from my pocket some chocolate-cakes and sweets which I had brought with me.

"That is so nice!" said Jeanne; "there will be enough to go round the whole school."

The Lady of the Pelerine intervened.

"Mademoiselle Alexandre," she said, "thank Monsieur for his generosity."

Jeanne looked at her for an instant in a sullen way; then, turning to me, said with remarkable firmness,

"Monsieur, I thank you for your kindness in coming to see me."

"Jeanne," I said, pressing both her hands, "remain always a good, truthful, brave girl. Goodby."

As she left the room with her packages of chocolate and confectionery, she happened to strike the handles of her skipping-rope against the back of a chair. Mademoiselle Préfère, full of indignation, pressed both hands over her heart, under her pelerine; and I almost expected to see her give up her scholastic ghost.

When we found ourselves alone, she recovered her composure; and I must say, without considering myself thereby flattered, that she smiled upon me with one whole side of her face.

"Mademoiselle," I said, taking advantage of her good humor, "I noticed that Jeanne Alexandre looks a little pale. You know better than I how much consideration and care a young girl requires at her age. It would only be doing you an injustice by implication to recommend her still more earnestly to your vigilance."

These words seemed to ravish her with delight. She lifted her eyes, as in ecstasy, to the paper spirals of the ceiling, and, clasping her hands, exclaimed,

"How well these eminent men know the art of considering the most trifling details!"

I called her attention to the fact that the health of a young girl was not a trifling detail, and made my farewell bow. But she stopped me on the threshold to say to me, very confidentially,

"You must excuse me, Monsieur. I am a woman, and I love glory. I cannot conceal from you the fact that I feel myself greatly honored by the presence of a Member of the Institute in my humble institution."

I duly excused the weakness of Mademoiselle Préfère; and, thinking only of Jeanne, with the blindness of egotism, kept asking myself all along the road, "What are we going to do with this child?"

June 3.

I HAD escorted to the Cimétière des Marnes that day a very aged colleague of mine who, to use the words of Goethe, had consented to die. The great Goethe, whose own vital force was something extraordinary, actually believed that one never dies until one really wants to die—that is to say, when all those energies which resist dissolution, and the sum of which make up life itself, have been totally destroyed. In other words he believed that people only die when it is no longer possible for them to live. Good! it is merely a question of properly understanding one another; and when fully comprehended, the magnificent idea of Goethe only brings us quietly back to the song of La Palisse.

Well, my excellent colleague had consented to die —thanks to several successive attacks of extremely persuasive apoplexy—the last of which proved unanswerable. I had been very little acquainted with him during his lifetime; but it seems that I became his friend the moment he was dead, for our colleagues assured me in the most serious manner, with deeply sympathetic countenances, that I should act as one of the pall-bearers, and deliver an address over the tomb.

After having read very badly a short address I had written as well as I could—which is not saying much for it—I started out for a walk in the woods of Ville-d'Avray, and followed, without leaning too much on the Captain's cane, a shaded path on which the sunlight fell, through foliage, in little disks of gold. Never had the scent of grass and fresh leaves,—never had the beauty of the sky over the trees, and the serene might of noble vegetal forms, so deeply affected my senses and all my being; and the pleasure I felt in that silence, broken only by faintest tinkling sounds, was at once of the senses and of the soul.

I sat down in the shade of the roadside under a

11

clump of young oaks. And there I made a promise
to myself not to die, or at least not to consent to die,
before I should be again able to sit down under an
oak, where—in the great peace of the open conntry—
I could meditate on the nature of the soul and the
ultimate destiny of man. A bee, whose brown corsage gleamed in the sun like an armor of old-gold,
came to light upon a mallow-flower close by me—
darkly rich in color, and fully opened upon its tufted
stalk. It was certainly not the first time I had wit-
nessed so common an incident; but it was the first
time that I watched it with such comprehensive and
friendly curiosity. I could discern that there were all
sorts of sympathies between the insect and the flower
—a thousand singular little relationships which I had
never before even suspected.

Satiated with nectar, the insect rose and buzzed
away in a straight line, while I lifted myself up as
best I could, and readjusted myself upon my legs.

"Adieu!" I said to the flower and to the bee.
"Adieu! Heaven grant I may live long enough to
discover the secret of your harmonies. I am very
tired. But man is so made that he can only find
relaxation from one kind of labor by taking up another. The flowers and insects will give me that
relaxation, with God's will, after my long researches
in philology and diplomatics. How full of meaning
is that old myth of Antæus! I have touched the
Earth and I am a new man; and now, at seventy

years of age, new feelings of curiosity take birth in my mind, even as young shoots sometimes spring up from the hollow trunk of an aged oak!"

June 4.

I LIKE to look out of my window at the Seine and its quays on those soft gray mornings which give such an infinite tenderness of tint to everything. I have seen that azure sky which flings so luminous a calm over the Bay of Naples. But our Parisian sky is more animated, more kindly, more spiritual. It smiles, threatens, caresses—takes an aspect of melancholy or a look of merriment like a human gaze. At this moment it is pouring down a very gentle light on the men and beasts of the city as they accomplish their daily tasks. Over there, on the opposite bank, the stevedores of the Port Saint-Nicholas are unloading a cargo of cows' horns; while two men standing on a gangway are tossing sugar-loaves from one to the other, and thence to somebody in the hold of a steamer. On the north quay, the cab-horses, standing in a line under the shade of the plane-trees, each with its head in a nose-bag, are quietly munching their oats, while the rubicund drivers are drinking at the counter of the wine-seller opposite, but all the while keeping a sharp lookout for early customers.

The dealers in second-hand books put their boxes on the parapet. These good retailers of Mind, who are

always in the open air, with blouses loose to the
breeze, have become so weatherbeaten by the wind,
the rain, the frost, the snow, the fog, and the great
sun, that they end by looking very much like the old
statues of cathedrals. They are all friends of mine,
and I scarcely ever pass by their boxes without picking out of one of them some old book which I had
always been in need of up to that very moment, without any suspicion on my part of the fact.

Then on my return home I have to endure the outcries of my housekeeper, who accuses me of bursting
all my pockets and filling the house with waste paper
to attract the rats. Thérèse is wise about that, and it
is because she is wise that I do not listen to her; for
in spite of my tranquil mien, I have always preferred
the folly of the passions to the wisdom of indifference.
But just because my own passions are not of that sort
which burst out with violence to devastate and kill,
the common mind is not aware of their existence.
Nevertheless, I am greatly moved by them at times,
and it has more than once been my fate to lose my
sleep for the sake of a few pages written by some forgotten monk or printed by some humble apprentice of
Peter Schœffer. And if these fierce enthusiasms are
slowly being quenched in me, it is only because I am
being slowly quenched myself. Our passions are ourselves. My old books are Me. I am just as old and
thumbworn as they are.

A light breeze sweeps away, along with the dust of

the pavements, the winged seeds of the plane-trees, and the fragments of hay dropped from the mouths of the horses. The dust is nothing remarkable in itself; but as I watch it flying, I remember a moment in my childhood when watching just such a whirl of dust; and my old Parisian soul is much affected by that sudden recollection. All that I see from my window—that horizon which extends to the left as far as the hills of Chaillot, and enables me to distinguish the Arc de Triomphe like a die of stone, the Seine, river of glory, and its bridges, the ash-trees of the terrace of the Tuileries, the Louvre of the Renaissance, cut and graven like goldsmith-work; and on my right, towards the Pont-Neuf (*pons Lutetia novus dictus*, as it is named on old engravings), all the old and venerable part of Paris, with its towers and spires:—all that is my life, it is myself; and I would be nothing but for all those things which are thus reflected in me, through my thousand varying shades of thought, inspiring me and animating me. That is why I love Paris with an immense love.

And nevertheless I am weary, and I know that there can be no rest for me in the heart of this great city which thinks so much, which has taught me to think, and which forever urges me to think more. And how avoid being excited among all these books which incessantly tempt my curiosity without ever satisfying it? At one moment it is a date I have to look for; at another it is the name of a place I have to make

sure of, or some quaint term of which it is important
to determine the exact meaning.   Words?—why, yes!
words.   As a philologist, I am their sovereign; they
are my subjects, and, like a good king, I devote my
whole life to them.   But will I not be able to abdicate
some day?   I have an idea that there is somewhere
or other, quite far from here, a certain little cottage
where I could enjoy the quiet I so much need, while
awaiting that day in which a greater quiet — that
which can be never broken — shall come to wrap me
all about.   I dream of a bench before the threshold,
and of fields spreading away out of sight.   But I must
have a fresh smiling young face beside me, to reflect
and concentrate all that freshness of nature.   I could
then imagine myself a grandfather, and all the long
void of my life would be filled. . . .

I am not a violent man, and yet I become easily
vexed, and all my works have caused me quite as much
pain as pleasure.   And I do not know how it is that
I still keep thinking about that very conceited and
very inconsiderate impertinence which my young
friend of the Luxembourg took the liberty to utter
about me some three months ago.   I do not call him
" friend " in irony, for I love studious youth with all
its temerities and imaginative eccentricities.   Still,
my young friend certainly went beyond all bounds.
Master Ambroise Paré, who was the first to attempt
the ligature of arteries, and who, having commenced
his profession at a time when surgery was only per-

formed by quack barbers, nevertheless succeeded in lifting the science to the high place it now occupies, was assailed in his old age by all the young sawbones' apprentices. Being grossly abused during a discussion by some young addlehead who might have been the best son in the world, but who certainly lacked all sense of respect, the old master answered him in his treatise *De la Mumie, de la Licorne, des Venins et de la Peste.* " I pray him," said the great man—" I pray him, that if he desire to make any contradictions to my reply, he abandon all animosities, and treat the good old man with gentleness." This answer seems admirable from the pen of Ambroise Paré; but even had it been written by a village bonesetter, grown gray in his calling, and mocked by some young stripling, it would still be worthy of all praise.

It might perhaps seem that my memory of the incident had been kept alive only by a base feeling of resentment. I thought so myself at first, and reproached myself for thus dwelling on the saying of a boy who could not yet know the meaning of his own words. But my reflections on this subject subsequently took a better course: that is why I now note them down in my diary. I remembered that one day when I was twenty years old (that was more than half a century ago) I was walking about in that very same garden of the Luxembourg with some comrades. We were talking about our old professors; and one of us happened to name Monsieur Petit-Radel, an estimable and learned man, who was the first to throw some light upon the origin of early Etruscan civilization, but who had been unfortunate enough to prepare a chronological table of the lovers of Helen. We all laughed a great deal about that chronological table; and I cried out, " Petit-Radel is an ass, not in three letters, but in twelve whole volumes !"

This foolish speech of my adolescence was uttered too lightly to be a weight on my conscience as an old man. May God kindly prove to me some day that I never used any less innocent shaft of speech in the battle of life! But I now ask myself whether I really never wrote, at any time in my life, something quite as unconsciously absurd as the chronological table of the lovers of Helen. The progress of science renders useless the very books which have been the greatest aids to that progress. As those works are no longer useful, modern youth is naturally inclined to believe they never had any value; it despises them, and ridicules them if they happen to contain any superannuated opinion whatever. That was why, in my twentieth year, I amused myself at the expense of Monsieur Petit-Radel and his chronological table; and that was why, the other day, at the Luxembourg, my young and irreverent friend . . .

" *Rentre en toi-même, Octave, et cesse de te plaindre.*
    Quoi! tu veux qu'on t'épargne et n'as rien épargné !" *

---

* " Look into thyself, Octavius, and cease complaining.
    What! thou wouldst be spared, and thou thyself hast spared
        none !"

June 6.

It was the first Thursday in June. I shut up my books, and took my leave of the holy Abbot Drocto-veus, who being now in the enjoyment of celestial bliss, cannot feel very impatient to behold his name and works glorified on earth through the humble compilation being prepared by my hands. Must I confess it? That mallow-plant I saw visited by a bee the other day has been occupying my thoughts much more than all the ancient abbots who ever bore crosiers or wore mitres. There is in one of Sprengel's books which I read in my youth, at that time when I used to read anything and everything, some ideas about "the loves of flowers" which now return to memory after having been forgotten for half a century, and which to-day interest me so much that I regret not to have devoted the humble capacities of my mind to the study of insects and of plants.

And only a while ago my housekeeper surprised me at the kitchen window, in the act of examining some wallflowers through a magnifying-glass. . . .

It was while looking for my cravat that I made these reflections. But after searching to no purpose in a great number of drawers, I found myself obliged, after all, to have recourse to my housekeeper. Thérèse came limping in.

" Monsieur," she said, " you ought to have told me you were going out, and I would have given you your cravat !"

" But Thérèse," I replied, " would it not be a great deal better to put it some place where I could find it without your help?"

Thérèse did not deign to answer me.

Thérèse no longer allows me to arrange anything. I cannot even have a handkerchief without asking her for it; and as she is deaf, crippled, and, what is worse, beginning to lose her memory, I languish in perpetual destitution.   But she exercises her domestic authority with such quiet pride that I do not feel the courage to attempt a *coup d'état* against her government.

" My cravat! Thérèse!—do you hear?—my cravat! if you drive me wild like this with your slow ways, it will not be a cravat I shall need, but a rope to hang myself!"

" You must be in a very great hurry, Monsieur," replied Thérèse.   " Your cravat is not lost.   Nothing is ever lost in this house, because I have charge of everything.   But please allow me the time at least to find it."

" Yet here," I thought to myself—" here is the result of half a century of devotedness and self-sacrifice! . . . Ah! if by any happy chance, this inexorable Thérèse had once in her whole life, only once, failed in her duty as a servant—if she had ever been at fault for one single instant, she could never have assumed this inflexible authority over me, and I would at least have the courage to resist her.   But how can one resist virtue?   The people who have no weaknesses are terrible; there is no way of taking advantage of them. Just look at Thérèse, for example; she has not a single fault for which you can blame her! She has no doubt of herself, nor of God, nor of the world. She is the valiant woman, the wise virgin of Scripture; others may know nothing about her, but I know her worth. In my fancy I always see her carrying a lamp, an humble kitchen lamp, illuminating the beams of some rustic roof—a lamp which will never go out while suspended from that meagre arm of hers, scraggy and strong as a vine-branch.

"Thérèse, my cravat! Don't you know, wretched woman, that to-day is the first Thursday in June, and that Mademoiselle Jeanne will be waiting for me? The schoolmistress has certainly had the parlor floor vigorously waxed: I am sure one can look at one's self in it now; and it will be quite a consolation for me when I slip and break my old bones upon it—which is sure to happen sooner or later—to see my rueful countenance reflected in it as in a looking-glass. Then taking for my model that amiable and admirable hero whose image is carved upon the handle of Uncle Victor's walking-stick, I will control myself so as not to make too ugly a grimace. . . . See what a splendid sun! The quays are all gilded by it, and the Seine smiles in countless little flashing wrinkles. The city is gold: a dust-haze, blonde and gold-toned as a woman's hair, floats above its beautiful contours. . . . Thérèse, my cravat! . . . Ah! I can now comprehend the wisdom of that old Chrysal who used to keep his neckbands in a big Plutarch. Hereafter I shall follow his example by laying all my neckties away between the leaves of the 'Acta Sanctorum.'"

Thérèse lets me talk on, and keeps looking for the necktie in silence. I hear a gentle ringing at our door-bell.

"Thérèse," I exclaim; "there is somebody ringing the bell! Give me my cravat, and go to the door; or, rather, go to the door first, and then, with the help of Heaven, you will give me my cravat. But please do not stand there between the clothes-press and the door like an old hack horse between two saddles."

Thérèse marched to the door as if advancing upon an enemy. My excellent housekeeper becomes more inhospitable the older she grows. Every stranger is an object of suspicion to her. According to her own assertion, this disposition is the result of a long experience with human nature. I had not the time to consider whether the same experience on the part of another experimenter would produce the same results. Maître Mouche was waiting to see me in the anteroom.

Maître Mouche is still more yellow than I had believed him to be. He wears blue glasses, and his eyes keep moving uneasily behind them, like mice running about behind a screen.

Maître Mouche excuses himself for having intruded

upon me at a moment when . . . He does not characterize the moment; but I think he means to say a moment in which I happen to be without my cravat. It is not my fault, as you very well know. Maître Mouche, who does not know, does not appear to be at all shocked, however. He is only afraid that he might have dropped in at the wrong moment. I succeed in partially reassuring him at once upon that point. He then tells me it is as the guardian of Mademoiselle Alexandre that he has come to talk with me. First of all, he desires that I shall not hereafter pay any heed to those restrictions he had at first deemed it necessary to put upon the permit given to visit Mademoiselle Jeanne at the boarding-school. Henceforth the establishment of Mademoiselle Préfère will be open to me any day that I may choose to call—between the hours of midday and four o'clock. Knowing the interest I have taken in the young girl, he considers it his duty to give me some information about the person to whom he has confided his ward. Mademoiselle Préfère, whom he has known for many years, is in possession of his utmost confidence. Mademoiselle Préfère is, in his estimation, an enlightened person, of excellent morals, and capable of giving excellent counsel.

"Mademoiselle Préfère," he said to me, " has principles; and principles are rare in these days, Monsieur. Everything has been totally changed; and this epoch of ours cannot compare with the preceding ones.'

"My stairway is a good example, Monsieur," I replied; "twenty-five years ago it used to allow me to climb it without any trouble, and now it takes my breath away, and wears my legs out before I have climbed half a dozen steps. It has had its character spoiled. Then there are those journals and books I used once to devour without resistance by moonlight: to-day, even in the brightest sunlight, they mock my curiosity, and exhibit nothing but a blur of white and black when I have not got my spectacles on. Then the gout has got into my limbs. That is another malicious trick of the times!"

"Not only that, Monsieur," gravely replied Maître Mouche, "but what is really unfortunate in our epoch is that no one is satisfied with his position. From the top of society to the bottom, in every class, there prevails a discontent, a restlessness, a love of comfort . . ."

"*Mon Dieu*, Monsieur!" I exclaimed. "You think this love of comfort is a sign of the times? Men have never had at any epoch a love of discomfort. They have always tried to better their condition. This constant effort produces constant changes, and the effort is always going on—that is all there is about it!"

"Ah! Monsieur," replied Maître Mouche, "it is easy to see that you live in your books—out of the business world altogether. You do not see, as I see them, the conflicts of interest, the struggle for money.

It is the same effervescence in all minds, great or small. The wildest speculations are being everywhere indulged in. What I see around me simply terrifies me!"

I wondered within myself whether Maître Mouche had called upon me only for the purpose of expressing his virtuous misanthropy; but all at once I heard words of a more consoling character issue from his lips. Maître Mouche began to speak to me of Virginie Préfère as a person worthy of respect, of esteem, and of sympathy,—highly honorable, capable of great devotedness, cultivated, discreet,—able to read aloud remarkably well, extremely modest, and skilful in the art of applying blisters. Then I began to understand that he had only been painting that dismal picture of universal corruption in order the better to bring out, by contrast, the virtues of the school-mistress. I was further informed that the institution in the Rue Demours was well patronized, prosperous, and enjoyed a high reputation with the public. Maître Mouche lifted up his hand—with a black woollen glove on it—as if making oath to the truth of these statements. Then he added:

"I am enabled, by the very character of my profession, to know a great deal about people. A notary is, to a certain extent, a father-confessor. I deemed it my duty, Monsieur, to give you this agreeable information at the moment when a lucky chance enabled you to meet Mademoiselle Préfère. There is only one thing more which I would like to say. This lady—who is, of course, quite unaware of my action in the matter—spoke to me of you the other day in terms of the deepest sympathy. I could only weaken their expression by repeating them to you; and, furthermore, I could not repeat them without betraying, to a certain extent, the confidence of Mademoiselle Préfère."

"Do not betray it, Monsieur; do not betray it!" I responded. "To tell you the truth, I had no idea that Mademoiselle Préfère knew anything whatever about me. But since you have the influence of an old friend with her, I will take advantage of your good will, Monsieur, to ask you to exercise that influence in behalf of Mademoiselle Jeanne Alexandre. The child—for she is still a child—is overloaded with work. She is at once a pupil and a mistress—she is overtasked. Besides, she is punished in petty disgusting ways; and hers is one of those generous natures which will be forced into revolt by such continual humiliation."

"Alas!" replied Maître Mouche, "she must be trained to take her part in the struggle of life. One does not come into this world simply to amuse one's self, and to do just what one pleases."

"One comes into this world," I responded, rather warmly, "to enjoy what is beautiful and what is good, and to do as one pleases, when the things one wants to do are noble, intelligent, and generous. An education which does not cultivate the will, is an education that depraves the mind. It is a teacher's duty to teach the pupil *how* to will."

I perceived that Maître Mouche began to think me a rather silly man. With a great deal of quiet self-assurance, he proceeded :

" You must remember, Monsieur, that the education of the poor has to be conducted with a great deal of circumspection, and with a view to that future state of dependence they must occupy in society. Perhaps you are not aware that the late Noël Alexandre died a bankrupt, and that his daughter is being educated almost by charity ?"

" Oh ! Monsieur !" I exclaimed, " do not say it ! To say it is to pay one's self back, and then the statement ceases to be true."

" The liabilities of the succession," continued the notary, " exceeded the assets. But I was able to effect a settlement with the creditors in favor of the minor."

He undertook to explain matters in detail. I declined to listen to these explanations, being incapable of understanding business methods in general, and those of Maître Mouche in particular. The notary then took it upon himself to justify Mademoiselle Préfère's educational system, and observed by way of conclusion,

" It is not by amusing one's self that one can learn."

" It is only by amusing one's self that one can learn,"

12

I replied. " The whole art of teaching is only the art of awakening the natural curiosity of young minds for the purpose of satisfying it afterwards; and curiosity itself can be vivid and wholesome only in proportion as the mind is contented and happy. Those acquirements crammed by force into the minds of children simply clog and stifle intelligence. In order that knowledge be properly digested, it must have been swallowed with a good appetite. I know Jeanne! If that child were intrusted to my care, I should make of her—not a learned woman, for I would look to her future happiness only—but a child full of bright intelligence and full of life, in whom everything beautiful in art or nature would awaken some gentle responsive thrill. I would teach her to live in sympathy with all that is beautiful—comely landscapes, the ideal scenes of poetry and history, the emotional charm of noble music. I would make lovable to her everything I would wish her to love. Even her needlework I would make pleasurable to her, by a proper choice of the tissues, the style of embroideries, the designs of lace. I would give her a beautiful dog, and a pony to teach her how to manage animals; I would give her birds to take care of, so that she could learn the value of even a drop of water and a crumb of bread. And in order that she should have a still higher pleasure, I would train her to find delight in exercising charity. And inasmuch as none of us may escape pain, I should teach her that Christian wisdom which elevates us above all suffering, and gives a beauty even to grief itself.   That is my idea of the right way to educate a young girl."

" I yield, Monsieur," replied Maître Mouche, joining his black-gloved hands together.

And he rose.

" Of course you understand," I remarked, as I went to the door with him, " that I do not pretend for a moment to impose my educational system upon Mademoiselle Préfère; it is necessarily a private one, and quite incompatible with the organization of even the best-managed boarding-schools.   I only ask you to persuade her to give Jeanne less work and more play, and not to punish her except in case of absolute necessity, and to let her have as much freedom of mind and body as the regulations of the institution permit."

It was with a pale and mysterious smile that Maître Mouche informed me that my observations would be taken in good part, and should receive all possible consideration.

Therewith he made me a little bow, and took his departure, leaving me with a peculiar feeling of discomfort and uneasiness.   I have met a great many strange characters in my time, but never any at all resembling either this notary or this schoolmistress.

July 6.

Maître Mouche had so much delayed me by his visit that I gave up going to see Jeanne that day. Professional duties kept me very busy for the rest of the week. Although at the age when most men retire altogether from active life, I am still attached by a thousand ties to the society in which I have lived. I have to preside at meetings of academies, scientific congresses, assemblies of various learned bodies. I am overburdened with honorary functions; I have seven of these in one government department alone. The *bureaux* would be very glad to get rid of me, and I should be very glad to get rid of them. But habit is stronger than both of us together, and I continue to hobble up the stairs of various government buildings. Old clerks point me out to each other as I go by like a ghost wandering through the corridors. When one has become very old one finds it extremely difficult to disappear. Nevertheless, it is time, as the old song says, " *de prendre ma retraite et de songer à faire un fin* "—to retire on my pension and prepare myself to die a good death.

An old marchioness, who used to be a friend of Helvetius in her youth, and whom I once met at my father's house when a very old woman, was visited during her last sickness by the priest of her parish, who wanted to prepare her to die.

" Is that really necessary?" she asked. " I see

everybody else manage it perfectly well the first time."

My father went to see her very soon afterwards, and found her extremely ill.

"Good-evening, my friend!" she said, pressing his hand. "I am going to see whether God improves upon acquaintance."

So were wont to die the *belles amies* of the philosophers. Such an end is certainly not vulgar nor impertinent, and such levities are not of the sort that emanate from dull minds. Nevertheless, they shock me. Neither my fears nor my hopes could accommodate themselves to such a mode of departure. I would like to make mine with a perfectly collected mind; and that is why I must begin to think, in a year or two, about some way of belonging to myself; otherwise, I should certainly risk . . . But, hush! let Him not hear His name and turn to look as He passes by! I can still lift my fagot without His aid.

. . . I found Jeanne very happy indeed. She told me that, on the Thursday previous, after the visit of her guardian, Mademoiselle Préfère had set her free from the ordinary regulations and lightened her tasks in several ways. Since that lucky Thursday she could walk in the garden — which only lacked leaves and flowers — as much as she liked; and she had even been given facilities to work at her unfortunate little figure of Saint-George.

She said to me, with a smile,

"I know very well that I owe all this to you."

I tried to talk with her about other matters, but I remarked that she could not attend to what I was saying, in spite of her effort to do so.

"I see you are thinking about something else," I said. "Well, tell me what it is; for, if you do not, we shall not be able to talk to each other at all, which would be very unworthy of both of us."

She answered,

"Oh! I was really listening to you, Monsieur; but it is true that I was thinking about something else. You will excuse me, won't you? I could not help thinking that Mademoiselle Préfère must like you very, very much indeed, to have become so good to me all of a sudden."

Then she looked at me in an odd, smiling, frightened way, which made me laugh.

"Does that surprise you?" I asked.

"Very much," she replied.

"Please tell me why?"

"Because I can see no reason, no reason at all . . . but there! . . . no reason at all why you should please Mademoiselle Préfère so much."

"So, then, you think I am very displeasing, Jeanne?"

She bit her lips, as if to punish them for having made a mistake; and then, in a coaxing way, looking at me with her great soft eyes, gentle and beautiful as a spaniel's, she said,

"I know I said a foolish thing; but, still, I do not

see any reason why you should be so pleasing to Mademoiselle Préfère. And, nevertheless, you seem to please her a great deal—a very great deal. She called me one day, and asked me all sorts of questions about you."

" Really ?"

" Yes ; she wanted to find out all about your house. Just think ! she even asked me how old your servant was !"

And Jeanne burst out laughing.

" Well, what do you think about it ?" I asked.

She remained a long while with her eyes fixed on the worn-out cloth of her shoes, and seemed to be thinking very deeply. Finally, looking up again, she answered,

" I am distrustful. Isn't it very natural to feel uneasy about what one cannot understand ? I know I am foolish ; but you won't be offended with me, will you ?"

" Why, certainly not, Jeanne. I am not a bit offended with you."

I must acknowledge that I was beginning to share her surprise ; and I began to turn over in my old head the singular thought of this young girl—" One is uneasy about what one cannot understand."

But, with a fresh burst of merriment, she cried out,

" She asked me . . . guess ! I will give you a hundred guesses—a thousand guesses. You give it up ? . . . She asked me if you liked good eating."

" And how did you receive this shower of interrogations, Jeanne?"

" I replied, 'I don't know, Mademoiselle.' And Mademoiselle then said to me, 'You are a little fool. The least details of the life of an eminent man ought to be observed. Please to know, Mademoiselle, that Monsieur Sylvestre Bonnard is one of the glories of France!'"

" Stuff!" I exclaimed. "And what did *you* think about it, Mademoiselle?"

" I thought that Mademoiselle Préfère was right." But I don't care at all ... (I know it is naughty what I am going to say) ... I don't care a bit, not a bit, whether Mademoiselle Préfère is or is not right about anything."

" Well, then, content yourself, Jeanne, Mademoiselle Préfère was not right."

" Yes, yes, she was quite right that time; but I wanted to love everybody who loved you — everybody without exception—and I cannot do it, because it would never be possible for me to love Mademoiselle Préfère."

" Listen, Jeanne," I answered, very seriously, "Mademoiselle Préfère has become good to you; try now to be good to her."

She answered sharply,

" It is very easy for Mademoiselle Préfère to be good to me, and it would be very difficult indeed for me to be good to her."

I then said, in a still more serious tone:

" My child, the authority of a teacher is sacred. You must consider your schoolmistress as occupying the place to you of the mother whom you lost."

I had scarcely uttered this solemn stupidity when I bitterly regretted it. The child turned pale, and the tears sprang to her eyes.

"Oh, Monsieur!" she cried, "how could you say such a thing—*you?* You never knew mamma!"

Ay, just Heaven! I did know her mamma. And how indeed could I have been foolish enough to have said what I did?

She repeated, as if to herself:

"Mamma! my dear mamma! my poor mamma!"

A lucky chance prevented me from playing the fool any further. I do not know how it happened that at that moment I looked as if I was going to cry. At my age one does not cry. It must have been a bad cough which brought the tears into my eyes. But, anyhow, appearances were in my favor. Jeanne was deceived by them. Oh! what a pure and radiant smile suddenly shone out under her beautiful wet eyelashes—like sunshine among branches after a summer shower! We took each other by the hand and sat a long while without saying a word—absolutely happy. Those celestial harmonies which I once thought I heard thrilling through my soul while I knelt before that tomb to which a saintly woman had guided me, suddenly awoke again in my heart, slow-swelling through the blissful moments with infinite softness. Doubtless the child whose hand pressed my own also heard them; and then, elevated by their enchantment above the material world, the poor old man and the artless young girl both knew that a tender ghostly Presence was making sweetness all about them.

"My child," I said at last, "I am very old, and many secrets of life which you will only learn little by little, have been revealed to me. Believe me, the future is shaped out of the past. Whatever you can do to live contentedly here, without impatience and without fretting, will help you to live some future day in peace and joy in your own home. Be gentle, and learn how to suffer. When one suffers patiently one suffers less. If you should ever happen to have a serious cause of complaint I shall be there to take your part. If you should be badly treated, Madame De Gabry and I would both consider ourselves badly treated in your person." . . .

"Is your health very good indeed, dear Monsieur?"

It was Mademoiselle Préfère, approaching stealthily behind us, who had asked the question, with her peculiar smile. My first idea was to tell her to go to the devil; my second, that her mouth was as little suited for smiling as a frying-pan for musical purposes; my third was to answer her politely and assure her that I hoped she was very well.

She sent the young girl out to take a walk in the garden; then, pressing one hand upon her pelerine and extending the other towards the *Tableau d'Honneur*, she showed me the name of Jeanne Alexandre written at the head of the list in large text.

"I am very much pleased," I said to her, "to find that you are satisfied with the behavior of that child. Nothing could delight me more; and I am inclined to attribute this happy result to your affectionate vigilance. I have taken the liberty to send you a few books which I think may serve both to instruct and to amuse young girls. You will be able to judge by glancing over them whether they are adapted to the perusal of Mademoiselle Alexandre and her companions."

The gratitude of the schoolmistress not only overflowed in words, but seemed about to take the form of tearful sensibility. In order to change the subject I observed,

"What a beautiful day this is!"

"Yes," she replied; "and if this weather continues, those dear children will have a nice time for their enjoyment."

"I suppose you are referring to the holidays. But Mademoiselle Alexandre, who has no relatives, cannot go away. What in the world is she going to do all alone in this great big house?"

"Oh, we will do everything we can to amuse her. . . . I will take her to the museums and—"

She hesitated, blushed, and continued,

"—and to your house, if you will permit me."

"Why, of course!" I exclaimed. "That is a first-rate idea."

We separated very good friends with one another, I with her, because I had been able to obtain what I desired; she with me, for no appreciable motive—which fact, according to Plato, elevated her into the highest rank of the Hierarchy of Souls.

. . . And nevertheless it is not without a presentiment of evil that I find myself on the point of introducing this person into my house. And I would be very glad indeed to see Jeanne in charge of anybody else rather than of her. Maître Mouche and Mademoiselle Préfère are characters whom I cannot at all understand. I never can imagine why they say what they do say, nor why they do what they do; they have a mysterious something in common which makes me feel uneasy. As Jeanne said to me a little while ago: "One is uneasy about what one cannot understand."

Alas! at my age one has learned only too well how little sincerity there is in life; one has learned only too well how much one loses by living a long time in this world; and one feels that one can no longer trust any except the young.

————

August 12.

I WAITED for them. In fact, I waited for them very impatiently. I exerted all my powers of insinuation and of coaxing to induce Thérèse to receive them kindly; but my powers in this direction are very limited. They came. Jeanne was neater and prettier than I had ever expected to see her. She has not, it is true, anything approaching the charm of her mother. But to-day, for the first time, I observed that she has a pleasing face; and a pleasing face is of great advantage to a woman in this world. I think that her hat was a little on one side; but she smiled, and the City of Books was all illuminated by that smile.

I watched Thérèse to see whether the rigid manners of the old housekeeper would soften a little at the sight of the young girl. I saw her turning her lustreless eyes upon Jeanne; I saw her long wrinkled face, her toothless mouth, and that pointed chin of hers—like the chin of some puissant old fairy. And that was all I could see.

Madcmoiselle Préfère made her appearance all in blue—advanced, retreated, skipped, tripped, cried out, sighed, cast her eyes down, rolled her eyes up, bewildered herself with excuses—said she dared not, and nevertheless dared—said she would never dare again, and nevertheless dared again—made courtesies innumerable—made, in short, all the fuss she could.

" What a lot of books!" she screamed. " And have you really read them all, Monsieur Bonnard ?"

" Alas! I have," I replied, " and that is just the reason that I do not know anything; for there is not a single one of those books which does not contradict some other book; so that by the time one has read them all one does not know what to think about anything. That is just my condition, Madame."

Thereupon she called Jeanne for the purpose of communicating her impressions. But Jeanne was looking out of the window.

"How beautiful it is!" she said to us. "How I love to see the river flowing! It makes you think about all kinds of things."

Mademoiselle Préfère having removed her hat and exhibited a forehead tricked out with blonde curls, my housekeeper sturdily snatched up the hat at once, with the observation that she did not like to see people's clothes scattered over the furniture. Then she approached Jeanne and asked her for her "things," calling her "my little lady!" Whereupon the little lady giving up her cloak and hat, exposed to view a very graceful neck and a lithe figure, whose outlines were beautifully relieved against the great glow of the open window; and I could have wished that some one else might have seen her at that moment—some one very different from an aged housekeeper, a schoolmistress frizzled like a sheep, and this old humbug of an archivist and paleographer.

"So you are looking at the Seine," I said to her. "See how it sparkles in the sun!"

"Yes," she replied, leaning over the window-bar, "it looks like a flowing of fire. But see how nice and cool it looks on the other side over there, under the shadow of the willows! That little spot there pleases me better than all the rest."

"Good!" I answered. "I see that the river has a charm for you. How would you like, with Mademoi-

selle Préfère's permission, to make a trip to Saint
Cloud? We would certainly be able to take the steam-
boat just below the Pont-Royal."

Jeanne was delighted with my suggestion, and Mademoiselle Préfère willing to make any sacrifice. But
my housekeeper was not at all willing to let us go off
so unconcernedly. She summoned me into the dining-
room, whither I followed her in fear and trembling.

"Monsieur," she said to me as soon as we found ourselves alone, "you never think about anything, and
it is always I who have to think about everything.
Luckily for you I have a good memory."

I did not think that it was a favorable moment for
any attempt to dispel this wild illusion. She continued:

"So you were going off without saying a word to me
about what this little lady likes to eat? At her age
one does not know anything, one does not care about
anything in particular, one eats like a bird. You yourself, Monsieur, are very difficult to please; but at least
you know what is good: it is very different with these
young people—they do not know anything about cooking. It is often the very best thing which they think
the worst, and what is bad seems to them good, because
their stomachs are not quite formed yet—so that one
never knows just what to do for them. Tell me if the
little lady would like a pigeon cooked with green pease,
and whether she is fond of vanilla ice-cream."

"My good Thérèse," I answered, "just do whatever
you think best, and whatever that may be I am sure

it will be very nice.   Those ladies will be quite con
tented with our humble ordinary fare."

Thérèse replied, very dryly,

"Monsieur, I am asking you about the little lady:
she must not leave this house without having enjoyed
herself a little.   As for that old frizzle-headed thing,
if she doesn't like my dinner she can suck her thumbs.
I don't care what she likes !"

My mind being thus set at rest, I returned into the
City of Books, where Mademoiselle Préfère was cro-
cheting as calmly as if she were at home.   I almost
felt inclined myself to think she was.   She did not
take up much room, it is true, in the angle of the window.   But she had chosen her chair and her footstool
so well that those articles of furniture seemed to have
been made expressly for her.

Jeanne, on the other hand, devoted her attention to
the books and pictures—gazing at them in a kindly,
expressive, half-sad way, as if she were bidding them
an affectionate farewell.

"Here," I said to her, "amuse yourself with this
book, which I am sure you cannot help liking, because it is full of beautiful engravings."   And I threw
open before her Vecellio's collection of costume-
designs—not the commonplace edition, by your leave,
so meagrely reproduced by modern artists, but in truth
a magnificent and venerable copy of that *editio prin-
ceps* which is noble as those noble dames who figure
upon its yellowed leaves, made beautiful by time.

While turning over the engravings with artless curiosity, Jeanne said to me,

"We were talking about taking a walk; but this is a great journey you are making me take. And I would like to travel very, very far away!"

"In that case, Mademoiselle," I said to her, "you must arrange yourself as comfortably as possible for travelling. But you are now sitting on one corner of your chair, so that the chair is standing upon only one leg, and that Vecellio must tire your knees. Sit down comfortably; put your chair on its four feet, and put your book on the table."

She obeyed me with a laugh.

I watched her. She cried out suddenly,

"Oh, come look at this beautiful costume!" (It was that of the wife of a Doge of Venice). "How noble it is! What magnificent ideas it gives one of that life! Oh, I must tell you—I adore luxury!"

"You must not express such thoughts as those, Mademoiselle," said the schoolmistress, lifting up her little shapeless nose from her work.

"Nevertheless, it was a very innocent utterance," I replied. "There are splendid souls in whom the love of splendid things is natural and inborn."

The little shapeless nose went down again.

"Mademoiselle Préfère likes luxury too," said Jeanne; "she cuts out paper trimmings and shades for the lamps. It is economical luxury; but it is luxury all the same."

13

Having returned to the subject of Venice, we were just about to make the acquaintance of a certain patrician lady attired in an embroidered dalmatic, when I heard the bell ring. I thought it was some peddler with his basket; but the gate of the City of Books opened, and . . . Well, Master Sylvestre Bonnard, you were wishing awhile ago that the grace of your *protegée* might be observed by some other eyes than old withered eyes behind spectacles. Your wishes have been fulfilled in a most unexpected manner, and a voice cries out to you, as to the imprudent Theseus,

> "Craignez, Seigneur, craignez que le Ciel rigoureux
> Ne vous haïsse assez pour exaucer vos vœux !
> Souvent dans sa colère il reçoit nos victimes,
> Ses présents sont souvent la peine de nos crimes." *

The gate of the City of Books had opened, and a handsome young man made his appearance, ushered in by Thérèse. That good old soul only knows how to open the door for people and to shut it behind them; she has no idea whatever of the tact requisite for the waiting-room and for the parlor. It is not in her nature either to make any announcements or to make anybody wait. She either throws people out on the lobby, or simply pitches them at your head.

---

* "Beware, my lord! Beware lest stern Heaven hate you enough to hear your prayers! Often 'tis in wrath that Heaven receives our sacrifices; its gifts are often the punishment of our crimes."

And here is this handsome young man already inside; and I cannot really take the girl at once and hide her like a secret treasure in the next room. I wait for him to explain himself; he does it without the least embarrassment; but it seems to me that he has already observed the young girl who is still bending over the table looking at Vecellio. As I observe the young man it occurs to me that I have seen him somewhere before, or else I must be very much mistaken. His name is Gélis. That is a name which I have heard somewhere,—I can't remember where. At all events, Monsieur Gélis (since there is a Gélis) is a fine-looking young fellow. He tells me that this is his third class-year at the École des Chartes, and that he has been working for the past fifteen or eighteen months upon his graduation thesis, the subject of which is the Condition of the Benedictine Abbeys in 1700. He has just read my works upon the "Monasticon;" and he is convinced that he cannot terminate his thesis successfully without my advice, to begin with, and in the second place without a certain manuscript which I possess, and which is nothing less than the "Register of the Accounts of the Abbey of Citaux from 1683 to 1704."

Having thus explained himself, he hands me a letter of introduction bearing the signature of one of the most illustrious of my colleagues.

Good! Now I know who he is! Monsieur Gélis is the very same young man who last year under the chestnut-trees called me an idiot! And while unfolding his letter of introduction I think to myself:

"Aha! my unlucky youth, you are very far from suspecting that I overheard what you said, and that I know what you think of me—or, at least, what you did think of me that day, for these young minds are so fickle! I have got you now, my friend! You have fallen into the lion's den, and so unexpectedly, in good sooth, that the astonished old lion does not know what to do with his prey. But come now, old lion! do not act like an idiot! Is it not possible that you were an idiot? If you are not one now, you certainly were one! You were a fool to have been listening to Monsieur Gélis at the foot of the statue of Marguerite de Valois; you were doubly a fool to have heard what he said; and you were trebly a fool not to have forgotten what it would have been much better never to have heard."

Having thus scolded the old lion, I exhorted him to show clemency. He did not appear to require much coaxing, and gradually became so good-natured that he had some difficulty in restraining himself from bursting out into joyous roarings. From the way in which I had read my colleague's letter one might have supposed me a man who did not know his alphabet. I took a long while to read it; and Monsieur Gélis might have become very tired under different circumstances; but he was watching Jeanne, and endured the trial with exemplary patience. Jeanne occasionally turned her face in our direction. Well, you could not expect a person to remain perfectly motionless, could you? Mademoiselle Préfère was arranging her curls, and her bosom occasionally swelled with little sighs. It may be observed that I have myself often been honored with these little sighs.

"Monsieur," I said, as I folded up the letter, "I shall be very happy to be of any service to you. You are occupied with researches in which I myself have always felt a very lively interest. I have done all that lay in my power. I know, as you do—and still better than you can know—how much there remains to do. The manuscript you asked for is at your disposal; you may take it home with you, but it is not a manuscript of the smallest kind, and I am afraid—"

"Oh, Monsieur," said Gélis, "big books have never been able to make me afraid of them."

I begged the young man to wait for me, and I went into the next room to get the Register, which I could not find at first, and which I almost despaired of finding, as I discerned, from certain familiar signs, that Thérèse had been setting the room in order. But the Register was so big and so heavy that, luckily for me, Thérèse had not been able to put it in order as she had doubtless wished to do. I could scarcely lift it up myself; and I had the pleasure of finding it quite as heavy as I could have hoped.

"Wait, my boy," I said, with a smile which must have been very sarcastic—"wait! I am going to give you something to do which will break your arms first, and afterwards your head.   That will be the first vengeance of Sylvestre Bonnard.   Later on we shall see what else there is to be done."

When I returned to the City of Books I heard Monsieur Gélis and Mademoiselle Jeanne chatting—chatting together, if you please! as if they were the best friends in the world.   Mademoiselle Préfère, being full of decorum, did not say anything; but the other two were chattering like birds.   And what about? About the blond tint used by Venetian painters!   Yes, about the "Venetian blond."   That little serpent of a Gélis was telling Jeanne the secret of the dye with which the women of Titian and of Veronese tinted their hair according to the best authorities.   And Mademoiselle Jeanne was expressing her opinion very prettily about the blond of honey and the blond of gold.   I understood that that scamp of a Vecellio was responsible—that they had been bending over the book together, and that they had been admiring either that Doge's wife we had been looking at awhile before, or some other patrician woman of Venice.

Never mind!   I appeared with my enormous old book, thinking that Gélis was going to make a grimace.   It was as much as one could have asked a porter to carry, and my arms were all sore just lifting it. But the young man caught it up like a feather, and slipped it under his arm with a smile.   Then he thanked me with that sort of brevity which I like, reminded me that he had need of my advice, and, having made an appointment to meet me another day, took his departure after bowing to us with the most perfect self-possession conceivable.

" He seems quite a genteel lad," I said.

Jeanne turned over a few more pages of Vecellio, and made no answer.

" Aha !" I thought to myself. . . . And then we went to Saint-Cloud.

———

September—December.

THE regularity with which visit succeeded visit to the old man's house thereafter made me feel very grateful to Mademoiselle Préfère, who succeeded at last in winning her right to occupy a special corner in the City of Books. She now says " *my* chair," " *my* footstool," " *my* pigeon-hole." Her pigeon-hole is really a small shelf properly belonging to the Poets of La Champagne, whom she expelled therefrom in order to obtain a lodging for her work-bag. She is very amiable, and I must really be a monster not to like her. I can only endure her—in the severest sig- nification of the word. But what would one not en- dure for Jeanne's sake ? Her presence lends to the City of Books a charm which seems to hover about it still after she has gone. She is very ignorant ; but she is so finely gifted that whenever I show her any- thing beautiful I am astounded to find that I had never really seen it before, and that it is she who makes me see it. I have found it impossible so far to make her follow some of my ideas, but I have often found pleasure in following the whimsical and delicate course of her own.

A more practical man than I would attempt to teach her to make herself useful; but is not the capacity of being amiable a useful thing in life? Without being pretty, she charms; and the power to charm is perhaps, after all, worth quite as much as the ability to darn stockings. Furthermore, I am not immortal; and I doubt whether she will have become very old when my notary (who is not Maître Mouche) shall read to her a certain paper which I signed a little while ago.

I do not wish that any one except myself should provide for her, and give her her dowry. I am not, however, very rich, and the paternal inheritance did not gain bulk in my hands. One does not accumulate money by poring over old texts. But my books—at the price which such noble merchandise fetches to-day —are worth something. Why, on that shelf there are some poets of the sixteenth century for which bankers would bid against princes! And I think that those " Heures " of Simon Vostre would not be readily overlooked at the Hotel Silvestre any more than would those *Preces Piæ* compiled for the use of Queen Claude. I have taken great pains to collect and to preserve all those rare and curious editions which

people the City of Books; and for a long time I used
to believe that they were as necessary to my life as
air and light. I have loved them well, and even now
I cannot prevent myself from smiling at them and
caressing them. Those morocco bindings are so delightful to the eye! Those old vellums are so soft
to the touch! There is not a single one among those
books which is not worthy, by reason of some special
merit, to command the respect of an honorable man.
What other owner would ever know how to dip into
them in the proper way? Can I be even sure that
another owner would not leave them to decay in neg-
lect, or mutilate them in the moment of some ignorant whim? Into whose hands will fall that incomparable copy of the " Histoire de l'Abbaye de Saint-
Germain-des-Prés," on the margins of which the
author himself, in the person of Jacques Bouillard,
made such substantial notes in his own handwriting?
. . . Master Bonnard, you are an old fool! Your
housekeeper—poor soul!—is nailed down upon her
bed with a merciless attack of rheumatism. Jeanne
is to come with her chaperon, and, instead of thinking how you are going to receive them, you are thinking about a thousand stupidities. Sylvestre Bonnard,
you will never succeed at anything in this world, and
it is I myself who tell you so!

And at this very moment I catch sight of them from
my window, as they get out of the omnibus. Jeanne
leaps down like a kitten: but Mademoiselle Préfère

intrusts herself to the strong arm of the conductor, with the shy grace of a Virginia recovering after the shipwreck, and this time quite resigned to being saved. Jeanne looks up, sees me, laughs, and Mademoiselle Préfère has to prevent her from waving her umbrella at me as a friendly signal. There is a certain stage of civilization to which Mademoiselle Jeanne never can be brought. You can teach her all the arts if you like (it is not exactly to Mademoiselle Préfère that I am now speaking); but you will never be able to teach her perfect manners. As a charming girl she makes the mistake of being charming only in her own way. Only an old fool like myself could forgive her pranks. As for young fools—and there are several of them still to be found—I do not know what they would think about it; and what they might think is none of my business. Just look at her running along the sidewalk, wrapped up in her cloak, with her hat tilted back on her head, and her feather fluttering in the wind, like a schooner in full rig! And really she has a grace of poise and motion which suggests a fine sailing vessel—so much so, indeed, that she makes me remember seeing one day, when I was at Havre . . . But, Bonnard, my friend, how many times is it necessary to tell you that your housekeeper is in bed, and that you must go and open the door yourself?

Open, Old Man Winter! 'tis Spring who rings the bell.

It is Jeanne herself—Jeanne all flushed like a rose.

Mademoiselle Préfère, indignant and out of breath, has still another whole flight to climb before reaching our lobby.

I explained the condition of my housekeeper, and proposed that we should dine at a restaurant. But Thérèse—all-powerful still, even upon her sick-bed— decided that we should dine at home, whether we wanted to or no. Respectable people, in her opinion, never dined at restaurants. Moreover, she had made all necessary arrangements — the dinner had been bought; the concierge would cook it.

The audacious Jeanne insisted upon going to see whether the old woman wanted anything. As you might suppose, she was sent back to the parlor in short order, but not so harshly as I had feared.

"If I want anybody to do anything for me, which, thank God, I do not," Thérèse had replied, "I would get somebody less delicate and dainty than you are. What I want is rest. That is a merchandise which is not sold at fairs under the sign of *Motus-un-doigt-sur-la-bouche.* Go and have your fun, and don't stay here—for old age might be catching."

Jeanne, after telling us what she had said, added that she liked very much to hear old Thérèse talk. Whereupon Mademoiselle Préfère reproached her for expressing such unladylike tastes.

I tried to excuse her by citing the example of Molière. Just at that moment it came to pass that, while climbing the ladder to get a book, she upset a whole shelf-row. There was a heavy crash; and Mademoiselle Préfère, being, of course, a very delicate person, almost fainted. Jeanne quickly followed the books to the foot of the ladder. She made one think of a kitten suddenly transformed into a woman, catching mice which had been transformed into old books. While picking them up, she found one which happened to interest her, and she began to read it, squatting down upon her heels. It was the " Prince Grenouille," she told us. Mademoiselle Préfère took occasion to complain that Jeanne had so little taste for poetry. It was impossible to get her to recite Casimir de Lavigne's poem on the death of Joan of Arc without mistakes. It was the very most she could do to learn " Le Petit Savoyard." The schoolmistress did not think that any one should read the " Prince Grenouille" before learning by heart the stanzas to Duperrier; and, carried away by her enthusiasm, she began to recite them in a voice sweeter than the bleating of a sheep:

> " 'Ta douleur, Duperrier, sera donc éternelle,
>   Et les tristes discours
>   Que te met en l'esprit l'amitié paternelle
>   L'augmenteront toujours;

> . . . . . .

> " 'Je sais de quels appas son enfance etait pleine,
>   Et n'ai pas entrepris,
>   Injurieux ami, de consoler ta peine
>   Avecque son mépris.' "

Then in ecstasy she exclaimed,

"How beautiful that is! What harmony! How is it possible for any one not to admire such exquisite, such touching verses! But why did Malherbe call that poor Monsieur Duperrier his '*injurieux ami*' at a time when he had been so severely tried by the death of his daughter? *Injurieux ami*—you must acknowledge that the term was very harsh."

I explained to this poetical person that the phrase "*Injurieux ami,*" which shocked her so much was an apposition, etc., etc. What I said, however, had so little effect towards clearing her head that she was seized with a severe and prolonged fit of sneezing. Meanwhile it was evident that the history of "Prince Grenouille" had proved extremely funny; for it was all that Jeanne could do, as she crouched down there on the carpet, to keep herself from bursting into a wild fit of laughter. But when she had finished with the prince and princess of the story, and the multitude of their children, she assumed a very suppliant expression, and begged me as a great favor to allow her to put on a white apron and go to the kitchen to help in getting the dinner ready.

"Jeanne," I replied, with the gravity of a master, "I think that if it is a question of breaking plates, knocking off the edges of dishes, denting all the pans, and smashing all the skimmers, the person whom Thérèse has set to work in the kitchen already will be able to perform her task without assistance; for it seems to me at this very moment I can hear disastrous noises in that kitchen. But anyhow, Jeanne, I will charge you with the duty of preparing the dessert. So go and get your white apron; I will tie it on for you."

Accordingly, I solemnly knotted the linen apron about her waist; and she rushed into the kitchen, where she proceeded at once—as we discovered later on—to prepare various dishes unknown to Vatel, unknown even to that great Carême who began his treatise upon *pièces montées* with these words: "*The Fine Arts are five in number: Painting, Music, Poetry, Sculpture, and Architecture — whereof the principal branch is Confectionery.*" But I had no reason to be pleased with this little arrangement—for Mademoiselle Préfère, on finding herself alone with me, began to act after a fashion which filled me with frightful anxiety. She gazed upon me with eyes full of tears and flames, and uttered enormous sighs.

"Oh, how I pity you!" she said. "A man like you —a man so superior as you are—having to live alone with a coarse servant (for she is certainly coarse, that is incontestable)! How cruel such a life must be! You have need of repose—you have need of comfort, of care, of every kind of attention; you might fall sick. And yet there is no woman who would not deem it an honor to bear your name, and to share your existence. No, there is none; my own heart tells me so."

And she squeezed both hands over that heart of hers—always so ready to fly away.

I was driven almost to distraction. I tried to make Mademoiselle Préfère comprehend that I had no intention whatever of changing my habits at so advanced an age, and that I found just as much happiness in life as my character and my circumstances rendered possible.

"No, you are not happy!" she cried. "You need to have always beside you a mind capable of comprehending your own. Shake off your lethargy, and cast your eyes about you. Your professional connections are of the most extended character, and you must have charming acquaintances. One cannot be a Member of the Institute without going into society. See, judge, compare. No sensible woman would refuse you her hand. I am a woman, Monsieur; my instinct never deceives me—there is something within me which assures me that you would find happiness in marriage. Women are so devoted, so loving (not all, of course, but some)! And, then, they are so sensitive to glory. Remember, that at your age one has need, like Œdipus, of an Egeria! Your cook has no more strength—she is deaf, she is infirm. If anything should happen to you at night! Oh! it makes me shudder even to think of it!"

And she really shuddered—she closed her eyes, clenched her hands, stamped on the floor. Great was my dismay. With awful intensity she resumed,

"Your health—your dear health! The health of a Member of the Institute! How joyfully I would shed the very last drop of my blood to preserve the life of a scholar, of a *littérateur*, of a man of worth. And any woman who would not do as much, I would despise her! Let me tell you, Monsieur—I used to know the wife of a great mathematician, a man who used to fill whole blank-books with calculations—so many blank-books that they filled all the closets in the house. He had heart-disease, and he was visibly pining away. And I saw that wife of his, sitting there beside him, perfectly calm! I could not endure it. I said to her one day, 'My dear, you have no heart! If I were in your place I would do . . . I would do . . . I do not know what I would do!'"

She paused for want of breath. My situation was terrible. As for telling Mademoiselle Préfère what I really thought about her advice—that was something which I could not even dream of daring to do. For to fall out with her was to lose the chance of seeing Jeanne. So I resolved to take the matter quietly. In any case, she was in my house: that consideration helped me to treat her with something of courtesy.

"I am very old, Mademoiselle," I answered her, "and I am very much afraid that your advice comes to me rather too late in life. Still, I will think about it. In the meanwhile let me beg of you to be calm. I think a glass of *eau sucrée* would do you good!"

To my great surprise, these words calmed her at once; and I saw her sit down very quietly in *her* corner, close to *her* pigeon-hole, upon *her* chair, with her feet upon *her* footstool.

The dinner was a complete failure. Mademoiselle Préfère, who seemed lost in a brown study, never noticed the fact. As a rule I am very sensitive about such misfortunes; but this one caused Jeanne so much delight that at last I could not help enjoying it myself. Even at my age I had not been able to learn before that a chicken, raw on one side and burned on the other, was a funny thing; but Jeanne's bursts of laughter taught me that it was. That chicken caused us to say a thousand very witty things, which I have forgotten; and I was enchanted that it had not been properly cooked. Jeanne put it back to roast again; then she broiled it; then she stewed it with butter. And every time it came back to the table it was much less comestible and much more hilarious than before. When we did eat it, at last, it had become a thing for which there is no name in any *cuisine*.

The almond cake was much more extraordinary. It was brought to the table in the pan, because it never could have been got out of it. I invited Jeanne to help us all to a piece, thinking that I was going to embarrass her; but she broke the pan and gave each of us a fragment. To think that anybody at my age could eat such things was an idea possible only to **a** very artless mind. Mademoiselle Préfère, suddenly awakened from her dream, indignantly pushed away the sugary splinter of earthenware, and deemed it opportune to inform me that she herself was exceedingly skilful in making confectionery.

"Ah!" exclaimed Jeanne, with an air of surprise not altogether without malice.

Then she wrapped all the fragments of the pan in a piece of paper, for the purpose of giving them to her little playmates—especially to the three little Mouton girls, who are naturally inclined to gluttony.

Secretly, however, I was beginning to feel very uneasy. It did not now seem in any way possible to keep much longer upon good terms with Mademoiselle Préfère since her matrimonial fury had thus burst forth. And that lady gone, good-by to Jeanne! I took advantage of a moment while the sweet soul was busy putting on her cloak, in order to ask Jeanne to tell me exactly what her own age was. She was eighteen years and one month old. I counted on my fingers, and found she would not come of age for another two years and eleven months. And how would we be able to manage during all that time?

At the door Mademoiselle Préfère squeezed my hand with so much meaning that I fairly shook from head to foot.

"Good by," I said very gravely to the young girl. "But listen to me a moment: your friend is very old, and might perhaps fail you when you need him most

Promise me never to fail in your duty to yourself, and then I shall have no fear.   God keep you, my child!"

After closing the door behind them, I opened the window to get a last look at her as she was going away.   But the night was dark, and I could see only two vague shadows flitting across the quay.   I heard the vast deep hum of the city rising up about me; and I suddenly felt a great sinking at my heart.

Poor child!

———

December 15.

THE King of Thulé kept a goblet of gold which his dying mistress had bequeathed him as a souvenir. When about to die himself, after having drank from it for the last time, he threw the goblet into the sea. And I keep this diary of memories even as that old prince of the mist-haunted seas kept his carven goblet; and even as he flung away at last his love-trinket, so will I burn this my book of souvenirs.   Assuredly it is not through any arrogant avarice, nor through any egotistical pride, that I shall destroy this record of an humble life—it is only because I fear lest those things which are dear and sacred to me might appear to others, because of my inartistic manner of expression, either commonplace or absurd.

I do not say this in view of what is going to follow. Absurd I certainly must have been when, having been invited to dinner by Mademoiselle Préfère. I took my seat in a *bergère* (it was really a *bergère*) at the right hand of that alarming person. The table had been set in a little parlor; and I could observe from the poor appearance of the display that the schoolmistress was one of those ethereal souls who soar above terrestrial things. Chipped plates, unmatched glasses, knives with loose handles, forks with yellow prongs—there was absolutely nothing wanting to spoil the appetite of an honest man.

I was assured that the dinner had been cooked for me—for me alone—although Maître Mouche had also been invited. Mademoiselle Préfère must have imagined that I had Sarmatian tastes on the subject of butter; for the butter which she offered me, served up in little thin pats, was excessively rancid.

The roast very nearly poisoned me. But I had the pleasure of hearing Maître Mouche and Mademoiselle Préfère discourse upon virtue. I said the pleasure— I ought to have said the shame: for the sentiments to which they gave expression soared far beyond the range of my vulgar nature.

What they said proved to me as clear as day that devotedness was their daily bread, and that self-sacrifice was not less necessary to their existence than air and water. Observing that I was not eating, Mademoiselle Préfère made a thousand efforts to overcome that which she was good enough to term my "discretion." Jeanne was not of the party, because, I was told, her presence at it would have been contrary to the rules, and would have wounded the feelings of the other school-children, among whom it was necessary to maintain a certain equality. I secretly congratulated her upon having escaped from the Merovingian butter; from the huge radishes, empty as funeral-urns; from the coriaceous roast, and from various other curiosities of diet to which I had exposed myself for the love of her.

The extremely disconsolate-looking servant served up some liquid to which they gave the name of cream —I do not know why—and vanished away like a ghost.

Then Mademoiselle Préfère related to Maître Mouche, with extraordinary transports of emotion, all that she had said to me in the City of Books, during the time that my housekeeper was sick in bed. Her admiration for a Member of the Institute, her terror of seeing me sick and alone, and the certainty she felt that any intelligent woman would be proud and happy to share my existence—she concealed nothing, but, on the contrary, added many fresh follies to the recital. Maître Mouche kept nodding his head in approval while cracking nuts. Then, after all this verbiage, he demanded, with an agreeable smile, what my answer had been.

Mademoiselle Préfère, pressing one hand upon her heart and extending the other towards me, cried out,

" He is so affectionate, so superior, so good, and so great! He answered.   But I could never, because

I am only an humble woman—I could never repeat the words of a Member of the Institute. I can only utter the substance of them. He answered, 'Yes, I understand you—yes.'"

And with these words she reached out and seized one of my hands. Then Maître Mouche, also overwhelmed with emotion, arose and seized my other hand.

"Monsieur," he said, "permit me to offer my congratulations."

Several times in my life I have known fear; but never before had I experienced any fright of so nauseating a character. A sickening terror came upon me.

I disengaged my two hands, and, rising to my feet, so as to give all possible seriousness to my words, I said,

"Madame, either I explained myself very badly when you were at my house, or I have totally misunderstood you here in your own. In either case, a positive declaration is absolutely necessary. Permit me, Madame, to make it now, very plainly. No—I never did understand you; I am totally ignorant of the nature of this marriage project that you have been planning for me—if you really have been planning one. In any event, I would not think of marrying. It would be an unpardonable folly at my age, and even now, at this moment, I cannot conceive how a sensible person like you could ever have advised me to marry.

Indeed, I am strongly inclined to believe that I must have been mistaken, and that you never said anything of the kind before. In the latter case, please to excuse an old man totally unfamiliar with the usages of society, unaccustomed to the conversation of ladies, and very contrite for his mistake."

Maître Mouche went back very softly to his place, where, not finding any more nuts to crack, he began to whittle a cork.

Mademoiselle Préfère, after staring at me for a few moments with an expression in her little round dry eyes which I had never seen there before, suddenly resumed her customary sweetness and graciousness. Then she cried out, in honeyed tones,

"Oh! these learned men!—these studious men! They are all like children. Yes, Monsieur Bonnard, you are a real child!"

Then, turning to the notary, who still sat very quietly in his corner, with his nose over his cork, she exclaimed, in beseeching tones,

"Oh, do not accuse him! Do not accuse him! Do not think any evil of him, I beg of you! Do not think it at all! Must I ask you upon my knees?"

Maître Mouche continued to examine all the various aspects and surfaces of his cork without making any further manifestation.

I was very indignant; and I know that my cheeks must have been extremely red, if I could judge by the flush of heat which I felt rise to my face. This would enable me to explain the words I heard through all the buzzing in my ears:

"I am frightened about him! our poor friend! . . . Monsieur Mouche, be kind enough to open a window! It seems to me that a compress of arnica would do him some good."

I rushed out into the street with an unspeakable feeling of shame.

"My poor Jeanne!"

December 20.

I PASSED eight days without hearing anything further in regard to the Préfère establishment. Then, feeling myself unable to remain any longer without some news of Clémentine's daughter, and feeling furthermore that I owed it as a duty to myself not to cease my visits to the school without more serious cause, I took my way to Aux Ternes.

The parlor seemed to me more cold, more damp, more inhospitable, and more insidious than ever before; and the servant much more silent and much more scared. I asked to see Mademoiselle Jeanne; but, after a very considerable time, it was Mademoiselle Préfère who made her appearance instead — severe and pale, with lips compressed and a hard look in her eyes.

"Monsieur," she said, folding her arms over her pelerine, "I regret very much that I cannot allow you to see Mademoiselle Alexandre to-day ; but I cannot possibly do it."

"Why not ?" I asked, in astonishment.

"Monsieur," she replied, "the reasons which compel me to request that your visits shall be less frequent hereafter are of an excessively delicate nature ; and I must beg you to spare me the unpleasantness of mentioning them."

"Madame," I replied, "I have been authorized by Jeanne's guardian to see his ward every day. Will you please to inform me of your reasons for opposing the will of Monsieur Mouche ?"

"The *guardian* of Mademoiselle Alexandre," she replied (and she dwelt upon that word "guardian" as upon a solid support), "desires, quite as strongly as I myself do, that your assiduities may come to an end as soon as possible."

"Then, if that be the case," I said, "be kind enough to let me know his reasons and your own."

She looked up at the little spiral of paper on the ceiling, and then replied, with stern composure,

"You insist upon it ? Well, although such explanations are very painful for a woman to make, I will yield to your exactions. This house, Monsieur, is an honorable house. I have my responsibility. I have to watch like a mother over each one of my pupils. Your assiduities in regard to Mademoiselle Alexandre could not possibly be continued without serious injury to the young girl herself ; and it is my duty to insist that they shall cease."

"I do not really understand you," I replied—and I was telling the plain truth. Then she deliberately resumed :

"Your assiduities in this house are being interpreted, by the most respectable and the least suspicious persons, in such a manner that I find myself obliged, both in the interest of my establishment and in the interest of Mademoiselle Alexandre, to see that they end at once."

"Madame," I cried, "I have heard a great many silly things in my life, but never anything so silly as what you have just said !"

She answered me very quietly,

"Your words of abuse will not affect me in the slightest. When one has a duty to accomplish, one is strong enough to endure all."

And she pressed her pelerine over her heart once more — not perhaps on this occasion to restrain, but doubtless only to caress that generous heart.

"Madame," I said, shaking my finger at her, "you have wantonly aroused the indignation of an aged man. Be good enough to act in such a fashion that the old man may be able at least to forget your existence, and do not add fresh insults to those which I have already sustained from your lips. I give you fair warning that I shall never cease to look after Mademoiselle Alexandre ; and that should you attempt to do her any harm, in any manner whatsoever, you will have serious reason to regret it !"

The more I became excited, the more she became cool; and she answered in a tone of superb indifference :

"Monsieur, I am much too well informed in regard to the nature of the interest which you take in this young girl, not to withdraw her immediately from that very surveillance with which you threaten me. After observing the more than equivocal intimacy in which you are living with your housekeeper, I ought to have taken measures at once to render it impossible for you ever to come into contact with an innocent child. In the future I shall certainly do it. If up to this time I have been too trustful, it is for Mademoiselle Alexandre, and not for you, to reproach me with it. But she is too artless and too pure—thanks to me! —ever to have suspected the nature of that danger into which you were trying to lead her. I scarcely suppose that you will place me under the necessity of enlightening her upon the subject."

"Come, my poor old Bonnard," I said to myself, as I shrugged my shoulders—"so you had to live as long as this in order to learn for the first time exactly what a wicked woman is. And now your knowledge of the subject is complete."

I went out without replying; and I had the pleasure of observing, from the sudden flush which overspread the face of the schoolmistress, that my silence had wounded her far more than my words.

As I passed through the court I looked about me in

every direction for Jeanne. She was watching for me, and she ran to me

"If anybody touches one little hair of your head, Jeanne, you write me! Good-by!"

"No, not good-by."

I replied.

"Well, no—not good-by! Write to me!"

I went straight to Madame de Gabry's residence.

"Madame is at Rome with Monsieur. Did not Monsieur know it?"

"Why, yes," I replied. Madame wrote me." . . .

She had indeed written me in regard to her leaving home; but my head must have become very much confused, so that I had forgotten all about it. The servant seemed to be of the same opinion, for he looked at me in a way that seemed to signify, "Monsieur Bonnard is doting"—and he leaned down over the balustrade of the stairway to see if I was not going to do something extraordinary before I got to the bottom. But I descended the stairs rationally enough; and then he drew back his head in disappointment.

On returning home I was informed that Monsieur Gélis was waiting for me in the parlor. (This young man has become a constant visitor. His judgment is at fault betimes; but his mind is not at all commonplace.) On this occasion, however, his usually welcome visit only embarrassed me. "Alas!" I thought to myself, "I will be sure to say something very stupid to

my young friend to-day, and he also will think that
my faculties are becoming impaired. But still I cannot really explain to him that I had first been demanded in wedlock, and subsequently traduced as a
man wholly devoid of morals—that even Thérèse had
become an object of suspicion—and that Jeanne remains in the power of the most rascally woman on
the face of the earth. I am certainly in an admirable
state of mind for conversing about Cistercian abbeys
with a young and mischievously minded man. Nevertheless, we shall see—we shall try." ...

But Thérèse stopped me :

"How red you are, Monsieur!" she exclaimed, in
a tone of reproach.

"It must be the spring," I answered.

She cried out,

"The spring!—in the month of December?"

That is a fact! this is December. Ah! what is the
matter with my head? what a fine help I am going
to be to poor Jeanne!

"Thérèse, take my cane; and put it, if you possibly
can, some place where I shall be able to find it again."

"Good-day, Monsieur Gélis. How are you?"

———

Undated.

NEXT morning the old boy wanted to get up; but
the old boy could not get up. A merciless invisible

hand kept him down upon his bed. Finding himself immovably riveted there, the old boy resigned himself to remain motionless; but his thoughts kept running in all directions.

He must have had a very violent fever; for Mademoiselle Préfère, the Abbots of Saint-Germain-des-Prés, and the servant of Madame de Gabry appeared to him in divers fantastic shapes. The figure of the servant in particular lengthened weirdly over his head, grimacing like some gargoyle of a cathedral. Then it seemed to me that there were a great many people, much too many people, in my bedroom.

This bedroom of mine is furnished after the antiquated fashion. The portrait of my father in full uniform, and the portrait of my mother in her cashmere dress, are suspended on the wall. The wall-paper is covered with green foliage-designs. I am aware of all this, and I am even conscious that everything is faded, very much faded. But an old man's room does not require to be pretty; it is enough that it should be clean, and Thérèse sees to that. At all events my room is sufficiently decorated to please a mind like mine, which has always remained somewhat childish and dreamy. There are things hanging on the wall or scattered over the tables and shelves which usually please my fancy and amuse me. But to-day it would seem as if all those objects had suddenly conceived some kind of ill-will against me. They have all become garish, grimacing, menacing. That statuette, modelled after one of the Theological Virtues of Notre-Dame de Brou, always so ingenuously graceful in its natural condition, is now making contortions and putting out its tongue at me. And that beautiful miniature—in which one of the most suave pupils of Jehan Fouquet depicted himself, girdled with the cord-girdle of the Sons of St. Francis, offering his book, on bended knee, to the good Duke d'Angoulême—who has taken it out of its frame and put in its place a great ugly cat's head, which stares at me with phosphorescent eyes? And the designs on the wallpaper have also turned into heads—hideous green heads. . . . But no—I am sure that wall-paper must have foliage-designs upon it at this moment just as it had twenty years ago, and nothing else. . . . But no, again—I was right before—they are heads, with eyes, noses, mouths—they are heads! . . . Ah! now I understand! they are both heads and foliage-designs at the same time. I wish I could not see them at all.

And there, on my right, the pretty miniature of the Franciscan has come back again; but it seems to me as if I can only keep it in its frame by a tremendous effort of will, and that the moment I get tired the ugly cat-head will appear in its place. Certainly I am not delirious; I can see Thérèse very plainly, standing at the foot of my bed; I can hear her speaking to me perfectly well, and I would be able to answer her quite satisfactorily if I were not kept so busy in trying to compel the various objects about me to maintain their natural aspect.

Here is the doctor coming. I never sent for him, but it gives me pleasure to see him. He is an old neighbor of mine; I have never been of much service to him, but I like him very much. Even if I do not say much to him, I have at least full possession of all my faculties, and I even find myself extraordinarily crafty and observing to-day, for I note all his gestures, his every look, the least wrinkling of his face. But the doctor is very cunning, too, and I cannot really tell what he thinks about me. The deep thought of Goethe suddenly comes to my mind, and I exclaim,

"Doctor, the old man has consented to allow himself to become sick; but he does not intend, this time at least, to make any further concessions to nature."

Neither the doctor nor Thérèse laugh at my little joke. I suppose they cannot have understood it.

The doctor goes away; evening comes; and all sorts of strange shadows begin to shape themselves about my bed-curtains, forming and dissolving by turns. And other shadows—ghosts—throng by before me; and through them I can see distinctly the impassive face of my faithful servant. And suddenly a cry, a shrill cry, a great cry of distress, rends my ears. Was it you who called me, Jeanne?

The day is over; and the shadows take their places at my bedside to remain with me all through the long night.

Then morning comes—I feel a peace, a vast peace, wrapping me all about.

Art Thou about to take me into Thy rest, my dear Lord God?

————

February, 186—.

The doctor is quite jovial. It seems that I am doing him a great deal of credit by being able to get out of bed. If I must believe him, innumerable disorders must have pounced down upon my poor old body all at the same time.

These disorders, which are the terror of ordinary mankind, have names which are the terror of philologists. They are hybrid names, half Greek, half Latin, with terminations in " ite," indicating the inflammatory condition, and in " algia," indicating pain. The doctor gives me all their names, together with a corresponding number of adjectives ending in " ic," which serve to characterize their detestable qualities. In short, they represent a good half of that most perfect copy of the Dictionary of Medicine contained in the too-authentic box of Pandora.

" Doctor, what an excellent common-sense story the story of Pandora is!—if I were a poet I would put it into French verse. Shake hands, doctor! You have brought me back to life; I forgive you for it. You have given me back to my friends; I thank you for it. You say I am quite strong. That may

15

be, that may be; but I have lasted a very long time. I am a very old article of furniture; I might be very satisfactorily compared to my father's arm-chair. It was an arm-chair which the good man had inherited, and in which he used to lounge from morning until evening. Twenty times a day, when I was quite a baby, I used to climb up and seat myself on one of the arms of that old-fashioned chair. So long as the chair remained intact, nobody paid any particular attention to it. But it began to limp on one foot; and then folks began to say that it was a very good chair. Afterwards it became lame in three legs, squeaked with the fourth leg, and lost nearly half of both arms. Then everybody would exclaim, ' What a strong chair !' They wondered how it was that after its arms had been worn off and all its legs knocked out of plumb, it could yet preserve the recognizable shape of a chair, remain nearly erect, and still be of some service. The horse-hair came out of its body at last, and it gave up the ghost. And when Cyprien, our servant, sawed up its mutilated members for fire-wood, everybody redoubled their cries of admiration. ' Oh! what an excellent—what a marvellous chair ! It was the chair of Pierre Sylvestre Bonnard, the dry-goods merchant —of Epéminède Bonnard, his son—of Jean-Baptiste Bonnard, the Pyrrhonian philosopher and Chief of the Third Maritime Division. Oh! what a robust and venerable chair !' In reality it was a dead chair. Well, doctor, I am that chair. You think I am solid because

I have been able to resist an attack which would have killed many people, and which only killed me three fourths. Much obliged! I feel none the less that I am something which has been irremediably damaged."

The doctor tries to prove to me, with the help of enormous Greek and Latin words, that I am really in a very good condition. It would, of course, be useless to attempt any demonstration of this kind in so lucid a language as French. However, I allow him to persuade me at last; and I see him to the door.

"Good! good!" exclaimed Thérèse; "that is the way to put the doctor out of the house! Just do the same thing once or twice again, and he will not come to see you any more—and so much the better!"

"Well, Thérèse, now that I have become such a hearty man again, do not refuse to give me my letters. I am sure there must be quite a big bundle of letters, and it would be very wicked to keep me any longer from reading them."

Thérèse, after some little grumbling, gave me my letters. But what did it matter?—I looked at all the envelopes, and saw that no one of them had been addressed by the little hand which I so much wish I could see here now, turning over the pages of the Vecellio. I pushed the whole bundle of letters away: they had no more interest for me.

April–June.

I⟶ was a hotly contested engagement.

"Wait, Monsieur, until I have put on my clean things," exclaimed Thérèse, "and I will go out with you this time also; I will carry your folding-stool as I have been doing these last few days, and we will go and sit down somewhere in the sun."

Thérèse actually thinks me infirm. I have been sick, it is true, but there is an end to all things! Madame Malady has taken her departure quite a while ago, and it is now more than three months since her pale and gracious-visaged handmaid, Dame Convalescence, politely bade me farewell. If I were to listen to my housekeeper, I would become a veritable *Monsieur Argant*, and I would wear a nightcap with ribbons for the rest of my life. . . . No more of this!—I propose to go out by myself! Thérèse will not hear of it. She takes my folding-stool, and wants to follow me.

"Thérèse, to-morrow, if you like, we will take our seats on the sunny side of the wall of La Petite Provence, and stay there just as long as you please. But to-day I have some very important affairs to attend to."

"So much the better! But your affairs are not the only affairs in this world."

I beg, I scold; I make my escape.

It is quite a pleasant day. With the aid of a cab, and the help of God, I trust to be able to fulfil my purpose.

There is the wall on which is painted in great blue letters the words "*Pensionnat de Demoiselles tenu par Mademoiselle Virginie Préfère.*" There is the iron gate which would give free entrance into the court-yard if it were ever opened. But the lock is rusty, and sheets of zinc put up behind the bars protect from indiscreet observation those dear little souls to whom Mademoiselle Préfère doubtless teaches modesty, sincerity, justice, and disinterestedness. There is a window, with iron bars before it, and panes daubed over with white paint—the window of the bath-rooms, like a glazed eye—the only aperture of the building opening upon the exterior world. As for the house-door, through which I entered so often, but which is now closed against me forever, it is just as I saw it the last time, with its little iron-grated wicket. The single stone step in front of it is deeply worn, and, without having very good eyes behind my spectacles, I can see the little white scratches on the stone which have been made by the nails in the shoes of the girls going in and out. And why cannot I also go in? I have a feeling that Jeanne must be suffering a great deal in this dismal house, and that she calls my name in secret. I cannot go away from the gate! A strange anxiety takes hold of me. I pull the bell. The scared-looking servant comes to the door, even much more scared-looking than when I saw her the last time. Strict orders have been given: I am not to be allowed to see Mademoiselle Jeanne. I beg the servant to be so kind as to tell me how the child is. The servant, after looking to her right and then to her left, tells me that Mademoiselle Jeanne is well, and then shuts the door in my face. And I am all alone in the street again."

How many times since then have I wandered in the same way under that wall, and passed before the little door,—full of shame and despair to find myself even weaker than that poor child, who has no other help or friend except myself in the world !

Finally I overcame my repugnance sufficiently to call upon Maître Mouche. The first thing I remarked was that his office is much more dusty and much more mouldy this year than it was last year. The notary made his appearance after a moment, with his familiar stiff gestures, and his restless eyes quivering behind his eye-glasses. I made my complaints to him. He answered me. . . . But why should I write down, even in a blank-book which I am going to burn, my recollections of a downright scoundrel ? He takes sides with Mademoiselle Préfère, whose intelligent mind and irreproachable character he has long appreciated. He does not feel himself in a position to decide the nature of the question at issue; but he must assure me that appearances have been greatly against me. That of course makes no difference to me. He adds— (and this does make some difference to me)—that the small sum which had been placed in his hands to defray the expenses of the education of his ward has been expended, and that, in view of the circumstances, he cannot but greatly admire the disinterestedness of Mademoiselle Préfère in consenting to allow Mademoiselle Jeanne to remain with her.

A magnificent light, the light of a perfect day, floods the sordid place with its incorruptible torrent, and illuminates the person of that man!

And outside it pours down its splendor upon all the wretchedness of a populous quarter.

How sweet it is,—this light with which my eyes have so long been filled, and which ere long I must forever cease to enjoy! I wander out with my hands behind me, dreaming as I go, following the line of the fortifications; and I find myself after a while, I know not how, in an out-of-the-way suburb full of miserable little gardens. By the dusty roadside I observe a plant whose flower, at once dark and splendid, seems worthy of association with the noblest and purest mourning for the dead. It is a columbine. Our fathers called it "Our Lady's Glove"—*le gant de Notre-Dame.* Only such a "Notre-Dame" as might make herself very, very small, for the sake of appearing to little children, could ever slip her dainty fingers into the narrow capsule of that flower.

And there is a big bumble-bee who tries to force himself into the flower, brutally; but his mouth cannot reach the nectar, and the poor glutton strives and strives in vain. He has to give up the attempt, and comes out of the flower all smeared over with pollen.

He flies off in his own heavy lumbering way; but there are not many flowers in this portion of the suburbs, which has been defiled by the soot and smoke of factories. So he comes back to the columbine again, and this time he pierces the corolla and sucks the honey through the little hole which he has made: I should never have thought that a bumble-bee had so much sense! Why, that is admirable! The more I observe them, the more do insects and flowers fill me with astonishment. I am like that good Rollin who went wild with delight over the flowers of his peach-trees. I wish I could have a fine garden, and live at the verge of a wood.

August, September.

IT occurred to me one Sunday morning to watch for the moment when Mademoiselle Préfère's pupils were leaving the school in procession to attend mass at the parish church. I watched them passing two by two,—the little ones first with very serious faces. There were three of them all dressed exactly alike— dumpy, plump, important-looking little creatures, whom I recognized at once as the Mouton girls. Their elder sister is the artist who drew that terrible head of Tatius, King of the Sabines. Beside the column, the assistant school-teacher, with her prayer-book in her hand, was gesturing and frowning. Then came the next oldest class, and finally the big girls, all whispering to each other, as they went by. But I did not see Jeanne.

I went to police-headquarters and inquired whether they did not have, filed away somewhere or other, any information regarding the establishment in the Rue Demours. I succeeded in inducing them to send some female inspectors there. These returned bringing with them the most favorable reports about the establishment. In their opinion the Préfère School was a model school. It is evident that if I were to force an investigation, Mademoiselle Préfère would receive academic honors.

October 3.

THIS Thursday being a school-holiday I had the chance of meeting the three little Mouton girls in the vicinity of the Rue Demours. After bowing to their mother, I asked the eldest, who appears to be about ten years old, how was her playmate, Mademoiselle Jeanne Alexandre.

The little Mouton girl answered me, all in a breath, " Jeanne Alexandre is not my playmate. She is only kept in the school for charity—so they make her sweep the class-rooms. It was Mademoiselle who said so. And Jeanne Alexandre is a bad girl : so they lock her up in the dark room—and it serves her right—and I am a good girl—and I am never locked up in the dark room."

The three little girls resumed their walk, and Ma. dame Mouton followed close behind them, looking back over her broad shoulder at me, in a very suspicious manner.

Alas! I find myself reduced to expedients of a questionable character. Madame de Gabry will not come back to Paris for at least three months more, at the very soonest. Without her, I have no tact, I have no common-sense—I am nothing but a cumbersome, clumsy, mischief-making machine.

Nevertheless, I cannot possibly permit them to make Jeanne a boarding-school servant!

December 28.

THE idea that Jeanne was obliged to sweep the rooms had become absolutely unbearable.

The weather was dark and cold. Night had already begun. I rang the school-door bell with the tranquillity of a resolute man. The moment that the timid servant opened the door, I slipped a gold piece into her hand, and promised her another if she would arrange it so that I could see Mademoiselle Alexandre. Her answer was,

" In one hour from now, at the grated window."

And she slammed the door in my face so rudely that she knocked my hat into the gutter. I waited for one very long hour in a violent snow-storm; then I approached the window. Nothing! The wind raged, and the snow fell heavily. Workmen passing by with their implements on their shoulders, and their heads bent down to keep the snow from coming in their faces, rudely jostled me. Still nothing. I began to fear I had been observed. I knew that I had done wrong in bribing a servant, but I was not a bit sorry for it. Woe to the man who does not know how to break through social regulations in case of necessity! Another quarter of an hour passed. Nothing. At last the window was partly opened.

"Is that you, Monsieur Bonnard?"

"Is that you, Jeanne?—tell me at once what has become of you."

"I am well—very well."

"But what else!"

"They have put me in the kitchen, and I have to sweep the school-rooms."

"In the kitchen! Sweeping—you! Gracious goodness!"

"Yes, because my guardian does not pay for my schooling any more."

"Gracious goodness! Your guardian seems to me to be a thorough scoundrel."

"Then you know—"

"What?"

"Oh! don't ask me to tell you that!—but I would rather die than find myself alone with him again."

"And why did you not write to me?"

"I was watched."

At that instant I formed a resolve which nothing in this world could have induced me to change. I did, indeed, have some idea that I might be acting contrary to law; but I did not give myself the least concern about that idea. And, being firmly resolved, I was able to be prudent. I acted with remarkable coolness.

"Jeanne," I asked, "tell me! does that room you are in open into the court-yard?"

"Yes."

"Can you open the street-door from the inside yourself?"

"Yes,—if there is nobody in the porter's lodge."

"Go and see if there is any one there, and be careful that nobody observes you."

Then I waited, keeping a watch on the door and window.

In six or seven seconds Jeanne reappeared behind the bars, and said,

"The servant is in the porter's lodge."

"Very well," I said, "have you a pen and ink?"

"No."

"A pencil?"

"Yes."

"Pass it out here."

I took an old newspaper out of my pocket, and—in a wind which blew almost hard enough to put the street-lamps out, in a downpour of snow which almost blinded me—I managed to wrap up and address that paper to Mademoiselle Préfère.

While I was writing I asked Jeanne,

"When the postman passes he puts the papers and letters in the box, doesn't he? He rings the bell and goes away? Then the servant opens the letter-box and takes whatever she finds there to Mademoiselle Préfère immediately : is not that about the way the thing is managed whenever any mail comes?"

Jeanne thought it was.

"Then we shall soon see. Jeanne, go and watch again; and, as soon as the servant leaves the lodge, open the door and come out here to me."

Having said this, I put my newspaper in the box, gave the bell a tremendous pull, and then hid myself in the embrasure of a neighboring door.

I might have been there several minutes, when the little door quivered, then opened, and a young girl's head made its appearance through the opening. I took hold of it; I pulled it towards me.

"Come, Jeanne! come!"

She stared at me uneasily. Certainly she must have been afraid that I had gone mad; but, on the contrary, I was very rational indeed.

"Come, my child! come!"

"Where?"

"To Madame de Gabry's."

Then she took my arm. For some time we ran like a couple of thieves. But running is an exercise ill-suited to one as corpulent as I am, and, finding myself out of breath at last, I stopped and leaned upon something which turned out to be the stove of a dealer in roasted chestnuts, who was doing business at the corner of a wine-seller's shop, where a number of cabmen were drinking. One of them asked us if we did not want a cab. Most assuredly we wanted a cab! The driver, after setting down his glass on the zinc counter, climbed upon his seat and urged his horse forward. We were saved.

"Phew!" I panted, wiping my forehead. For, in spite of the cold, I was perspiring profusely.

What seemed very odd was that Jeanne appeared to be much more conscious than I was of the enormity which we had committed. She looked very serious indeed, and was visibly uneasy.

"In the kitchen!" I cried out, with indignation.

She shook her head, as if to say, "Well, there or anywhere else, what does it matter to me?" And, by the light of the street-lamps, I observed with pain that her face was very thin and her features all pinched. I did not find in her any of that vivacity, any of those bright impulses, any of that quickness of expression, which used to please me so much. Her gaze had become timid, her gestures constrained, her whole attitude melancholy. I took her hand—a little cold hand, which had become all hardened and bruised. The poor child must have suffered very much. I questioned her. She told me very quietly that Mademoiselle Préfère had summoned her one day, and called her a little monster and a little viper, for some reason which she had never been able to learn.

She had added, "You shall not see Monsieur Bonnard any more; for he has been giving you bad advice, and he has conducted himself in a most shameful manner towards me." "I then said to her, 'That, Mademoiselle, you will never be able to make me believe.' Then Mademoiselle slapped my face and sent me back to the school-room. The announcement that I would never be allowed to see you again made me feel as if night had come down upon me. Don't you know those evenings when one feels so sad to see the darkness come?—well, just imagine such a moment stretched out into weeks—into whole months! Don't you remember my little Saint-George? Up to that time I had worked at it as well as I could—just simply to work at it—just to amuse myself. But when I lost all hope of ever seeing you again I took my little wax figure, and I began to work at it in quite another way. I did not try to model it with wooden matches any more, as I had been doing, but with hair-pins. I even made use of *épingles à la neige.* But perhaps you do not know what *épingles à la neige* are? Well, I became more particular about it than you can possibly imagine. I put a dragon on Saint-George's helmet; and I passed hours and hours in making a head and eyes and a tail for the dragon. Oh, the eyes! the eyes, above all! I never stopped working at them till I got them so that they had red pupils and white eyelids and eye-brows and everything! I know I am very silly; I had an idea that I was going to die as soon as my little Saint-George would be finished. I worked at it during recreation-hours, and Mademoiselle Préfère used to let me alone. One day I learned that you were in the parlor with the schoolmistress; I watched for you; we said *Au revoir!* that day to each other. I was a little consoled by seeing you. But, some time after that, my guardian came and wanted to make me go out with him one Thursday. I refused to go to his house,—but please don't ask me why, Monsieur. He answered me, quite gently, that I was a very whimsical little girl. And then he left me alone. But the next day Mademoiselle Préfère came to me with such a wicked look on her face that I was really afraid. She had a letter in her hand. 'Mademoiselle,' she said to me, 'I am informed by your guardian that he has spent all the money which belonged to you. Don't be afraid! I do not intend to abandon you; but, you must acknowledge yourself, it is only right that you should earn your own livelihood.' Then she put me to work house-cleaning; and whenever I made a mistake she would lock me up in the garret for days together. And that is what happened to me since I saw you last. Even if I had been able to write to you, I do not know whether I should have done it, because I did not think you could possibly take me away from the school; and, as Maître Mouche did not come back to see me, there was no hurry. I thought I could wait for a while in the garret and the kitchen."

"Jeanne," I cried, "even if we should have to flee

to Oceanica, the abominable Préfère shall never get hold of you again. I will take a great oath on that! And why should we not go to Oceanica? The climate is very healthy; and I read in a newspaper the other day that they have pianos there. But, in the meantime, let us go to the house of Madame de Gabry, who returned to Paris, as luck would have it, some three or four days ago; for you and I are two innocent fools, and we have great need of some one to help us."

Even as I was speaking Jeanne's features suddenly became pale, and seemed to shrink into lifelessness; her eyes became all dim; her lips, half open, contracted with an expression of pain. Then her head sank sideways on her shoulder;—she had fainted.

I lifted her in my arms, and carried her up Madame de Gabry's staircase like a little baby asleep. But I was myself on the point of fainting, from emotional excitement and fatigue together, when she came to herself again.

"Ah! it is you," she said: "so much the better!"

Such was our condition when we rang our friend's door-bell.

———

Same day.

IT was eight o'clock. Madame de Gabry, as might be supposed, was very much surprised by our unexpected appearance. But she welcomed the old man and the child with that glad kindness which always

expressed itself in her beautiful gestures. It seems
to me,—if I might use that language of devotion so
familiar to her,—it seems to me as though some heav-
enly grace streams from her hands whenever she opens
them; and even the perfume which impregnates her
robes seems to inspire the sweet calm zeal of charity
and good works. Surprised she certainly was; but
she asked us no questions,—and that silence seemed
to me admirable.

"Madame," I said to her, "we have both come to
place ourselves under your protection. And, first of
all, we are going to ask you to give us some supper—
or to give Jeanne some, at least; for a moment ago,
in the carriage, she fainted from weakness. As for
myself, I could not eat a bite at this late hour without passing a night of agony in consequence. I hope
that Monsieur de Gabry is well."

"Oh, he is here!" she said.

And she called him immediately.

"Come in here, Paul! Come and see Monsieur Bonnard and Mademoiselle Alexandre."

He came. It was a pleasure for me to see his frank
broad face, and to press his strong square hand. Then
we went, all four of us, into the dining-room; and while
some cold meat was being cut for Jeanne—which she
never touched notwithstanding—I related our advent-
ure. Paul de Gabry asked me permission to smoke
his pipe, after which he listened to me in silence.
When I had finished my recital he scratched the short

stiff beard upon his chin, and uttered a tremendous
"*Sacrebleu!*" But, seeing Jeanne stare at each of us
in turn, with a frightened look in her face, he added:

"We will talk about this matter to-morrow morning. Come into my study for a moment; I have an
old book to show you that I want you to tell me something about."

I followed him into his study, where the steel of
shot-guns and hunting-knives, suspended against the
dark hangings, glimmered in the lamp-light. There,
pulling me down beside him upon a leather-covered
sofa, he exclaimed,

"What have you done? Great God! Do you
know what you have done? Corruption of a minor,
abduction, kidnapping! You have got yourself into a
nice mess! You have simply rendered yourself liable
to a sentence of imprisonment of not less than five
nor more than ten years."

"Mercy on us!" I cried; "ten years imprisonment
for having saved an innocent child."

"That is the law!" answered Monsieur de Gabry.
"You see, my dear Monsieur Bonnard, I happen to
know the Code pretty well—not because I ever stud-
ied law as a profession, but because, as mayor of Lusance, I was obliged to teach myself something about
it in order to be able to give information to my sub-
ordinates. Mouche is a rascal; that woman Préfère is
a vile hussy; and you are a . . . Well! I really cannot
find any word strong enough to signify what you are!"

After opening his book-case, where dog-collars, riding-whips, stirrups, spurs, cigar-boxes, and a few books of reference were indiscriminately stowed away, he took out of it a copy of the Code, and began to turn over the leaves.

"'CRIMES AND MISDEMEANORS' . . . 'SEQUESTRATION OF PERSONS'—that is not your case. . . . 'ABDUCTION OF MINORS'—here we are. . . . 'ARTICLE 354:— *Whosoever shall, either by fraud or violence, have abducted or have caused to be abducted any minor or minors, or shall have enticed them, or turned them away from, or forcibly removed them, or shall have caused them to be enticed, or turned away from, or forcibly removed from the places in which they have been placed by those to whose authority or direction they have been submitted or confided, shall be liable to the penalty of imprisonment. See* PENAL CODE, *21 and 28.*' Here is 21:—'*The term of imprisonment shall not be less than five years.*' 28.— '*The sentence of imprisonment shall be considered as involving a loss of civil rights.*' Now all that is very plain, is it not, Monsieur Bonnard?"

"Perfectly plain."

"Now let us go on: 'ARTICLE 356:— *In case the abductor be under the age of 21 years at the time of the offence, he shall only be punished with*' . . . But we certainly cannot invoke this article in your favor. ARTICLE 357:—*In case the abductor shall have married the girl by him abducted, he can only be prosecuted at the instance of such persons as, according to the Civil*

*Code, may have the right to demand that the marriage
shall be declared null; nor can he be condemned until
after the nullity of the marriage shall have been pronounced.*' I do not know whether it is a part of your
plans to marry Mademoiselle Alexandre! You can
see that the Code is good-natured about it; it leaves
you one door of escape. But no—I ought not to joke
with you, because really you have put yourself in a
very unfortunate position! And how could a man
like you imagine that here in Paris, in the middle of
the nineteenth century, a young girl can be abducted
with absolute impunity? We are not living in the
Middle Ages now; and such things are no longer permitted by law."

"You need not imagine," I replied, "that abduction
was lawful under the ancient Code. You will find in
Baluze a decree issued by King Childebert at Cologne,
either in 593 or 594, on the subject: moreover, everybody knows that the famous *Ordonnance de Blois*, of
May, 1579, formally enacted that any persons convict-
ed of having suborned any son or daughter under the
age of twenty-five years, whether under promise of
marriage or otherwise, without the full knowledge,
will, or consent of the father, mother, and guardians,
should be punished with death; and the ordinance
adds: '*Et pareillement seront punis extraordinaire-
ment tous ceux qui auront participé audit rapt, et qui
auront prêté conseil, confort, et aide en aucune manière
que ce soit.*' (And in like manner shall be extraordi-

narily punished all persons whomsoever, who shall
have participated in the said abduction, and who shall
have given thereunto counsel, succor, or aid in any
manner whatsoever.) Those are the exact, or very
nearly the exact, terms of the ordinance. As for that
article of the Code-Napoléon which you have just told
me of, and which excepts from liability to prosecution
the abductor who marries the young girl abducted by
him, it reminds me that according to the laws of Bre-
tagne, forcible abduction, followed by marriage, was
not punished. But this usage, which involved various
abuses, was suppressed in 1720—at least I give you
the date within ten years My memory is not very
good now, and the time is long passed when I could
repeat by heart without even stopping to take breath,
fifteen hundred verses of Girart de Roussillon.

" As far as regards the Capitulary of Charlemagne,
which fixes the compensation for abduction, I have not
mentioned it because I am sure that you must remember it. So, my dear Monsieur de Gabry, you see abduction was considered as a decidedly punishable offence under the three dynasties of Old France. It is a
very great mistake to suppose that the Middle Ages
represent a period of social chaos. You must remember, on the contrary—"

Monsieur de Gabry here interrupted me :

" So," he exclaimed, " you know the *Ordonnance de
Blois*, you know Baluze, you know Childebert, you
know the Capitularies—and you don't know anything
about the Code-Napoléon !"

I replied that, as a matter of fact, I never had read the Code; and he looked very much surprised.

"And now do you understand," he asked, "the extreme gravity of the action you have committed?"

I had not indeed been yet able to understand it fully. But little by little, with the aid of Monsieur Paul's very sensible explanations, I reached the conviction at last that I would not be judged in regard to my motives, which were innocent, but only according to my action, which was punishable. Thereupon I began to feel very despondent, and to utter divers lamentations.

"What am I to do?" I cried out, "what am I to do? Am I then irretrievably ruined?—and have I also ruined the poor child whom I wanted to save?"

Monsieur de Gabry silently filled his pipe, and lighted it so slowly that his kind broad face remained for at least three or four minutes glowing red behind the light, like a blacksmith's in the gleam of his forge-fire. Then he said,

"You want to know what to do? Why, don't do anything, my dear Monsieur Bonnard! For God's sake, and for your own sake, don't do anything at all! Your situation is bad enough as it is; don't try to meddle with it now, unless you want to create new difficulties for yourself. But you must promise me to sustain me in any action that I may take. I shall go to see Monsieur Mouche the very first thing to-morrow morning; and if he turns out to be what we think he is—that is to say, a consummate rascal—I shall very soon find means of making him harmless, even if the devil himself should take part with him. For everything depends on him. As it is too late this evening to take Mademoiselle Jeanne back to her boarding-school, my wife will keep the young lady here to-night. This of course plainly constitutes the misdemeanor of complicity; but it saves the girl from anything like an equivocal position. As for you, my dear Monsieur, you just go back to the Quai Malaquais as quickly as you can; and if they come to look for Jeanne there, it will be very easy for you to prove she is not in your house."

While we were thus talking, Madame de Gabry was preparing to make her young lodger comfortable for the night. When she bade me good-by at the door, she was carrying a pair of clean sheets, scented with lavender, thrown over her arm.

"That," I said, "is a sweet honest smell."

"Well, of course," answered Madame de Gabry, "you must remember we are peasants."

"Ah!" I answered her, "Heaven grant that I also may be able one of these days to become a peasant! Heaven grant that one of these days I may be able, as you are at Lusance, to inhale the sweet fresh odor of the country, and live in some little house all hidden among trees; and if this wish of mine be too ambitious on the part of an old man whose life is nearly closed, then I will only wish that my winding sheet may be as sweetly scented with lavender as that linen you have on your arm."

It was agreed that I should come to breakfast the following morning. But I was positively forbidden to show myself at the house before midday. Jeanne, as she kissed me good-by, begged me not to take her back to the school any more. We felt much affected at parting, and very anxious.

I found Thérèse waiting for me on the landing, in such a condition of worry about me that it had made her furious. She talked of nothing less than keeping me under lock and key in the future.

What a night I passed! I never closed my eyes for one single instant. From time to time I could not help laughing like a boy at the success of my prank; and then again, an inexpressible feeling of horror would come upon me at the thought of being dragged before some magistrate, and having to take my place upon the prisoner's bench, to answer for the crime which I had so naturally committed. I was very much afraid; and nevertheless I felt no remorse or regret whatever. The sun, coming into my room at last, merrily lighted upon the foot of my bed, and then I made this prayer:

"My God, 'Thou who didst make the sky and the dew,' as it is said in *Tristan*, judge me in Thine equity, not indeed according unto my acts, but according only to my motives, which Thou knowest have been upright and pure; and I will say: Glory to Thee in

heaven, and peace on earth to men of good-will. I
give into Thy hands the child I stole away. Do that
for her which I have not known how to do : guard her
from all her enemies ;—and blessed forever be Thy
name !"

* * *

December 29.

WHEN I arrived at Madame de Gabry's, I found
Jeanne completely transfigured.

Had she also, like myself, at the first light of dawn,
called upon Him " who made the sky and the dew "?
She smiled with such a sweet calm smile !·

Madame de Gabry called her away to arrange her
hair ; for the amiable lady had insisted upon combing
and plaiting, with her own hands, the hair of the child
confided to her care. As I had come a little before
the hour agreed upon, I had interrupted this charming toilet. By way of punishment I was told to go
and wait in the parlor all by myself. Monsieur de
Gabry joined me there in a little while. He had
evidently just come in, for I could see on his forehead
the mark left by the lining of his hat. His frank face
wore an expression of joyful excitement. I thought I
had better not ask him any questions ; and we all
went to breakfast. When the servants had finished
waiting on the table, Monsieur Paul, who was keeping
his good story for the dessert, said to us,

" Well ! I went to Levallois."

"Did you see Maître Mouche?" excitedly inquired Madame de Gabry.

"No," he replied, curiously watching the expression of disappointment upon our faces.

After having amused himself with our anxiety for a reasonable time, the good fellow added:

"Maître Mouche is no longer at Levallois. Maître Mouche has gone away from France. The day after to-morrow will make just eight days since he decamped, taking with him all the money of his clients—a tolerably large sum. I found the office closed. A woman who lived close by told me all about it with an abundance of curses and imprecations. The notary did not take the 7.55 train all by himself; he took with him the daughter of the hair-dresser of Levallois, a young person quite famous in that part of the country for her beauty and her accomplishments;—they say she could shave better than her father. Well, anyhow Mouche has run away with her; the Commissaire de Police confirmed the fact for me. Now, really, could it have been possible for Maître Mouche to have left the country at a more opportune moment? If he had only deferred his escapade one week longer, he would have been still the representative of society, and would have had you dragged off to jail, Monsieur Bonnard, like a criminal. At present we have nothing whatever to fear from him. Here is to the health of Maître Mouche!" he cried, pouring out a glass of white wine.

I would like to live a long time if it were only to remember that delightful morning. We four were all assembled in the big white dining-room around the waxed oak-table. Monsieur Paul's mirth was of the hearty kind,—even perhaps a little riotous; and the good man quaffed deeply. Madame de Gabry smiled at me, with a smile so sweet, so perfect, and so noble, that I thought such a woman ought to keep smiles like that simply as a reward for good actions, and thus make everybody who knew her do all the good of which they were capable. Then, to reward us for our pains, Jeanne, who had regained something of her former vivacity, asked us in less than a quarter of an hour one dozen questions to answer which would have required an exhaustive exposition of the nature of man, the nature of the universe, the science of physics and of metaphysics, the Macrocosm and the Micro-cosm—not to speak of the Ineffable and the Unknow-able. Then she drew out of her pocket her little Saint-George, who had suffered most cruelly during our flight. His legs and arms were gone; but he still had his gold helmet with the green dragon on it. Jeanne solemnly pledged herself to make a restoration of him in honor of Madame de Gabry.

Delightful friends! I left them at last overwhelmed with fatigue and joy.

On re-entering my lodgings I had to endure the very sharpest remonstrances from Thérèse, who said she had given up trying to understand my new way of living. In her opinion Monsieur had really lost his mind.

"Yes, Thérèse, I am a mad old man and you are a mad old woman. That is certain! May the good God bless us both, Thérèse, and give us new strength; for we now have new duties to perform. But let me lie down upon the sofa; for I really cannot keep myself on my feet any longer."

* * *

January 15, 186–.

"Good-morning, Monsieur," said Jeanne, letting herself in; while Thérèse remained grumbling in the corridor because she had not been able to get to the door in time.

"Mademoiselle, I beg you will be kind enough to address me very solemnly by my title, and to say to me, 'Good-morning, my guardian.'"

"Then it has all been settled? Oh, how nice!" cried the child, clapping her hands.

"It has all been arranged, Mademoiselle, in the *Salle-commune* and before the Justice of the Peace; and from to-day you are under my authority. . . . What are you laughing about, my ward? I see it in your eyes. You have some crazy idea in your head this very moment—some more nonsense, eh?"

"Oh, no! Monsieur. . . . I mean, my guardian. I was looking at your white hair. It curls out from

under the edge of your hat like honeysuckle on a bal-
cony. It is very handsome, and I like it very much!"

"Be good enough to sit down, my ward, and, if you
can possibly help it, stop saying ridiculous things, because I have some very serious things to say to you.
Listen. I suppose you are not going to insist upon
being sent back to the establishment of Mademoiselle
Préfère? . . . No. Well, then, what would you say
if I should take you here to live with me, and to finish
your education, and keep you here until . . . what
shall I say?—forever, as the song has it?"

"Oh, Monsieur!" she cried, flushing crimson with
pleasure.

I continued,

"Back there we have a nice little room, which my
housekeeper cleaned up and furnished for you. You
are going to take the place of the books which used to
be in it; you will succeed them as day succeeds night.
Go with Thérèse and look at it, and see if you think you
will be able to live in it. Madame de Gabry and I have
made up our minds that you can sleep there to-night."

She had already started to run; I called her back
for a moment.

"Jeanne, listen to me a moment longer! You have
always until now made yourself a favorite with my
housekeeper, who, like all very old people, is apt to
be cross at times. Be gentle and forbearing. Make
every allowance for her. I have thought it my duty
to make every allowance for her myself, and to put up

with all her fits of impatience. Now, let me tell you,
Jeanne:—Respect her! And when I say that, I do
not forget that she is my servant and yours; neither
will she ever allow herself to forget it for a moment.
But what I want you to respect in her is her great age
and her great heart. She is an humble woman who
has lived a very, very long time in the habit of doing
good; and she has become hardened and stiffened in
that habit. Bear patiently with the harsh ways of
that upright soul. If you know how to command, she
will know how to obey. Go now, my child; arrange
your room in whatever way may seem to you best
suited for your studies and for your repose."

Having started Jeanne, with this viaticum, upon her
domestic career, I began to read a Review, which, although conducted by very young men, is excellent.
The tone of it is somewhat unpolished, but the spirit
zealous. The article I read was certainly far superior,
in point of precision and positivism, to anything of the
sort ever written when I was a young man. The author of the article, Monsieur Paul Meyer, points out
every error with a remarkably lucid power of incisive
criticism.

We used not in my time to criticise with such strict
justice. Our indulgence was vast. It went even so
far as to confound the scholar and the ignoramus in
the same burst of praise. And nevertheless one must
learn how to find fault; and it is even an imperative
duty to blame when the blame is deserved.

I remember little Raymond (that was the name we gave him); he did not know anything, and his mind was not a mind capable of absorbing any solid learning; but he was very fond of his mother. We took very good care never to utter a hint of the ignorance of so perfect a son; and, thanks to our forbearance, little Raymond made his way to the highest positions. He had lost his mother then; but honors of all kinds were showered upon him. He became omnipotent— to the grievous injury of his colleagues and of science. . . . But here comes my young friend of the Luxembourg.

"Good-evening, Gélis. You look very happy to-day. What good fortune has come to you, my dear lad?"

His good fortune is that he has been able to sustain his thesis very creditably, and that he has taken a high rank in his class. He tells me this with the additional information that my own works, which were incidentally referred to in the course of the examination, had been spoken of by the college professors in terms of the most unqualified praise.

"That is very nice," I replied; "and it makes me very happy, Gélis, to find my old reputation thus associated with your own youthful honors. I was very much interested, you know, in that thesis of yours; but some domestic arrangements have been keeping me so busy lately that I quite forgot this was the day on which you were to sustain it."

Mademoiselle Jeanne made her appearance very op-

portunely, as if in order to suggest to him something
about the nature of those very domestic arrangements.
The giddy girl burst into the City of Books like a
fresh breeze, crying out at the top of her voice that
her room was a perfect little wonder. Then she became very red indeed on seeing Monsieur Gélis there.
But none of us can escape our destiny.

Monsieur Gélis asked her how she was with the tone
of a young fellow who presumes upon a previous acquaintance, and who proposes to put himself forward
as an old friend. Oh, never fear!—she had not forgotten him at all: that was very evident from the fact
that then and there, right under my nose, they resumed their last year's conversation on the subject of
the "Venetian-blond"! They continued the discussion
after quite an animated fashion. I began to ask myself what right I had to be in the room at all. The
only thing I could do in order to make myself heard
was to cough. As for getting in a word, they never
even gave me a chance. Gélis discoursed enthusiasti-
cally, not only about the Venetian colorists, but also
upon all other matters relating to nature or to mankind. And Jeanne kept answering him, "Yes, Monsieur, you are right." . . . "That is just what I supposed, Monsieur." . . . "Monsieur, you express so
beautifully just what I feel." . . . "I am going to
think a great deal about what you have just told me.
Monsieur."

When *I* speak, Mademoiselle never answers me in

17

that tone. It is only with the very tip of her tongue that she will even taste any intellectual food which I set before her. Usually she will not touch it at all. But Monsieur Gélis seems to be in her opinion the supreme authority upon all subjects. It was always, " Oh, yes !"—" Oh, of course !"—to all his empty chatter. And, then, the eyes of Jeanne! I had never seen them look so large before; I had never before observed in them such fixity of expression; but her gaze otherwise remained what it always is—artless, frank, and brave. Gélis evidently pleased her; she likes Gélis, and her eyes betrayed the fact. They would have published it to the entire universe! All very fine, Master Bonnard!—you have been so deeply interested in observing your ward, that you have been forgetting you are her guardian! You began only this morning to exercise that function; and you can already see that it involves some very delicate and difficult duties. Bonnard, you must really try to devise some means of keeping that young man away from her; you really ought. . . . Eh! how am I to know what I am to do? . . .

I have picked up a book at random from the nearest shelf; I open it, and I enter respectfully into the middle of a drama of Sophocles. The older I grow, the more I learn to love the two civilizations of the antique world; and now I always keep the poets of Italy and of Greece on a shelf within easy reach of my arm in the City of Books.

Monsieur and Mademoiselle finally condescend to take some notice of me, now that I seem too busy to take any notice of them. I really think that Mademoiselle Jeanne has even asked me what I am reading. No, indeed, I will not tell her what it is. What I am reading, between ourselves, is the chant of that suave and luminous Chorus which rolls out its magnificent melopœıa through a scene of passionate violence—the Chorus of the Old Men of Thebes—Ερως ανικατε. . . . "*Invincible Love, O Thou who descendest upon rich houses,—Thou who dost rest upon the delicate cheek of the maiden,—Thou who dost traverse all seas,—surely none among the Immortals can escape Thee, nor indeed any among men who live but for a little space; and he who is possessed by Thee, there is a madness upon him.*" And when I had re-read that delicious chant, the face of Antigone appeared before me in all its passionless purity. What images! Gods and goddesses who hover in the highest height of heaven! The blind old man, the long-wandering beggar-king, led by Antigone, has now been buried with holy rites; and his daughter, fair as the fairest dream ever conceived by human soul, resists the will of the tyrant and gives pious sepulture to her brother. She loves the son of the tyrant, and that son loves her also. And as she goes on her way to execution, the victim of her own sweet piety, the old men sing, "*Invincible Love, O Thou who dost descend upon rich houses,—Thou who dost rest upon the delicate cheek of the maiden.*" . . .

"Mademoiselle Jeanne, are you really very anxious to know what I am reading? I am reading, Mademoiselle—I am reading that Antigone, having buried the blind old man, wove a fair tapestry embroidered with images in the likeness of laughing faces."

"Ah!" said Gélis, as he burst out laughing, "that is not in the text."

"It is a scolium," I said.

"Inedited," he added, getting up.

I am not an egotist. But I am prudent. I have to bring up this child; she is much too young to be married now. No! I am not an egotist, but I must certainly keep her with me for a few years more—keep her alone with me. She can surely wait until I am dead! Fear not, Antigone, old Œdipus will find holy burial soon enough.

In the meanwhile, Antigone is helping our housekeeper to scrape the carrots. She says she likes to do it—that it is in her line, being related to the art of sculpture.

————

May.

WHO would recognize the City of Books now? There are flowers everywhere—even upon all the articles of furniture. Jeanne was right: those roses do look very nice in that blue china vase. She goes to market every day with Thérèse, under the pretext of helping the old servant to make her purchases, but she never brings anything back with her except flowers. Flowers are really very charming creatures. And one of these days I must certainly carry out my plan, and devote myself to the study of them, in their own natural domain, in the country—with all the science and earnestness which I possess.

For what have I to do here? Why should I burn my eyes out over these old parchments which cannot now tell me anything worth knowing? I used to study them, those old texts, with the most ardent enjoyment. What was it which I was then so anxious to find in them? The date of a pious foundation—the name of some monkish *imagier* or copyist—the price of a loaf, of an ox, or of a field—some judicial or administrative enactment—all that, and yet something more, a Something vaguely mysterious and sublime which excited my enthusiasm. But for sixty years I have been searching in vain for that Something. Better men than I—the masters, the truly great, the Fauriels, the Thierrys, who found so many things— died at their task without having been able, any more than I have been, to find that Something which, being incorporeal, has no name, and without which, nevertheless, no great mental work would ever be undertaken in this world. And now that I am only looking for what I should certainly be able to find, I cannot find anything at all; and it is probable that I will never be able to finish the history of the Abbots of Saint-Ger main-des-Prés.

"Guardian, just guess what I have in my handkerchief."

"Judging from appearances, Jeanne, I should say flowers."

"Oh, no—not flowers.   Look!"

I look, and I see a little gray head poking itself out of the handkerchief. It is the head of a little gray cat. The handkerchief opens; the animal leaps down upon the carpet, shakes itself, pricks up first one ear and then the other, and begins to examine with due caution the locality and the inhabitants thereof.

Thérèse, out of breath, with her basket on her arm, suddenly makes her appearance in time to take an objective part in this examination, which does not appear to result altogether in her favor; for the young cat moves slowly away from her, without, however, venturing near my legs, or approaching Jeanne, who displays extraordinary volubility in the use of caressing appellations. Thérèse, whose chief fault is her inability to hide her feelings, thereupon vehemently reproaches Mademoiselle for bringing home a cat that she did not know anything about. Jeanne, in order to justify herself, tells the whole story. While she was passing with Thérèse before a drug-store, she saw the clerk kick a little cat into the street. The cat, astonished and frightened, seemed to be asking itself whether to remain in the street where it was being terrified and knocked about by the people passing by, or whether to go back into the drug-store even at the risk of being kicked out a second time. Jeanne thought it was in a very critical position, and understood its hesitation. It looked so stupid; and she knew it looked stupid only because it could not decide what to do. So she took it up in her arms. And as it had not been able to obtain any rest either in-doors or out-of-doors, it allowed her to hold it. Then she stroked and petted it to keep it from being afraid, and boldly went to the drug-clerk and said,

"If you don't like that animal, you mustn't beat it; you must give it to me."

"Take it," said the drug-clerk.

. . . "Now there!" adds Jeanne, by way of conclusion; and then she changes her voice again to a flute tone in order to say all kinds of sweet things to that cat.

"He is horribly thin," I observe, looking at the wretched animal;—"moreover, he is horribly ugly." Jeanne thinks he is not ugly at all, but she acknowledges that he looks even more stupid than he looked at first : this time she thinks it not indecision, but surprise, which gives that unfortunate aspect to his countenance. She asks us to imagine ourselves in his place; —then we are obliged to acknowledge that he cannot possibly understand what has happened to him. And then we all burst out laughing in the face of the poor little beast, which maintains the most comical look of gravity. Jeanne wants to take him up ; but he hides himself under the table, and cannot even be tempted to come out by the lure of a saucer of milk.

We all turn our backs and promise not to look; when we inspect the saucer again, we find it empty.

"Jeanne," I observe, "your *protégé* has a decidedly tristful aspect of countenance; he is of a sly and suspicious disposition; I trust he is not going to commit in the City of Books any such misdemeanors as might render it necessary for us to send him back to his drugstore. In the meantime we must give him a name. Suppose we call him 'Don Gris de Gouttière'; but perhaps that is too long. 'Pill,' 'Drug,' or 'Castoroil' would be short enough, and would further serve to recall his early condition in life. What do you think about it?"

"'Pill' would not sound bad," answers Jeanne, "but it would be very unkind to give him a name which would be always reminding him of the misery from which we saved him. It would be making him pay too dearly for our hospitality. Let us be more generous, and give him a pretty name, in hopes that he is going to deserve it. See how he looks at us! He knows that we are talking about him. And now that he is no longer unhappy, he is beginning to look a great deal less stupid. I am not joking! Unhappiness does make people look stupid,—I am perfectly sure it does."

"Well, Jeanne, if you like, we will call your *protégé* Hannibal. The appropriateness of that name does not seem to strike you at once. But the Angora cat who preceded him here as an inmate of the City of Books, and to whom I was in the habit of telling all my secrets—for he was a very wise and discreet person—used to be called Hamilcar. It is natural that this name should beget the other, and that Hannibal should succeed Hamilcar.

We all agreed upon this point.

"Hannibal!" cried Jeanne, "come here!"

Hannibal, greatly frightened by the strange sonority of his own name, ran to hide himself under a book-case in an orifice so small that a rat could not have squeezed himself into it.

A nice way of doing credit to so great a name!

I was in a good humor for working that day, and I had just dipped the nib of my pen into the ink-bottle when I heard some one ring. Should any one ever read these pages written by an unimaginative old man, he will be sure to laugh at the way that bell keeps ringing through my narrative, without ever announcing the arrival of a new personage or introducing any unexpected incident. On the stage things are managed on the reverse principle. Monsieur Scribe never has the curtain raised without good reason, and for the greater enjoyment of ladies and young misses. That is art! I would rather hang myself than write a play,—not that I despise life, but because I should never be able to invent anything amusing. Invent! In order to do that one must have received the gift of inspiration. It would be a very unfortunate thing for

me to possess such a gift. Suppose I were to invent
some monkling in my history of the Abbey of Saint-
Germain-des-Prés! What would our young erudites
say? What a scandal for the School! As for the
Institute, it would say nothing and probably not even
think about the matter either. Even if my colleagues
still write a little sometimes, they never read. They
are of the opinion of Parny, who said,

> *" Une paisible indifférence*
> *Est la plus sage des vertus."* *

To be the least wise in order to become the most
wise—this is precisely what those Buddhists are aim-
ing at without knowing it. If there is any wiser wisdom than that I will go to Rome to report upon it. . . .
And all this because Monsieur Gélis happened to ring
the bell!

This young man has latterly changed his manner
completely with Jeanne. He is now quite as serious
as he used to be frivolous, and quite as silent as he
used to be chatty. And Jeanne follows his example.
We have reached the phase of passionate love under
constraint. For, old as I am, I cannot be deceived
about it: these two children are violently and sincerely
in love with each other. Jeanne now avoids him—
she hides herself in her room when he comes into the
library—but how well she knows how to reach him
when she is alone! alone at her piano! Every even-

---

* " The most wise of the virtues is a calm indifference."

ing she talks to him through the music she plays with a rich thrill of passional feeling which is the new utterance of her new soul.

Well, why should I not confess it? Why should I not avow my weakness? Surely my egotism would not become any less blameworthy by keeping it hidden from myself? So I will write it. Yes! I was hoping for something else;—yes! I thought I was going to keep her all to myself, as my own child, as my own daughter—not always, of course, not even perhaps for very long, but just for a few years more. I am so old! Could she not wait? And, who knows? With the help of the gout, I would not have imposed upon her patience too much. That was my wish; that was my hope. I had made my plans—I had not reckoned upon the coming of this wild young man. But the mistake is none the less cruel because my reckoning happened to be wrong. And yet it seems to me that you are condemning yourself very rashly, friend Sylvestre Bonnard : if you did want to keep this young girl a few years longer, it was quite as much in her own interest as in yours. She has a great deal to learn yet, and you are not a master to be despised. When that miserable notary Mouche—who subsequently committed his rascalities at so opportune a moment—paid you the honor of a visit, you explained to him your ideas of education with all the fervor of high enthusiasm. Then you attempted to put that system of yours into practice;— Jeanne is certainly an ungrateful girl, and Gélis a much too seductive young man!

But still,—unless I put him out of the house, which would be a detestably ill-mannered and ill-natured thing to do,—I must continue to receive him. He has been waiting ever so long in my little parlor, in front of those Sèvres vases with which King Louis Philippe so graciously presented me. The *Moissonneurs* and the *Pêcheurs* of Léopold Robert are painted upon those porcelain vases, which Gélis nevertheless dares to call frightfully ugly, with the warm approval of Jeanne, whom he has absolutely bewitched.

" My dear lad, excuse me for having kept you waiting so long. I had a little bit of work to finish."

I am telling the truth. Meditation is work, but of course Gélis does not know what I mean; he thinks I am referring to something archæological, and, his question in regard to the health of Mademoiselle Jeanne having been answered by a " Very well indeed," uttered in that extremely dry tone which reveals my moral authority as guardian, we begin to converse about historical subjects. We first enter upon generalities. Generalities are sometimes extremely serviceable. I try to inculcate into Monsieur Gélis some respect for that generation of historians to which I belong. I say to him,

" History, which was formerly an art, and which afforded place for the fullest exercise of the imagination, has in our time become a science, the study of which demands absolute exactness of knowledge."

Gélis asks leave to differ from me on this subject.

He tells me he does not believe that history is a science, or that it could possibly ever become a science.

" In the first place," he says to me, " what is history ? The written representation of past events. But what is an event ? Is it merely a commonplace fact ? Is it any fact ? No ! You say yourself it is a noteworthy fact. Now, how is the historian to tell whether a fact is noteworthy or not ? He judges it arbitrarily, according to his tastes and his caprices and his ideas—in short, like an artist ? For facts cannot by reason of their own intrinsic character be divided into historical facts and non-historical facts. But any fact is something exceedingly complex. Will the historian represent facts in all their complexity ? No, that is impossible. Then he will represent them stripped of the greater part of the peculiarities which constituted them, and consequently lopped, mutilated, different from what they really were. As for the inter-relation of facts, needless to speak of it ! If a so-called historical fact be brought into notice—as is very possible—by one or more facts which are not historical at all, and are for that very reason unknown, how is the historian going to establish the relation of these facts one to another ? And in saying this, Monsieur Bonnard, I am supposing that the historian has positive evidence before him, whereas in reality he feels confidence only in such or such a witness for sympathetic reasons. History is not a science ; it is an art, and one can succeed in that art only through the exercise of his faculty of imagination."

Monsieur Gélis reminds me very much at this moment of a certain young fool whom I heard talking wildly one day in the garden of the Luxembourg, under the statue of Marguerite of Navarre. But at another turn of the conversation we find ourselves face to face with Walter Scott, whose work my disdainful young friend pleases to term "rococo, troubadourish, and only fit to inspire somebody engaged in making designs for cheap bronze clocks." Those are his very words!

"Why!" I exclaim, zealous to defend the magnificent creator of "The Bride of Lammermoor," and "The Fair Maid of Perth," "the whole past lives in those admirable novels of his;—that is history, that is epopee!"

"It is frippery," Gélis answers me.

And,—will you believe it?—this crazy boy actually tells me that no matter how learned one may be, one cannot possibly know just how men used to live five or ten centuries ago, because it is only with the very greatest difficulty that one can picture them to one's self even as they were only ten or fifteen years ago. In his opinion, the historical poem, the historical novel, the historical painting, are all, according to their kind, abominably false as branches of art.

"In all the arts," he adds, "the artist can only reflect his own soul. His work, no matter how it may be dressed up, is of necessity contemporary with him-

self, being the reflection of his own mind. What do
we admire in the 'Divine Comedy' unless it be the
great soul of Dante? And the marbles of Michael
Angelo, what do they represent to us that is at all
extraordinary unless it be Michael Angelo himself?
The artist either communicates his own life to his creations, or else merely whittles out puppets and dresses
up dolls."

What a torrent of paradoxes and irreverences! But
boldness in a young man is not displeasing to me.
Gélis gets up from his chair and sits down again. I
know perfectly well what is worrying him, and who
he is waiting for. And now he begins to talk to me
about his being able to make fifteen hundred francs a
year, to which he can add the revenue he derives from
a little property that he has inherited—two thousand
francs a year or more. And I am not in the least deceived as to the purpose of these confidences on his
part. I know perfectly well that he is only making
his little financial statements in order to persuade me
that he is comfortably circumstanced, steady, fond of
home, comparatively independent—or, to put the matter in the fewest words possible, able to marry. *Quod
erat demonstrandum,*—as the geometricians say.

He has got up and sat down just twenty times.
He now rises for the twenty-first time; and, as he has
not been able to see Jeanne, he goes away feeling as
unhappy as possible.

The moment he has gone, Jeanne comes into the

City of Books, under the pretext of looking for Hannibal. She is also quite unhappy; and her voice becomes singularly plaintive as she calls her pet to give him some milk. Look at that sad little face, Bonnard! Tyrant, gaze upon thy work! Thou hast been able to keep them from seeing each other; but they have now both of them the same expression of countenance, and thou mayest discern from that similarity of expression that in spite of thee they are united in thought. Cassandra, be happy! Bartholo, rejoice! This is what it means to be a guardian! Just see her kneeling down there on the carpet with Hannibal's head between her hands!

Yes, caress the stupid animal!—pity him!—moan over him!—we know very well, you little rogue, the real cause of all those sighs and plaints! Nevertheless, it makes a very pretty picture. I look at it for a long time; then, throwing a glance around my library, I exclaim,

"Jeanne, I am tired of all those books; we must sell them."

———

September 20.

It is done!—they are betrothed. Gélis, who is an orphan, as Jeanne is, did not make his proposal to me in person. He got one of his professors, an old colleague of mine, highly esteemed for his learning and character, to come to me on his behalf. But what a love messenger! Great heavens! A bear,—

not a bear of the Pyrenees, but a literary bear,—and this latter variety of bear is much more ferocious than the former.

" Right or wrong (in my opinion wrong!) Gélis says that he does not want any dowry; he takes your ward with nothing but her chemise. Say yes, and the thing is settled! Make haste about it! I want to show you two or three very curious old tokens from Lorraine which I am sure you never saw before."

That is literally what he said to me. I answered him that I would consult Jeanne, and I found no small pleasure in telling him that my ward had a dowry.

Her dowry—there it is in front of me! It is my library. Henri and Jeanne have not even the faintest suspicion about it ; and the fact is I am commonly believed to be much richer than I am. I have the face of an old miser. It is certainly a lying face ; but its untruthfulness has often won for me a great deal of consideration. There is nobody so much respected in this world as a stingy rich man.

I have consulted Jeanne,—but what was the need of listening for her answer? It is done! They are betrothed.

It would ill become my character as well as my face to watch these young people any more for the mere purpose of noting down their words and gestures. *Noli me tangere :*—that is the maxim for all charming love affairs. I know my duty. It is to respect all

18

the little secrets of that innocent soul intrusted to me. Let these children love each other all they can! Never a word of their fervent outpouring of mutual confidences, never a hint of their artless self-betrayals, will be set down in this diary by the old guardian whose authority was so gentle and so brief.

At all events, I am not going to remain with my arms folded; and if they have their business to attend to, I have mine also. I am preparing a catalogue of my books, with a view to having them all sold at auction. It is a task which saddens and amuses me at the same time. I linger over it, perhaps a good deal longer than I ought to do; turning the leaves of all those works which have become so familiar to my thought, to my touch, to my sight—even out of all necessity and reason. But it is a farewell; and it has ever been in the nature of man to prolong a farewell.

This ponderous volume here, which has served me so much for thirty long years, how can I leave it without according to it every kindness that a faithful servant deserves? And this one again, which has so often consoled me by its wholesome doctrines, must I not bow down before it for the last time, as to a Master? But each time that I meet with a volume which ever led me into error, which ever afflicted me with false dates, omissions, lies, and other plagues of the archæologist, I say to it with bitter joy: "Go! impostor, traitor, false-witness! flee thou far away from me forever:—*vade retro!* all absurdly covered

with gold as thou art! and I pray it may befall thee--
thanks to thy usurped reputation and thy comely morocco attire—to take thy place in the cabinet of some
banker-bibliomaniac, whom thou wilt never be able
to seduce as thou hast seduced me, because he will
never read one single line of thee."

I laid aside some books I must always keep—those
books which were given to me as souvenirs. As I
placed among them the manuscript of the "Golden
Legend," I could not but kiss it in memory of Madame Trépof, who remained grateful to me in spite of
her high position and all her wealth, and who became
my benefactress merely to prove to me that she felt
I had once done her a kindness. . . . Thus I had made
a reserve. It was then that, for the first time, I felt
myself inclined to commit a deliberate crime. All
through that night I was strongly tempted; by morning the temptation had become irresistible. Everybody else in the house was still asleep. I got out of
bed and stole softly from my room.

Ye powers of darkness! ye phantoms of the night!
if while lingering within my home after the crowing
of the cock, you saw me stealing about on tiptoe in
the City of Books, you certainly never cried out, as
Madame Trépof did at Naples, "That old man has a
good-natured round back!" I entered the library;
Hannibal, with his tail perpendicularly erected, came to
rub himself against my legs and purr. I seized a volume from its shelf, some venerable Gothic text or

some noble poet of the Renaissance—the jewel, the treasure which I had been dreaming about all night, I seized it and slipped it away into the very bottom of the closet which I had reserved for those books I intended to retain, and which soon became full almost to bursting. It is horrible to relate: I was stealing the dowry of Jeanne! And when the crime had been consummated I set myself again sturdily to the task of cataloguing, until Jeanne came to consult me in regard to something about a dress or a trousseau. I could not possibly understand just what she was talking about, through my total ignorance of the current vocabulary of dressmaking and linen-drapery. Ah! if a bride of the fourteenth century had come to talk to me about the apparel of her epoch, then, indeed, I should have been able to understand her language! But Jeanne does not belong to my time, and I have to send her to Madame de Gabry, who on this important occasion will take the place of her mother.

. . . Night has come! Leaning from the window, we gaze at the vast sombre stretch of the city below us, pierced with multitudinous points of light. Jeanne presses her hand to her forehead as she leans upon the window-bar, and seems a little sad. And I say to myself as I watch her: All changes, even the most longed for, have their melancholy; for what we leave behind us is a part of ourselves: we must die in one life before we can enter into another!

And as if answering my thought, the young girl murmurs to me,

"My guardian, I am so happy; and still I feel as if I wanted to cry!"

THE LAST PAGE.

August 21, 1869.

PAGE eighty-seventh. . . . Only twenty lines more and I will have finished my book about insects and flowers. Page eighty-seventh and last. . . . "*As we have already seen, the visits of insects are of the utmost importance to plants; since their duty is to carry to the pistils the pollen of the stamens. It seems also that the flower itself is arranged and made attractive for the purpose of inviting this nuptial visit. I think I have been able to show that the nectary of the plant distils a sugary liquid which attracts the insect and obliges it to aid unconsciously in the work of direct or cross fertilization. The last method of fertilization is the more common. I have shown that flowers are colored and perfumed so as to attract insects, and interiorly so constructed as to offer those visitors such a mode of access that they cannot penetrate into the corolla without depositing upon the stigma the pollen with which they have been covered. My most venerated master Sprengel observes in regard to that fine down which lines the corolla of the wood-geranium: 'The wise Author of Nature has never created a single useless hair!' I say in my turn: If that Lily of the Valley whereof the Gospel makes mention is more richly clad than King Sol-*

*omon in all his glory, its mantle of purple is a wedding-garment, and that rich apparel is necessary to the perpetuation of the species.**

"BROLLES, *August 21, 1869.*"

———

Brolles! My house is the last one you pass in the single street of the village, as you go to the woods. It is a gabled house with a slate roof, which takes iridescent tints in the sun like a pigeon's breast. The weather-vane above that roof has won more consideration for me among the country people than all my works upon history and philology. There is not a single child who does not know Monsieur Bonnard's weather-vane. It is rusty, and squeaks very sharply in the wind. Sometimes it refuses to do any work at all—just like Thérèse, who now allows herself to be

———

* Monsieur Sylvestre Bonnard was not aware that several very illustrious naturalists were making researches at the same time as he in regard to the relation between insects and plants. He was not acquainted with the labors of Darwin, with those of Dr. Hermann Müller, nor with the observations of Sir John Lubbock. It is worthy of note that the conclusions of Monsieur Sylvestre Bonnard are very nearly similar to those reached by the three scientists above mentioned. Less important, but perhaps equally interesting, is the fact that Sir John Lubbock is, like Monsieur Bonnard, an archæologist who began to devote himself only late in life to the natural sciences.—*Note by the French Editor.*

assisted by a young peasant girl—though she grumbles a good deal about it. The house is not large, but I am very comfortable in it. My room has two windows, and gets the sun in the morning. The children's room is up-stairs. Jeanne and Henri come twice a year to occupy it.

Little Sylvestre's cradle used to be in it. He was a very pretty child, but very pale. When he used to play on the grass, his mother used to watch him very anxiously; and every little while she would stop her sewing in order to take him upon her lap. The poor little fellow never wanted to go to sleep. He used to say that when he was asleep he would go away, very far away, to some place where it was all dark, and where he saw things that made him afraid—things he did not want to see any more.

Then his mother would call me, and I would sit down beside his cradle. He would take one of my fingers into his little dry warm hand, and say to me,

"Godfather, you must tell me a story."

Then I would tell him all kinds of stories, which he would listen to very seriously. They all interested him, but there was one especially which filled his little soul with delight. It was "The Blue Bird." Whenever I finished that, he would say to me, "Tell it again! tell it again!" And I would tell it again until his little pale blue-veined head sank back upon the pillow in slumber.

The doctor used to answer all our questions by saying,

"There is nothing extraordinary the matter with him!"

No! There was nothing extraordinary the matter with little Sylvestre. One evening last year his father called me.

"Come," he said, "the little one is still worse."

I approached the cradle over which the mother hung motionless, as if tied down above it by all the powers of her soul.

Little Sylvestre turned his eyes towards me: their pupils had already rolled up beneath his eyelids, and could not descend again.

"Godfather," he said, "you are not to tell me any more stories."

No, I was not to tell him any more stories!

Poor Jeanne!—poor mother!

I am too old now to feel very deeply; but how strangely painful a mystery is the death of a child!

To-day, the father and mother have come to pass six weeks under the old man's roof. I see them now returning from the woods, walking arm in arm. Jeanne is closely wrapped in her black shawl, and Henri wears a crape about his straw hat; but they are both of them radiant with youth, and they smile very sweetly at each other. They smile at the earth which bears them; they smile at the air which bathes them; they smile at the light which each one sees in the eyes of the other. From my window I wave my handkerchief at them,—and they smile at my old age.

Jeanne comes running lightly up the stairs; she kisses me, and then whispers in my ear something which I divine rather than hear. And I make answer to her: "May God's blessing be with you, Jeanne, and with your husband, and with your children, and with your children's children forever!" . . . *Et nunc dimittis servum tuum, Domine!*"

THE END.

COMPLETE LIST OF TITLES IN
THE MODERN LIBRARY

For convenience in ordering please use number at right of title

CHEKHOV, ANTON (1860-1904)
Rothschild's Fiddle and Thirteen Other Stories (31)
CHESTERTON, G. K. (1874-   )
The Man Who Was Thursday (35)
CONTEMPORARY SCIENCE (99)
Edited with an Introduction by Dr. BENJ. HARROW
CRANE, STEPHEN (1870-1900)
Men, Women and Boats (102)
Introduction by VINCENT STARRETT
D'ANNUNZIO, GABRIELE (1864-   )
The Flame of Life (65)
The Child of Pleasure (98)
Introduction by ERNEST BOYD
The Triumph of Death (112)
Introduction by BURTON RASCOE
DAVIDSON, JOHN
Poems (60)   Introduction by R. M. WENLEY
DAUDET, ALPHONSE (1840-1897)
Sapho (85) In same volume with Prevost's "Manon Lescaut"
DOSTOYEVSKY, FIODOR (1821-1881)
Poor People (10)   Introduction by THOMAS SELTZER
DOUGLAS, NORMAN (1871-   )
South Wind (5)   Special Introduction for Modern Library
    Edition by the author
DOWSON, ERNEST (1867-1900)
Poems and Prose (74) Introduction by ARTHUR SYMONS
DREISER, THEODORE (1871-   )
Free and Other Stories (50)
Introduction by SHERWOOD ANDERSON
DUMAS, ALEXANDRE (1824-1895)
Camille (69) Introduction by SIR EDMUND GOSSE
DUNSANY, LORD (Edward John Plunkett) (1878-   )
A Dreamer's Tales (34) Introduction by PADRAIC COLUM
Book of Wonder (43)
ELLIS, HAVELOCK (1859-   )
The New Spirit (95) Introduction by the author
EVOLUTION IN MODERN THOUGHT (37)
A Symposium, including Essays by Haeckel, Thomson,
    Weismann, and others
FABRE, HENRI (1823-1915)
The Life of the Caterpillar (107)
Introduction by ROYAL DIXON
FLAUBERT, GUSTAVE (1821-1880)
Madame Bovary (28)
The Temptation of St. Anthony (92)
Translated by LAFCADIO HEARN
FLEMING, MARJORIE (1803-1811)
Marjorie Fleming's Book (93)
Introduction by CLIFFORD SMYTH

Modern Library of the World's Best Books

Modern Library of the World's Best Books

Modern Library of the World's Best Books

A SUBJECT INDEX OF TITLES IN
THE MODERN LIBRARY

FICTION

A SUBJECT INDEX OF TITLES IN
THE MODERN LIBRARY

SHORT STORIES

Winesburg, Ohio—Anderson
Balzac's Short Stories
Best Ghost Stories
Best American Humorous Short Stories
Best Russian Short Stories
Rothschild's Fiddle and Other Stories—Chekhov
Men, Women and Boats—Stephen Crane
Free and Other Stories—Theodore Dreiser
A Dreamer's Tales—Dunsany
Book of Wonder—Dunsany
Creatures That Once Were Men and Other Stories—Gorky
Soldiers Three—Kipling
Men in War—Latzko
Love and Other Stories—De Maupassant
Mlle. Fifi and Other Stories—De Maupassant
Tales of Mean Streets—Morrison
The Death of Ivan Ilyitch and Other Stories—Tolstoy

MODERN THOUGHT

Contemporary Science
Evolution in Modern Thought
Love's Coming of Age—Carpenter
The New Spirit—Havelock Ellis
Philosophy of William James
Beyond Good and Evil—Nietzsche
Genealogy of Morals—Nietzsche
Thus Spake Zarathustra—Nietzsche
Outline of Psychoanalysis
Studies in Pessimism—Schopenhauer
The Ego and His Own—Stirner
The Woman Question

DRAMA

Plays by W. S. Gilbert (2 volumes)
Plays by Ibsen (3 volumes)
Plays by Maeterlinck
Plays by Moliere
Plays by Eugene ONeill
Plays by Schnitzler
Plays by Strindberg
Plays by Tolstoy
Plays by Wilde (2 volumes)

POETRY

Prose and Poetry of Baudelaire
Poems of William Blake
Poems of John Davidson
Poems of Ernest Dowson
Poems of Swinburne
Poems of Francis Thompson
Poems of François Villon
Poems of Walt Whitman
Poems of Oscar Wilde

BELLES LETTRES

Marius the Epicurean—Pater
The Renaissance—Pater
Intentions—Oscar Wilde
Beyond Life—Cabell

CRITICISM

The Spirit of American Literature—Macy
A Modern Book of Criticisms—Edited by Ludwig Lewisohn

MISCELLANEOUS

The Art of Aubrey Beardsley

Art of Rodin

Jungle Peace—William Beebe

The Life of the Caterpillar—
Henri Fabre

Marjorie Fleming's Book

Confessions of a Young Man—
George Moore

Selections from the Writings
of Thomas Paine

Samuel Pepys' Diary

Ancient Man—Van Loon

Fairy Tales and Poems in
Prose—Wilde

Selected Addresses and Public Papers of Woodrow
Wilson

Irish Fairy and Folk Tales—
William Butler Yeats

FRENCH ROMANCES IN
THE MODERN LIBRARY

In no other country has the novel of romance and love
come to so fragrant and colorful a flowering as in France.
Love in all its troubled currents of sorrow, its pulsing
courses of pleasure, its flood-tides of exaltation, has been
more sympathetically understood and more lucidly revealed by the great writers of France than by the writers
of almost any other country. Not only has France
universalized the word "amour," she has also revealed
to us through her great novels, the very body and heartbeat of love.

Love and Other Stories—
Guy de Maupassant

Crime of Sylvestre Bonnard—
Anatole France

The Red Lily—
Anatole France

Madame Bovary—
Gustave Flaubert

Mlle. Fifi and Other Stories—
Guy de Maupassant

Mlle. de Maupin—
Theophile Gautier

Candide—Voltaire

Camille—Dumas

The Queen Pedauque—
Anatole France

Une Vie—Guy de Maupassant

Thais—Anatole France

Renée Mauperin—
E. and J. de Goncourt

Sapho—Alphonse Daudet and

Manon Lescaut — Antoine
François Prevost (the two
in one volume)

Madame Chrysanthème—
Pierre Loti

RUSSIAN LITERATURE IN
THE MODERN LIBRARY

The world has always regarded the Russian as some mysterious creature—half child, half genius. Out of Russia's soil has come a people, full of brooding, human pity and swift intuitions—a people sustained by the dreams of its idealists and brutalized by its despots. It is the soul of this creature, set against a background of racial hopes and sorrows, that the great writers of Russia have revealed to us in a literature that stands with the greatest literatures of the world.

The Seven That Were Hanged and The Red Laugh—Leonid Andreyev

Best Russian Short Stories— Edited by Thomas Seltzer

Rothschild's Fiddle and Other Stories—Anton Chekhov

Poor People— Fiodor Dostoyevsky

Creatures That Once Were Men and Other Stories— Maxim Gorky

Redemption and Other Plays Leo Tolstoy

The Death of Ivan Ilyitch and Other Stories— Leo Tolstoy

Fathers and Sons— Ivan Turgenev

Smoke—Ivan Turgenev

DISTINGUISHED WRITERS
WHO HAVE WRITTEN IN-
TRODUCTIONS TO TITLES IN
THE MODERN LIBRARY

In order to make each book in the Modern Library authoritative and helpful, we have, wherever possible, provided illuminating introductions by distinguished writers who are best qualified to write on their subject. These introductions are by some of the greatest writers and critics in the world. Of those who have written introductions to the Modern Library titles are such distinguished names as:

Ernest Boyd	Paul Elmer More
James Branch Cabell	George Jean Nathan
G. K. Chesterton	John Payne
Clarence Day, Jr.	Burton Rascoe
Floyd Dell	John Reed
Ashley Dukes	William Marion Reedy
Waldo Frank	Arthur B. Reeve
John Galsworthy	Ernest Rhys
Dr. Benjamin Harrow	Edgar Saltus
Albert Bushnell Hart	Carl Sandburg
Lafcadio Hearn	T. B. Saunders
Guy Holt	Thomas Seltzer
Arthur Hopkins	Vincent Starrett
Wm. Dean Howells	Clifford Smyth
Henry James	Arthur Symons
Alexander Jessup	John Garrett Underhill
Joyce Kilmer	Carl Van Doren
Richard Le Gallienne	Hendrik W. Van Loon
Ludwig Lewisohn	J. S. Van Teslaar
Phillip Littell	Carl Van Vechten
John Macy	Willard Huntington Wright
H. L. Mencken	Emile Zola